GW00771721

A GENTLEMAN OF SINISTER SCHEMES

THE LORD JULIAN MYSTERIES

BOOK EIGHT

GRACE BURROWES

GRACE BURROWES PUBLISHING

Cover image Cracked Light Studio, Inc.

Cover design by Wax Creative, Inc.

DEDICATION

Dedicated in memoriam to John "Bill" P., the truest of gentlemen. Bill was the sort of reader an author longs to clone ten thousand times over, but of course there was only one of him. In word and deed, Bill was unfailingly kind, good-humored, and compassionate, even as he faced the severe challenges of declining health. *Ave atque vale*, my friend. You will be remembered with great respect and will be much missed for a long, long time.

CHAPTER ONE

"Somebody is trying to kill me."

Gordon, Marquess of Dalhousie, drawled this announcement as if he'd been remarking upon the dreary March weather. "Two attempts that I can recognize as such. Surely, Lord Julian, you will agree that reinforcements are appropriate? Poor marksmanship foiled the first effort and a diminished appetite the second. Had I been the least bit peckish, I'd no doubt be strumming a harp by now."

He took a languid sip of his tea and set the saucer gently on the low table.

I was supposed to murmur assent, politely inform the marquess that I was at his disposal, and upend my life for his convenience. With winter yet in evidence and the Dalhousie seat some fifty miles distant, I was curiously reluctant to follow the expected path.

"Reinforcements, Dalhousie, of the bodyguard variety, perhaps. More tea?" We occupied Caldicott Hall's formal parlor—marquesses were something of a rarity, numbering a mere few dozen and lurking between dukes and earls in the order of precedence.

"No more tea, thank you. What I need is intelligence, my lord, and His Grace of Waltham has spoken highly of your ability to gather same. Who is doing this to me? Why now? When I know the who and the why, I will be in a position to put a stop to the nonsense."

Reasoning after my own heart, but if the murder of a peer had been attempted twice, the proceedings had progressed well past the nonsense stage.

I chose a piece of shortbread shaped to resemble a four-leaf clover. "You could remove yourself to the Continent for a time." Heaven knew I'd blown retreat often enough, both in uniform and after mustering out.

Dalhousie rose and began a circuit of the parlor. He was everything a peer should be—big, blond, handsome in a Viking sort of way, and turned out in the first stare of understated rural fashion. He was also impressed with his own consequence and assumed everybody else should be impressed with it too.

"The Continent does not appeal." The marquess stopped before an autumn landscape of Caldicott Hall. "I made my obeisance to Paris along with all the other lemmings. Came home after the first of the year, and never was I so glad to see the miasma of London's coal smoke. I am not now at liberty to resume overseas travel."

The shortbread was lovely. Buttery, just sweet enough, and fresh. I munched away patiently, though Dalhousie doubtless expected me to importune him for particulars.

"Planting isn't for several weeks," I said. "You doubtless have competent stewards and tenants. Lisbon is lovely in spring." Particularly if one carried no wartime memories of the place. Dalhousie had not served in uniform, which was understandable.

He was not only a peer, he also had no heir of the body. He was unmarried, and... *Ah.* Well, then. "You are expected in Town this spring."

"I am expected in Town every spring," he said. "Have been since I was first sent down from university for the usual excesses. I will turn five-and-thirty in the autumn, and it's time I tended to the succession."

To hear him tell it, procreation was the dullest duty ever devised by the mind of man. For some, that might be so, but for the past ten years Dalhousie had reigned at or near the top of Mayfair's list of eligibles. He was titled, wealthy, and healthy. He could have his pick of the diamonds, originals, and heiresses, and taking a bride would have no impact on his other amusements.

As I was debating another piece of shortbread, it occurred to me that Dalhousie was what I could have become had I not returned from the wars under a cloud of scandal. I was heir to my brother Arthur's dukedom, single, had all of my teeth, and had yet to take a bride.

Not for lack of trying, let it be said.

"Town might be safer for you than the family seat," I observed, leaving the remaining shortbread on the plate. "If your detractor is a disgruntled employee or tenant, then distance is your ally."

"Distance is an ally until I return home, my new marchioness at my side, and the attacks resume. I could not in good conscience ask immediate widowhood of a bride I esteemed, and besides that, the whole business is too tedious for words. I want it to stop."

Ergo, I must leap onto my horse and gallop to Dalhousie Manor, peer about with my spyglass, mutter knowledgeably over some tracks in the kitchen garden, and deliver an attempted murderer to the king's man.

"You want *me* to stop it," I said, "and while your faith in my abilities is flattering, my lord, my previous investigations have not involved matters of life or death." Not quite true, in that my life had been threatened once or twice. "I am hesitant to take on the investigation when others might be better suited to the task."

This, in fact, was the gravamen of my hesitation. A military officer dealt in matters of life and death by design, ordering his subordinates hither and thither into varying degrees of danger. I had both given and taken such orders, and I had fared badly with the whole business. I wanted nobody save myself relying on me to keep them safe ever again.

Dalhousie studied my late brother Harry's cavalry sword

mounted over the sideboard. The weapon had been gathering dust in Harry's old apartment. I'd moved it down to the first among Caldicott Hall's public rooms out of respect for my deceased brother. Also because the moment had come to evict his ghost from a perfectly lovely suite in the family wing.

"Others will bungle about," Dalhousie said, caressing the sword's pommel. "You are discreet. I must go courting next month—absolutely must—and I cannot have talk, my lord. This year of all years, I require latitude to maneuver in Town. I'll not be matched with some mercer's horse-faced daughter because the gossips have decided I'm doomed."

In my mind, the mercer's daughters, horse-faced or otherwise, breathed a collective sigh of relief. "Why not put off the courting for another year, Dalhousie? You've waited this long."

He turned a brooding eye on me. "I promised my mother that before the end of the year, I will wed. Her ladyship expects me to honor my word. I expect me to honor my word, and if you'd met my cousin Tam, you'd expect me to as well."

"Your heir?"

"My heir, my cousin, and some days, my penance. Tamerlane Dandridge pretends to scholarship while, in fact, the only subjects he studies with any assiduity are willing women and fine spirits. His step-cousin Susanna indulges his bookish inclinations, and bless her for that, or he'd likely already be dead of a pickled liver. He's also a passable violinist and basically a decent sort, though we do thank the heavenly intercessors that he's through his brilliant-composer phase."

"Could he be threatening your life?" If the relevant question was who benefited from the marquess's demise, Tamerlane surely would.

"Tam's not ambitious enough, not truly mean enough. He poses a threat to every decanter in sight and any friendly females, but he's otherwise harmless. Don't take my word for it. Make up your own mind about him when you come to Dalhousie Manor."

"Have I been invited?"

That Dalhousie sought my aid told me two things: First, he was annoyed by these threats on his life, perhaps even unnerved. One did not describe a peer in his prime as afraid, but Dalhousie could not persuade himself to ignore or deny the reality of the threats.

Second, he *expected* me to assist him. He'd presented himself in person at Caldicott Hall as a courtesy to my brother's title, not because he anticipated that I'd need convincing. I should leap at the opportunity to be useful to the marquess, and in this, he wasn't entirely wrong.

I had served under Wellington in the capacity of reconnaissance officer, gathering such intelligence as I was ordered to gather. My late brother Harry had served in the same capacity, though I had preferred to work in the villages and countryside, while Harry had been better suited to the cities and towns. As Wellington had begun to push north out of central Spain, Harry and I had found ourselves attached to the same camp.

He'd taken a stealthy leave one night against orders. Inspired by both curiosity and concern, I had followed him, and the pair of us had ended up prisoners in a certain notorious French chateau. I had survived captivity. Harry had not.

The conclusion reached by every military gossip in every allied army was that I'd betrayed my brother and my command. As best I could recall—I was interrogated repeatedly, at length, to the detriment of my cognitive and physical faculties—I had done no such thing. In fact, once Harry and I had been marched through the gates of the chateau, I hadn't seen him again, dead or alive.

I had learned of his demise from the polite French colonel responsible for my periodic misery and been subjected to the colonel's condolences on my loss.

Dalhousie reckoned that I would be eager to rehabilitate my reputation by spending time as the guest of a marquess. I might have been flattered had his motivation been social. Nothing less than threats on his handsome life had compelled him to extend hospitality to me. I was just irritated enough, just contrary enough, to be as insulted as I was intrigued.

Attempted murder of a marquess did not come along every day.

"I am inviting you to come to Dalhousie as my guest," the marquess said evenly. "To bide at your leisure while we await the arrival of spring, whereupon I will have no choice but to remove to Town. Somebody tried to put a bullet through my back, my lord, and somebody tried to send me to my Maker with poison. I haven't the luxury of drawing out a cat-and-mouse game, not with Tam as my heir. I'm sure you understand my concern."

The marquess was being genteelly snide. I was Arthur's sole heir, and neither Arthur nor I were married. I was engaged, true, and to the dearest, most lovely, insightful, darling woman God ever created, but engagements and secure successions were worlds apart, especially the engagement between me and Miss Hyperia West.

The thought of my dear Perry, and her calm, compassionate good sense, brought me up short.

She would tell me that Dalhousie needed my help, and if he didn't fear for his life, he ought to. I was in a position to look into his circumstances, and to refuse him aid would be petty.

Besides all that, I thrived on complicated, vexatious investigations.

"If I'm to involve myself in your situation, Dalhousie, you must understand that you will not control the course of my activities. I will poke my nose where you wish I wouldn't. I will question your staff and your neighbors. I will hare off for a morning without asking your permission, and I will expect your support and cooperation at every turn."

He had sense enough not to assume victory. "What sort of support?"

"You will invite Lady Ophelia Oliphant and Miss Hyperia West to join me at Dalhousie Manor. If you'd like to collect a few other guests for appearances' sake, feel free, but the ladies are my eyes and ears in places where a gentleman cannot intrude. They have been integral to the success of previous investigations, and I dare not take on such a serious matter without their assistance."

"*Miss West* assists you?" I'd surprised him.

"And at Yuletide, we became engaged, so Society should find nothing remarkable about inviting us both. Lady Ophelia is my godmother and serves as a chaperone when needed, though I trust your mother will be on hand as well."

"She will, and you must promise me—"

"No," I said gently. "I will not deceive your lady mother by supporting the pretense that my visit is merely social. Before the staff and neighbors, we can keep to that farce, but before your own mother, we will be honest."

Dalhousie opened his mouth, then shut it. He resumed his place on the sofa, shot his lacy cuffs, and took a piece of shortbread.

"Her ladyship knows everything that goes on in that house," he said. "Probably best to do as you say and explain matters to her honestly." He considered his sweet. "Congratulations on your engagement. Miss West is an estimable lady."

"She is also very sensible, so you must spare me any manly vapors when I tell you that before this investigation is over, I will know the names and present whereabouts of your every flirt, jilt, mistress, and amour, Dalhousie, and so will Miss West."

He stopped chewing. "That will be quite a list." Said without a hint of remorse.

"We will also know the names of anybody with whom you've dueled or declined to duel. Your creditors, be the debts commercial, personal, or debts of honor. Women scorned, jealous papas, angry neighbors, peers whose bills you refused to support in the Lords... anybody who might, in their darkest thoughts, wish you dead."

He rose again and simply stood before the sofa, as if in his busy, important life, he had somewhere else to be but had for the moment forgotten precisely where that was.

Then he looked at the half a piece of shortbread in his hand and sat back down. "Very well. I can make those lists on my way back to Hampshire. I trust you will follow posthaste?"

"You may trust that I will set out in three days. I have arrangements to make. My stewards will want written directions, as will the solicitors, and at the very least, I'll need some homing pigeons crated up to take along with me, to say nothing of packing a wardrobe that must allow for fickle weather. I should arrive by midday on Tuesday." I was capable of covering ground far more quickly than that, but I had learned to avoid forced marches if at all possible. "That schedule allows you time to invite the ladies and to explain the situation to your mother."

His lordship made a face as if he'd smelled a dead mouse behind the wainscoting. "The marchioness won't like it."

"She will like even less that you've been keeping the truth from her. I have a mother. One sympathizes, but you must be honest with her. Present the situation to her as a mere troubling possibility about which you seek her counsel, but don't be too fawning."

"Mother doesn't tolerate fawning." The admission of a man who spoke from experience.

"Until Tuesday, then. I'll see you out."

Five minutes later, we stood in the cavernous white marble foyer designed to impress visitors—also to chill them to the bone in winter —and waited for Dalhousie's coach to be brought around.

"When do you expect His Grace back from his travels?" Dalhousie asked.

"No definite date of return yet, but the general plan isn't until late spring or summer."

"You're managing?"

The question took me aback because it conveyed a hint of sympathy, and thus I answered honestly. "Barely. His Grace accomplishes more in a typical day than I do in a week, and he does it all without seeming to do much of anything. He's never hurried or harried, and he cannot get home soon enough to please me."

"He's the same way in the Lords. Has lunch at the club with this old viscount, hacks out with some uppish earl, and a bill has twenty more sponsors than it did a fortnight ago, but nobody quite knows how Waltham does it. He is proud of you. Says you've always been the cleverest sibling. Waltham does not make idle boasts."

The coach and four clattered up from the stable, a heavy traveling vehicle that would be comfortable in the cold weather, but hardly speedy.

"Safe journey, Dalhousie. Mind your back until reinforcements arrive."

"Until Tuesday." He sketched a bow and hopped into his coach.

I stood on the steps of the portico as the carriage lumbered around the empty fountain and on down the drive across the bleak winter landscape. Dirty snow remained along the hedges and stone walls. Gray-bellied clouds hung over the horizon. Inopportune weather for traveling.

What had I got myself into? Dalhousie was no retiring squire content to trot around his acres. His life had public, private, and financial spheres, and in any one of them, a deadly enemy might lurk. He was no boy just down from university either. His enemy might well have been nursing a grudge that went back fifteen years.

An icy wind swept dead leaves about my boots, my cue to return to the Hall and make my way to my apartment. All the while, I pondered another question:

Was Arthur truly proud of me? Truly? What an extraordinary notion.

CHAPTER TWO

"I can't say how long I'll be gone, but a fortnight to a month should see the business concluded." Unless, of course, Dalhousie was shot dead before I joined him.

Atticus, my erstwhile tiger, eyed me over the pages of his Shakespeare. "This ain't—isn't—a polite visit you're makin'. I should go with you." He was reading Lamb's version of the Bard's plays, simplified and sanitized for children. His literary education had been neglected, though the lad was painfully wise when it came to hard work and life's injustices.

I had challenged him to make a serious effort at the liberal arts, and he had decided to give the schoolroom a try. For now. The transformation from stable boy to scholar was subtle and very much a work in progress. Atticus's hair was more likely to be brushed of late and his boots clean, but he still wore the workaday clothes of the aspiring groom. He was also still growing like Jack Spriggins's enchanted beanstalk and had the appetite of a steeplechaser in racing season.

"Lady Ophelia and Miss West will join me," I said, tossing

another square of peat onto the library's hearth. "You need not fear that I'm on a solo mission."

"You shouldn't do that." He pushed his Shakespeare aside and rose from the reading table. "The footmen count the peats, and they know when you've been doing their work."

News to me. "I'm supposed to stand about shivering while I wait for one of them to heed the bell and do what I can jolly well do for myself?"

Atticus took up the poker and rearranged the peat and coals. "They can't have you getting your hands dirty, because then you might touch the walls and make more work for the maids, and nobody does the maids' cleaning chores no matter how cold he gets. Lord Dalhousie wouldn't ask you to investigate if his situation wasn't messy."

"Why do you say that?" The boy had a keen mind, else I might have been content to leave him to the stable work, which he enjoyed and did well.

"Because Dalhousie's a marquess, and you're a scandal. Your family outranks his, but *you* don't outrank *him*."

Somebody was developing an accurate grasp of precedence and courtesy titles. "God willing, I never shall. You are to remain here, apply yourself to your studies, and if it's not too much bother, keep an eye on Leander. He doesn't appear to be a natural scholar, but we can hope his academic proclivities improve as he matures." Was anybody under the age of seven a natural scholar?

Atticus studied the flames, which licked at the fresh fuel enthusiastically. "Lee don't want a governess. Doesn't, rather. He wants tutors, same as I have. The governess tries to treat him like he's still in dresses, and he's past that."

I had no idea how old Atticus was, because the deprivations of the poorhouse had doubtless stunted his growth. He put his age between eight and ten and had convincingly played both older and younger roles in the course of investigations.

"We thought a governess might ease the absence of a mother in

Leander's life." We being... myself, steward-at-large of the Waltham ducal affairs in Arthur's absence and uncle-without-a-clue when it came to Harry's by-blow. "Most boys have a governess until they reach the age of seven or so."

"No," Atticus said, replacing the hearth screen just so, "most boys don't. Not most boys where Leander comes from. If they're lucky, boys like Lee are apprenticed at seven or thereabouts. Miss Hunter is nice enough, and she means well, but she isn't Leander's ma, and she lets him get away with being a brat."

I'd hired Miss Amelia Hunter because she'd seemed kind and sensible. Not a besom. I'd had experience with a besom or two in my own nursery years, and between me and Harry, we'd run them all off.

Millicent, Leander's mother, had taken the sum of money Arthur had settled on her and made straight for a life of renewed respectability in her home shire, sans fils. She'd handed over guardianship of the boy to me, and not a single soul in all of polite society would judge her for those choices. The son she'd left in Caldicott Hall's nursery would likely judge her until he drew his last breath, and my own feelings on the matter were complicated.

Harry had obtained a special license on his last leave in London and had failed to make use of it in time to give his son legitimacy.

"Has Leander thrown his porridge?" I asked.

"He eats as much as he wants first, then throws the mostly empty bowl. Wastin' good food. Wastin' honey and cinnamon."

Miss Hunter had not reported the boy's rudeness to me. "Does this happen often?"

Atticus replaced the poker on the hearth stand. "Ask Miss Hunter. I'm not a snitch."

"You are a reliable reporter, and I appreciate that." The lad was also in a temper, which years in service had taught him to control. "I will trust to your good offices in my absence and will expect regular dispatches from the third floor."

"I don't write well enough yet to be reporting much of anything."

"You write well enough. It's your spelling that needs work. Greater men than you have been defeated in that task." I did not dare tousle the boy's hair, but I'd given him bad news—he was to be left behind at the Hall, whereas before he'd begun his studies, I would have taken him with me nearly everywhere. I wanted to soften the blow, to offer consolation, except that my objective was to keep Atticus out of danger.

If that meant he was also out of charity with me, I'd pay that price willingly.

"You said you'd take me with you when you went investigating." The words were spoken quietly. The stare aimed at my chest was lethal. "Gave me your word."

I could argue for the defense. I'd told him only that if an investigation required me to fly a kite in the park while on reconnaissance, I would involve him to the extent that a child's presence would make my performance more credible.

Turning up lawyerish was a sure sign of weak moral ground.

"This investigation isn't the usual inquiry, Atticus, and you cannot make progress with your education if you go at your studies only when the whim strikes you." To take on Dalhousie's situation would mean working far from home in the wilds of Hampshire. No busy house party would camouflage my presence or my purpose, and —not a detail—somebody was intent on *murdering* a peer.

A mind that contemplated not mere assault of a peer—a hanging felony in itself—but his intentional demise would think nothing of eliminating a child who asked too many questions or saw what he should not.

Atticus moved to the window, which overlooked garden walkways lined in drab privet hedges and lumpy piles of snow. "You think I can't manage belowstairs in a marquess's household? I manage here, and His Grace is a duke."

Atticus had not contended all that well, and only the fact that he'd arrived as my tiger had gained him what tolerance he'd been shown. The boy hailed from Town, and that alone rendered him worthy of suspicion to the retainers who'd served at the Hall since Noah had gone sailing.

Atticus had also bounced between the house and the stable, a foot in both inside and outside staff camps, and that, too, had made him an alien quantity. Now he was dwelling on the third floor, semi-supervised, and semi-miserable, and I did not see how jaunting off to Hampshire for a few weeks would ease his adjustment to his latest billet.

"You will stay here," I said as gently as I could without sounding apologetic. "You will attend your studies as you promised you would, and you will set an example for Leander in my absence. What lectures and punishments might eventually accomplish in terms of correcting his behavior, a bit of honest shaming-by-mature-example from you will achieve much more effectively."

Atticus absorbed the blow to his pride and ignored the sop to his dignity. "Leander needs a good hiding, and I'll not tend to that task for you, my lord. I daren't, when he hasn't the first notion how to defend himself. Enjoy your travels."

He bowed—the governess wasn't entirely wasted in the schoolroom—and withdrew, leaving Shakespeare faceup on the reading table.

I closed the book and set it back on the shelf reserved for youthful fare. An outing on horseback was in order. Nothing warded off a fit of the dismals like a good gallop, and the weather and my mood were both dismal indeed.

An officer subject to conflicting orders was in the worst possible position. Somebody might well die because he followed the wrong commands. The enemy might well gain. I felt honor-bound to keep Atticus safe, but in the boy's eyes, I was guilty of betrayal. He'd joined me on previous investigations and served me and my missions loyally and well.

I had consigned him to simplified comedies and proper spelling instead of allowing him to continue assisting with my inquiries. Well, so be it. If harm came to me in Hampshire, I'd rather Atticus lived to curse my highhandedness than put himself in danger on my account.

"The personage who accompanied you into the room is not good *ton*, Dalhousie." The Marchioness of Dalhousie hadn't flicked so much as a contemptuous glance in my direction. "Have the footmen remove him." A weighted beat of silence passed. "Please."

Dalhousie met her stare for stare. "Lord Julian is here as my guest, Mama. He will be shown every courtesy."

Two footmen, a matched set of Saxon-bred muscles, had turned to marble on either side of the double door. Dalhousie raised an eyebrow, and they withdrew in a gracefully choreographed allemande that ended with the doors closing in soundless unison.

Peers apparently went to Eyebrow School at some point. Arthur could clear a room in the same manner, and I'd seen my father do likewise on many an occasion.

"Dalhousie," the marchioness began patiently, "you think nobody is taking notice of who consorts or disports with whom because we have not yet removed to London, but I assure you—"

"Wellington vouches for him."

I mentally reviewed a map of Hampshire. We were perhaps ten miles from Stratfield Saye, the Duke of Wellington's estate. A short hack for a marquess with a potentially lethal problem to sort out.

The marchioness turned her back on us and settled on a green brocade sofa adorned with lavender velvet pillows. Her spine touched neither the sofa nor the pillows. She was tall enough to appear imposing even when sitting, but one could not call her graceful.

She was too brittle, too poised for battle. Too tightly stitched, so to speak.

"I'm sure His Grace," she began again, "being a consummate

gentleman, murmured a few platitudes, but that does not signify in the least. This man has been all but accused of—"

"Somebody," I said pleasantly, "is trying to kill your ladyship's only son. I'm here to stop them before they make another attempt. Might we be seated? I've been traveling in winter weather for hours, and though I am bad *ton* in the eyes of many, I'm also prone to fatigue, hunger, and thirst, the same as any other person."

The marchioness waved a hand, and Dalhousie took the place two feet from her on the sofa. I chose an upholstered wing chair and thanked heaven for well-stuffed cushions.

"Perhaps," her ladyship said to nobody in particular, "his visiting lordship has taken leave of his senses? Even the best families are sometimes dealt low cards when it comes to the mental faculties of the younger sons. One pities them, of course, but one does not befriend such persons."

Insults to me were fair game. Sneering at my family would not be tolerated. "Dalhousie, you will please tell your mother what's afoot, just as soon as you ring for a tray. Madam, you will listen to your son and cease insulting me for the sheer pleasure of bullying those too mannerly to correct your rudeness. When I am fed and rested, I will happily take you on, but you enjoy an unfair advantage at the moment. That makes you unsporting, by the way. Keep it up, and I will form a bad first impression of you."

Dalhousie stared at me as if I truly had taken leave of my senses. Then he rose and gave the bell-pull a double tug.

Her ladyship was at least looking at me. "Your father lacked a certain sense of decorum," she said. "He most definitely knew his own consequence, but he could be shockingly informal. Your brother, I am pleased to observe, did not inherit that unfortunate tendency."

No wonder Dalhousie had avoided marriage, if his mother was any example of what a wife became when married to a marquess.

I gave her my best imitation of Arthur's bland smile. "If you refer to the present Duke of Waltham, then surely you mean 'my only surviving brother'?"

She had the wits to swing her cannon to port. "What is this nonsense about somebody trying to kill you, Dalhousie?"

His lordship resumed a seat even farther down the sofa from his mother. "I have been shot at and poisoned."

"Shot at? Why haven't I heard of this?"

"I did not want to trouble you." He recited that bouncer with a straight face, which made it worse. In point of fact, Dalhousie had not wanted his dear mama troubling him, either by hovering or by dismissing his suspicions. Thirty-four years old and still under petticoat government.

That thought brought Leander to mind. He'd made me promise to write to him, and I'd made him promise not to throw his porridge even once while I was absent. When he'd equivocated, I'd threatened to hire two more governesses to abet Miss Hunter's efforts.

My avuncular skills wanted polishing, no doubt about it.

"This was at the Northbys' shoot?" the marchioness asked. "Somebody got tipsy and confused?"

"Somebody confused me for a grouse on the wing," Dalhousie replied. "That must be why my sable top hat now sports extra ventilation."

The duchess merely nodded. "Tamerlane was invited to that shooting party. He'd think it a great lark to knock the hat off your head, but that doesn't prove murderous intent. Unforgivable stupidity, yes, but in his case, that is hardly news or his greatest fault. He has reliable aim with a firearm, as a gentleman of country habits must."

Over any distance, reliable aim with a fowling piece was nonexistent. The whole point was to bring down a bird in flight, and thus scattered shot rather than a single bullet was the preferred ammunition.

"How do you explain the poisoning?" Dalhousie asked. "If aiming a bullet inches from my head was simply a lark, how do you explain that I nearly expired after eating that trifle?"

Her ladyship twitched at her elegantly draped skirts. "Stomach ailments strike where they will. Nobody else fell ill. Ergo, you were not poisoned."

"Ergo," I said, "the poisoner had access to the marquess's individual serving of trifle and knew he particularly liked it."

"I do like trifle," Dalhousie said. "Have since boyhood, but I've given orders it isn't to be served here until further notice."

"Who else was present at the table?" I asked.

Her ladyship glowered at me. "Half the shire. The hunt gathered here the following morning, so we hosted a number of overnight guests. Annual tradition, and one my late husband fully enjoyed."

Ergo, the present marquess was condemned to enjoy it as well. "I'll want a list, as well as a list of the kitchen staff, the footmen, the whole lot."

"You *cannot*," her ladyship said, a hand to her throat, "you *cannot possibly* intend to cause talk regarding his lordship's fanciful notions. I forbid it."

I was tired. My bum ached from too many hours in the coach, and Dalhousie had failed to enlist his mother as an ally when that option had been remotely possible. Now she was my sworn foe, determined to overlook even His Grace of Wellington's endorsement of my character.

I had nothing to lose by taking a firm line with her—she'd already plastered the walls with her figurative porridge—and much to gain.

"Very well," I said. "I'll rest for a day or two and then return to Caldicott Hall. When Dalhousie is murdered a few short weeks before he is to begin searching in earnest for a bride, we will all, especially his lordship's loving and devoted mother, be very glad I didn't run the risk of causing any *talk*."

She blinked, and then a soft tap on the door heralded the arrival of the tea tray. Whatever might be true of the marchioness's hospitality, the kitchen was on its mettle.

The three gleaming silver epergnes held sandwiches, macarons, shortbread, and both sweet and savory tarts. Two teapots in matching floral patterns, one pink, one blue, were swaddled in snowy linen. I

had just taken in the fact that the service was intended to accommodate a party of four when a young blond lady followed the footman
into the parlor.

"I heard we had company," she said. "You must be Lord Julian.
I'm Susanna Morton. Everybody calls me Suze, but I suppose that's
much too informal for a first acquaintance." She offered me her hand,
which I bowed over politely, and a smile, which I returned.

All the starch and sniffiness the marchioness worked so hard to
impose on each moment evaporated like so much fog rolling up the
mountainside on a summer morning. Susanna Morton's smile
conveyed good humor, intelligence, and genuine graciousness.

She was tallish for a lady, but not overly so, and about the
mouth, she bore a resemblance to smiling Renaissance madonnas.
She was pretty rather than beautiful, and her eyes were her best
feature. Gentian blue with an air of gentle, humorous inquisi-
tiveness.

"Shall I pour?" she asked, sidling into the space between the
marchioness and his lordship. "Do you prefer China black or
gunpowder, Lord Julian? Early in the day, Dalhousie likes his black
with a hint of bergamot. Her ladyship is partial to gunpowder with
lemon."

I had met Susanna Morton two minutes ago, but I already felt as
if I knew her and could trust her. She was the voice of reason, the
uncomplaining, sensible presence that steadied the more tempes-
tuous natures in any gathering. Her family doubtless overlooked her,
and she preferred it that way.

Freedom to organize her own affairs was ample compensation for
playing peacemaker, companion, good neighbor, as well as partner to
a procession of aging bachelors at whist and on the dance floor. She
doubtless ran every committee she sat on, though she was never the
chairwoman, and she was universally liked, though she would choose
her few friends carefully.

She would have made an excellent officer, and I could offer no
person higher praise than that.

"I'll have a cup of China black," I said, "and any and everything edible you choose to put on my plate."

"Traveling builds up an appetite." Miss Morton poured the marchioness's cup first, then passed mine to me. "You've come from Caldicott Hall?"

"I did, though Lady Ophelia and Miss West will be coming from Town."

The marchioness's saucer clattered to the table. "I beg your pardon." She hadn't spilled a drop. "Lady Ophelia Oliphant?"

"She is my godmother, and Dalhousie has invited both her and Miss West, my intended, to join us here." I took particular delight in referring to Perry as my intended.

"Hyperia West?" Miss Morton asked, handing Dalhousie his cup. "You are a lucky man, my lord. I needn't tell you that, I'm sure."

"Very lucky." Also very curious. The marchioness had picked up her tea and was sipping away, but mention of Godmama had thrown the ogress off stride. No small feat, that.

Miss Morton steered the talk to winter's interminable dreariness, the upcoming quarterly assembly, and an amusing anecdote involving a nanny goat and some local luminary's Christmas bonnet. Even as I silently applauded a masterful performance, I wondered what Miss Morton thought of the attempts on Dalhousie's life.

She'd doubtless be aware of the incidents, but did she attach lethal intent to them? Was she worried that her step-cousin logically figured at the top of the list of suspects?

As if my imagination had summoned him, Tamerlane Dandridge burst through the double doors without knocking.

"He is here! Lord Julian the Snoop, when he isn't Lord Julian the Traitor, though we're not supposed to say that part out loud." He grinned and bowed in my direction. "I'm Tam Dandridge, which if you say it fast enough, becomes Damn Dandridge after a pint or two. I mean no offense. I'm simply the black sheep up to my usual mischief. We have that black sheep bit in common."

I rose and bowed. "You are also the heir to the title, something else we have in common. Do you find that burden as uncomfortable as I do?"

Tamerlane was quick, but not quick enough to hide a flash of truth: He shared his pretty step-cousin's canniness, which blazed for an instant before disappearing in a grin that would have lit up all of Piccadilly.

"Burden?" He took a sip of Miss Morton's tea. "What burdens have I? Dalhousie is about to choose a bride, so this heir business won't be troubling me much longer. I shall be an uncle within the year. Depend upon it.

"I have my competence," he went on, "and Suze spoils me rotten. Not a care in the world, unless you count a great deal of frustration with sources relating to the mining of *lapis porphyrites*. Pliny the Elder mentions Egyptian origins, but that doesn't narrow the possibilities as much as you might think. His son is even less forthcoming, except on the topic of his dear pater's many literary accomplishments. Very frustrating."

Tamerlane prattled on, and Miss Morton overlooked his casual larceny. I was supposed to think the jester had made his entrance, but as I ingested nearly impolite quantities of sandwiches, I wondered if I had, in fact, met the villain of the piece.

CHAPTER THREE

"You disobeyed a direct order." I let the enormity of the transgression imbue my words with weight, but the urge to shout, to rant, was nigh overwhelming. "A *direct* order, Atticus. You were to bide at the Hall, attend your studies, and keep Leander from inspiring Miss Hunter to give notice."

Atticus disappeared into the dressing closet with my riding boots. "Miss Hunter won't hand in her notice. She's sweet on Young Jamison, and I am not Lee's minder. That's a paying job, that is, and a thankless one."

"Not his minder, you young idiot. His ally. His older, wiser friend in a changing and unkind world. He looks up to you, and you... Leave my clothing alone."

Atticus sent me a pitying glance, a pair of brocade slippers in hand. "You wasn't—weren't—honest with me, guv. Isn't there some sort of order about thou shalt not tell lies?"

"The proscribed behavior is perjury, lying under oath, and I told you no untruths in any case."

"You lied in what you didn't tell me. Somebody is trying to kill the marquess. If they'll kill the title, they will be twice as quick to kill anybody trying to protect the title. I can't have you dyin' on me."

He once again retreated to the dressing closet, leaving me thunderstruck.

"You think to *protect* me?"

My question was greeted with a short silence. Then Atticus emerged, holding a blue silk dressing gown.

"When the marquess called on you at the Hall, his coachy and groom passed the time in the servants' hall, and Young Jamison got them talking, which Young Jamison is good at. They explained as how his lordship Dalhousie has took a notion that somebody is trying to kill him. The coachy says the marquess is going batty in the upper story because he has to finally marry, but the groom said a bullet through a man's hat wasn't no joke whether he was courting a princess or already had six wives. The groom wasn't as sure about the trifle, but if I meant to poison a man, I'd put the poison in something sweet that he's likely to gobble right up. If you take those boots off, I'll get to cleaning them."

"You can't help it," I said slowly. "You are always on reconnaissance."

Atticus, perhaps sensing relenting on my part, hung the dressing gown on a hook on the nearest bedpost. "I keep my eyes and ears open. Doesn't everybody?"

"Not as well as you do." And what a penance that fate was. "Atticus, you still disobeyed a direct order. I cannot overlook such insubordination."

"Lee throws his porridge, and nobody makes him go without his nooning."

Ouch. "You are not Leander. For all we know, you are twice his age."

"I'm not throwing my porridge neither. Didn't you ever disobey a direct order?"

"When I followed my brother Harry from camp, I disobeyed

several standing orders, and the consequences were lethal to him and nearly so to me." And to my reputation, my pride, and my sanity.

Atticus dove into the trunk open before the hearth and emerged holding a hatbox. "I ain't Lord Harry."

No, Atticus was more like that fool Lord Julian, following his brother officer into the darkness because to sit idly by would be a violation of family loyalty and to blazes with the bleatings of various older, wiser generals.

"Atticus, what am I to do with you?"

He held the hatbox before him, putting me in mind of a drummer boy. "I brought extra copies of your cards, the ones you keep in your pocket. Jamison said you always have extra pairs of specs."

Blue spectacles to protect my weak eyes from strong sunlight. Cards for my pocket that explained a peculiar intermittent fault with my memory. Atticus was gently, and probably unintentionally, reminding me that I had vulnerabilities.

So, by God, did he. "I'm sending you back to Caldicott Hall, young man. You stowed away on the baggage coach to get here. You can accompany it back to the Hall tomorrow."

"I did not stow away. I traveled with your trunks like I sometimes do, and nobody asked me nothin'. This ain't the army, and following Lord Harry wasn't the first time you disobeyed an order."

On the one hand, I admired Atticus's courage. On the other hand, he needed to learn some damned deference. Some subtlety.

"An officer who disobeys orders can be stripped of rank and drummed out of the regiment."

Atticus took the hatbox to the wardrobe. "He can also live to follow better orders another day. You can't abide stupid orders. For me to stay at the Hall and watch Lee be a brat was stupid."

I could not have the boy loose on his own reconnaissance, ignoring my authority and disappearing from the Hall on a whim.

"Atticus, sit down."

He exercised some prudence and did as he was told. He took the capacious reading chair by the hearth, which made him look small and powerless. Blinking guileless eyes up at me rather overdid the innocent orphan act.

"I cannot afford a distraction," I said, drawing up the stool before the vanity. "I wanted to refuse the marquess's request. Very likely, he's making too much of unfortunate coincidences. One doesn't say that to a marquess, but if he's right, and somebody is trying to kill him, and I turned him away..."

"His death would be your fault. You'd be blamed for laughing at a man honestly in danger."

"More or less, and I cannot abide the notion of a peer's death on my conscience." Of anybody's death. Of anybody *else's* death, though I wasn't strictly or exclusively responsible for Harry's demise, or so I told myself. "Society already has a dim view of me, and I can't help that, but neither do I want more tarnish on my good name."

"It ain't tarnished, guv. Just dented a bit."

"If I investigate, and despite my best efforts, the marquess is killed, my good name won't be worth the mud on Atlas's horseshoes."

Atticus stared at his boots. "Damned if you investigate and damned if you don't?"

"Precisely, unless the marquess is a fool, and nobody is trying to kill him, in which case, I poke around Hampshire, endure the marchioness's rudeness, and return to the Hall in time for plowing and planting."

Atticus took less than a second to follow my reasoning. "You don't think he's a fool."

"I've met his heir. I cannot indulge in an abundance of optimism, Atticus."

"Damn Tam? The staff likes him."

Fast work, young man. "He's not at all what he seems. The marchioness has secrets of the sort Lady Ophelia will know, and Dalhousie hasn't been entirely honest with me. If you are to bide here, you must promise me on the soul of your sainted mother that you will exercise more caution than you have ever exercised in your short and peripatetic life. I cannot consistently guard your back."

And that drove me nigh to Bedlam.

"Me mam wasn't no saint, 'cause here I am," Atticus retorted. "Miss West will be here tomorrow with Lady Ophelia. We all guard each other's backs. You aren't on reconnaissance, all on your lonesome, fifty miles from camp, guv. I wish you'd figure that out."

"I'm still not happy with you, Atticus. I can't trust you to follow orders."

He began piling the trunk's shirts, breeches, and waistcoats on the bed. "You can trust me to ignore stupid orders. That won't change. You did likewise. I know you did, or you'd be dead three times over."

I wanted to hug him and swat his insightful little hindquarters. "I interpreted the occasional vague order to suit applicable circumstances."

"I interpreted orders too. Brought Shakespeare for reading, my copybook for writing, and I will send letters to Lee and Mr. Pringle on the regular. Miss West will help with my penmanship, and you can tell me what all the big words mean."

"They mean you have a lot more to learn."

He surveyed the heap of expensive tailoring on the bed. "I already know that. I can stay?"

"For now, but for heaven's sake, keep your head down, your mouth shut, and your tail tucked. We are in enemy territory and low on powder, shot, rum, and rations."

The prospect daunted me, given the seriousness of Dalhousie's situation. Atticus taking matters into his own hands confounded me. Loyalty was a fine quality, disobedience a singular fault, and I knew to my sorrow where the combination could lead.

"I will be in the library until it's time to change for supper," I said. "You will sleep on the cot in the dressing closet, get yourself a key to this apartment, and be otherwise the most invisible, unremarkable lad ever to mumble a tired grace before his supper."

"You looking over his lordship's book collection? Miss West says you can tell a lot about a man from his books."

I said that too. "I'm off to write to my mother."

"Her Grace? You saw her just yesterday."

"No matter. Some orders, my boy, are not open to any interpretation whatsoever. You'd best learn to discern them when you hear them."

I left on that admonitory note, dissatisfied with the whole exchange and also a little proud of Atticus's initiative. Vexed and worried, but proud too.

Miss Morton's tour of the Dalhousie Manor portrait gallery the next afternoon was both witty and informative, but my mind was on Atticus and the fact that I'd essentially let him off with a warning. To make him copy sonnets or subsist on bread and water would have been foolish. He needed sharp wits and to be seen going about the business of a tiger-cum-boot-boy.

Sonnets were punishment for naughty lordlings, and whatever else Atticus was, *lordling* did not apply. As Miss Morton maundered on about the current marquess's grandfather, it occurred to me that Society had no idea what to do with me, and I had no idea what to do with Atticus.

"I do see a resemblance about the eyes," I said. "A striking blue."

"Or a flattering blue on the part of the portraitist. My own father was said to be very like my grandpapa, but of course, I knew him later in life."

"Your parents are still extant?"

"Papa went to his reward four years ago, and I came to live with my step-aunt in the Dalhousie dower house." Miss Morton nodded in the direction of a couple done up in the magnificent plumage of the previous century. "Quite a coupe, for Aunt to marry a Dandridge spare. By rights, Tamerlane's mama should not have looked so high, but she was pretty and charming, and they were said to be a love match."

They certainly looked to be in love, but perhaps that was more artistic license. "What of you?" I asked. "Have you no interest in matrimony?"

Her smile lost some of its warmth. "If I'm to look after a man to earn my keep, my lord, I'd prefer to look after the devils I know. Tam appreciates me, and I'm not sure a husband would. I have a competence, not as generous as Tam's, but earning its modest way in the cent-per-cents. Dalhousie gives us the run of the family seat and assures me he always will, so I'm content."

Miss Morton was dishonest, at least in this detail. Busy, useful, independent, and cheerful she might be, but I doubted she was content.

"If you could marry without the threat of children, would the institution hold more appeal for you?"

"The *threat* of children?" Her graciousness faltered further. "An odd word choice, my lord."

"The threat of childbed, then, if I might be so indelicate."

She moved along to a portrait of the current marquess as a youth. The artist had tried to imbue the stripling with a dignity foreign to his years. The result was serious, stiff, and a little sad. Dalhousie probably wished the portrait hung in a more obscure location.

"One doesn't regard childbed as a threat," Miss Morton said. "To be fruitful and multiply is biblically ordained, a privilege, a divine honor. Marriage without a thought for procreation would be like buying an officer's commission with no intention of serving on the battlefield. A costume parade for cowards."

My question had touched a nerve, clearly, because that was direct speech from a woman who likely chose every word carefully.

"Is that what marriage is for the husband? A cowardly costume parade?" Certainly, the Regent's military honors qualified as such, and so fashionably too.

"A husband risks losing his esteemed wife in childbed, my lord, and surely we have wandered far afield from any topic the marchioness would consider appropriate in present company."

Present company being the ancestors, who, according to every elder I'd consulted, had been a rollicking, blasphemous, lusty lot in their most decorous moments. I had read some of my grandfather's memoirs, which dated from before the days of the present, mentally afflicted, king. The royal court had been a procession of scandals and intrigues, leavened by adultery, fornication, graft, and inebriation, while the king and queen tried in vain to set an example of decorum and devotion.

One had to give poor Mad George credit for attempting to break with previous royal tradition.

"If Dalhousie's wife dies in childbed, he'll marry again," I said. "And again and again. He'll have as many marchionesses as he pleases and likely grow richer with each wedding. You will forgive my choice of topic, but I'm only recently engaged, and thus the institution of marriage is much on my mind."

Miss Morton sent me one of those exactly-how-peculiar-is-Lord Julian? looks.

Somewhere among the beruffed and hose-clad earls, a sense of relief settled over me. Hyperia had arrived. I had heard no carriage wheels clattering on the cobbles. No swift passage of feet in the corridor, signaling footmen hustling along in anticipation of luggage to be unloaded.

I simply knew. My beloved was near, and my heart was lighter.

I'd had a similar, though less pleasant, experience when Arthur had taken ship for France. I'd been miles from the coast, we'd said our good-byes hours earlier, and yet, in the middle of an otherwise busy day, I'd been engulfed by a hollow ache. I had known to a moral certainty that my only surviving brother had left England's shores.

Miss Morton prattled gamely on, alluding to royal favors granted by King Charles II in exchange for personal favors extended by a countess-elevated-to-marchioness of the day. When the poacher wore a crown, his thievery became a matter of family pride in a mere century and a half.

"Miss Morton, while we've turned our attention to the general topic of mischief, what do you make of Dalhousie's concerns regarding his safety?"

She stopped before the blazing hearth, the only source of warmth in a large room with an abundance of windows.

"I have considered what to say in answer to that question, my lord, and decided that only blatant, unflattering honesty will serve. You must take the marquess's concerns seriously. He is a wealthy, powerful peer who has doubtless acquired enemies and detractors over the years. I realize that Tam must come under suspicion for form's sake, if nothing else, and I am confident whoever means Dalhousie ill is counting on Tam taking the blame."

"That theory has occurred to me, though it is lamentably true that Tamerlane will benefit enormously from Dalhousie dying without issue."

"There, you would be wrong, my lord." Miss Morton held slender hands out to the fire's heat. "Tam has all the freedom in the world now, to study, to ponder, to wander the estate, and to pass the time with anybody he pleases. He can marry anybody he likes, or never marry at all. If you hang the title around his neck, then he loses what he values most. He'll be expected to vote his seat, order a lot of lackeys about, and marry the heiress of his mama's choosing. He'd be miserable. If we think he's difficult now, I cannot imagine what he'd become if he inherits the title."

An interestingly fierce speech. Would the title cost Tam what he valued most—his freedom, ostensibly—or cost Miss Morton the post of manager and supporter-in-chief of her frivolous cousin?

I was spared the effort of a polite reply by one of the handsome footmen stepping through the open door.

"A carriage, Miss Morton, my lord. The marquess's other guests have arrived."

"Delightful," Miss Morton said, all smiles. "Please let the kitchen know, Shinley. Fancy trays in the formal parlor, braziers to heat the guest bedrooms if the hearths aren't sufficing. You'll inform the marchioness?"

"I'm on my way to her parlor next, miss."

"Excellent. To have some lively ladies on hand will be just the thing for the whole family. Thank you, Shinley."

She beamed at the footman as if he personally had conjured the miracle of good company, and he went smartly on his way.

"Will you greet your Miss West now, my lord? I cannot wait to renew my acquaintance with her, and Lady Ophelia is always a font of the most interesting news."

The best gossip, in other words. "I will most assuredly greet my intended with you. We spent the Yuletide holidays together, and I have limited myself to three letters a week ever since she left Caldicott Hall."

Hyperia had sent me three replies, and thus we did our part to keep the express riders in coin. Sometimes her epistles were brief, recounting a tiresome day of duty calls and at homes. Other times, she admitted to missing me. I treasured every jotting and intended that our grandchildren would as well... except that Hyperia did not want children.

With the marchioness and Dalhousie looking on, I limited my greeting to bowing over Hyperia's hand. A lavish, silent joy hummed between us nonetheless. I was likewise correct with Lady Ophelia, who presented her cheek for a kiss. The gesture was not lost on the marchioness, and I appreciated Godmama's display of support.

After tea, sandwiches, cakes, and more discussion of the insufferable winter roads, Hyperia asked me to accompany her to her room. She declared that she'd brought me some books from Town and would forget to pass them along if she did not see to this detail immediately.

I graciously assented to accompany her. We were engaged to be married, and such nonsense was both our right and expected of us.

"Jules," she said, leaning close as we gained the first landing. "Lady Ophelia says we're not to trust Lady Dalhousie any farther than you could throw the Regent."

His Royal Highness was a delicate flower of nearly twenty stone.

"Did she say why?"

"Details to follow when she can explain them to us both."

"Don't trust Tamerlane either," I said as we reached the first floor. "He professes to be an eccentric scholar but forgot that Pliny the Younger was nephew to the Elder rather than his son."

"He might have been testing your own attention to detail. Did you correct him?"

"Of course not. Let him think I'm as dim as a newel post. God above, I have missed you."

She squeezed my arm. "I've missed you too. Is Dalhousie truly in danger?"

"I believe he is. I will elaborate when you and I can be private with Lady Ophelia."

We reached the apartment designated for Hyperia's use, which happened to be next to my own. Miss Morton's doing, no doubt. The door was open, suggesting Hyperia's trunks were within and perhaps a maid or two as well.

"We'll have our hands full here, Perry, and whoever has made attempts on Dalhousie's life won't quibble at staging accidents for those intent on keeping the marquess safe."

"Precisely why this cannot be a solo investigation, Jules. Or do I mistake the matter?"

Such sternness. I kissed her cheek. "You mistake nothing. I'd best retrieve those books, or people might think you told a falsehood merely to find a moment alone with me."

She kissed me back. "Join Lady Ophelia and me for a nightcap in her sitting room after supper. I did bring books for Atticus."

My hopes for an exchange of more personal greetings were dashed by the presence of a maid and a footman ostensibly unpacking Hyperia's trunks while, in fact, flirting their eyelashes off. I took myself along to my own apartment, though waiting until the end of the day to report developments thus far would be frustrating.

I had my hand on the latch of my sitting room door when a piercing scream issued from within.

CHAPTER FOUR

"What is that, that *creature* doing here?" The question was howled by a pale, aging lady swaddled in lacy shawls and outrage. Her proportions were substantial, and her enormous shawl gave her the appearance of an amateur theatrical ghost clad in a tablecloth. "For that matter, sir, who are you and oh... you must be Lord Julian."

Atticus, the *creature* in question, stood in the doorway to the dressing closet, a polished boot in his hand, a thundering scowl on his face. He withdrew silently, showing commendable discretion.

"You must be Lady Albert," I said, bowing. "I apologize for the lack of a proper introduction. I trust you are feeling better?" She'd missed supper the previous evening, Miss Morton conveying regrets and explaining that dear Auntie had had a headache.

Lady Albert drew herself up in all her lacy glory. "I have the honor to be the relict of the late Lord Albert Dandridge. I trust you've been made comfortable? Dahlia delegates the drudgery of household management to my dear Susanna, and thus one can trust that the appropriate orders have been given respecting guest quarters."

"But one is not as certain the orders have been followed?" An excuse for snooping as flimsy as the trim on her ladyship's shawl.

"My lord is unfortunately correct. The staff is all smiles to Susanna's face, but they take their sweet time doing as she asks. Dahlia cannot be bothered to intervene—dreadful woman, and don't tell me to respect my betters, because in her case the admonition does not apply. If I've told Susanna once, I've told her a thousand times, we would be better off in the South of France, especially now that the Corsican has been dealt with. Tamerlane agrees with me, and he is a young man of rare discernment, though he hides it well. Has to, of course, what with Dalhousie having such a fragile sense of *amour propre.*"

Clearly, prattling ran in the family. Dalhousie's good opinion of himself was about as fragile as Yorkshire granite. "Dahlia would be the marchioness?"

Lady Albert aimed a sniff in what I presumed was the direction of the marchioness's quarters. "For now. She'll be the dowager marchioness ere long, and if she thinks I will give up the dower house or—perish the notion!—share it with her, she is in for a rude awakening. A very rude awakening. The late Lord Dalhousie promised me when I came here as a bride that I had the life estate in that dwelling. I have spent every spare groat I possess making it habitable. No small undertaking, my lord. Enormous, in fact. The place had bats and mice, and you would not believe the dust. And me all bereaved at the time with two grieving youngsters to raise."

Those youngsters would both have achieved their majorities four years ago. That neither of them chose to dwell with Lady Albert in the dower house was an interesting comment on the Dandridge family.

Atticus reappeared and laid a pristine white shirt on the bed, then returned to the dressing closet.

"I will leave you to change for supper," Lady Albert said, giving the gleaming andirons and spotless windows censorious looks. "If you have need of any service, my lord, any service at all, you will apply to Susanna, and she will see that the matter is dealt with. My word on it."

Her ladyship swept out, wanting only a lampshade on her head to add the proper touch to her exit. She was not the queen of the manor, nor was she the mother of the queen of the manor, and yet, she appropriated both roles as her right.

"What was she after?" I asked Atticus, who had returned with a burgundy waistcoat embroidered with green and lavender flowers.

"She were nose down in your jewelry box, guv. Went straight for the sparkly goods." He laid the waistcoat beside the shirt. "Are all the nobs thieves at heart?"

Many of them were. "Did she take anything?"

"Nah, I watched her for a bit before she saw me, and she hadn't made up her mind yet. You aren't much for fancy jewelry."

"The good pieces, what few I brought, are in the false bottom of my hatbox. We will leave them in hiding for now. These books are for you, with Miss West's compliments." I passed him *Tom Jones*, which he would struggle through as best he could for the sake of the racy bits, and a volume of Wordsworth, which he'd puzzle over when he had little else to do.

Atticus peered at the spine of *Tom Jones*. "I saw Lady Ophelia's carriage pull up."

Crests on display, matched grays in the traces. Godmama had made an entrance. "What have you learned from the staff?"

"The servants' hall is the usual seethin' cauldron of complaints and feuds. Good beer, good tucker. Dalhousie ain't a penny pincher, though nobody said much beyond that. I gather he flits through the kitchen of a morning on his way to the stable, and Cook don't seem to mind. The old marquess were a jolly fellow, and this lot... The servants don't care for either of the old besoms, they do like Tamerlane, and they have little to say about Miss Morton. If you brought the ruby cravat pin, you should wear it."

"Then Lady Albert will know she missed the best of the collection."

"If she realizes that much, she'll also know you outsmarted her."

"True, but it's too soon for tactical displays. Both Tamerlane and his mother are likely shrewder than they appear. I need to take their measures more thoroughly before I dangle bait before them."

"Lead me not into temptation," Atticus muttered. "That ruby is proper pretty."

Proper valuable, too, as was the ring that matched it. "Can you take a warning to our ladies for me?"

Atticus stood a little taller. "Aye."

"Let them know you found Lady Albert perusing my valuables and remind them to exercise all possible caution with their quarters. Lock everything that can be locked, leave a few pennies and the odd brooch in plain sight."

"More bait?"

"Distraction and reward." Or consolation. "If Lady Albert had pinched my sapphire cufflinks, do you think she'd come back for more?"

"She might, but she'd be pushing her luck. The better course would be to look for more pickin's elsewhere."

"Just so, and those who purposely appear daft often enjoy a profound instinct for self-preservation. Be off with you, and don't wait up for me when you've had your supper. The ladies and I are to finish the evening with a council of war. We might be late."

"Mind you get enough sleep, guv. You tried to put everything to rights at the Hall in less than two days, then you came galloping up here like the ghost of old Fiddy-Dippies was hot on your tail. Bad things happen when you get too tired."

That homily gave me a moment's pause. "Pheidippides," I said, "if you mean the fellow who brought the Athenians news of the Persian defeat at Marathon."

"That's what I said, Fiddy-Dippies. Means 'hot foot' in Greek, according to Pringle. Old Fiddy-Foot died after all that running around, and no matter that he brought good news."

The name meant *son of Pheidippos*. Pringle's version made for better telling. "Well, skip the dying part and get thee to the ladies with all due haste. They will soon be dressing for dinner, and then you won't be able to breach the castle walls for love nor flaming arrows. Convey the message discreetly."

"Now you're being insultin'. I'll wake you when the second bell rings."

He marched off, the oddest compendium of common sense, innocence, and mischief ever to need a haircut.

A nap was an excellent suggestion. Even a brief respite could be wonderfully restorative, and the prospect of a formal meal in honor of the ladies' arrival meant a very long evening indeed. I hung my formal kit on the wardrobe door, stripped to the skin, ran the warmer over the sheets, and climbed in for a snooze.

I did not precisely sleep, but I dozed, and in that lovely, peaceful state, several thoughts occurred to me: Lady Albert had a splendid motive for putting period to Dalhousie's mortal sojourn, even if—as Miss Morton insisted—Tamerlane did not.

If Tam inherited, Lady Albert's banishment to the dower house, her apparent penury, and her complete lack of familial consequence all changed overnight. Better still, her arch-nemesis

Dahlia the Dreadful Marchioness would come smartly down in the world. More than a few self-serving crimes had been committed in the name of maternal devotion.

And yet, I wanted Tam to be the villain. Simpler, easier to explain...

The next thought made no sense, and yet, I recalled it when I left the bed: Lady Albert had let forth a howl worthy of Mrs. Siddons when she'd clapped eyes on Atticus. Nobody had come running. Not the nearest footman, not a stray maid, and certainly not a member of the Dandridge family.

When we entertained at Caldicott Hall, the guest wing was always staffed with a footman in the corridor by day and a porter or underfootman by night. If Lady Albert had truly been in danger, the puzzling lack of response at Dalhousie Manor might have meant her demise.

"Tamerlane claims his mother is prone to seeing mice," Hyperia said as I showed her into Lady Ophelia's sitting room. "I can believe Lady Albert is prone to being discovered where she has no business poking her nose. A handy mouse would serve as a diversion."

"Mice," Lady Ophelia said from the sofa, "do not frequent guest rooms, when the kitchens and pantries are two floors below and full of food. Say what we might about the marquess's auntie, that was a fine, fine meal."

An interminable meal. I handed Hyperia into a wing chair and took the place beside Lady Ophelia. "The Dandridge family has the gift of chat," I said. "Even Dalhousie, when he bestirs himself, can pass time in idle conversation by the hour. I haven't the knack." Worse yet, I lacked the stamina to appear endlessly fascinated by the new fashion in parasols or the latest tally of the Regent's debts.

"But you can sit at a figurative mousehole for days," Lady Ophelia said. "Shall I ring for tea?"

I wanted my bed, preferably with Hyperia in it. We were not lovers, but we could be very affectionate sleeping companions. My manly humors had gone absent without leave to a significant extent, though I was increasingly hopeful that time would address the malady. Spring must follow winter, and all that.

"Tamerlane is either no scholar," Hyperia said, "or he's trying to create the impression that his scholarship is dodgy. The First Punic War lasted twenty-three years, not thirty."

"He's playacting," I said. "And no tea for me. The fewer people who know we are conferring, the better."

"You and I are engaged," Hyperia said, blowing me a kiss. "We're supposed to confer, and Lady Ophelia is supposed to nominally chaperone us while we do. What makes you think Tam is acting the fool, Jules?"

"Leander knows the Napoleonic battles by heart. He's six years old. His cousin Declan, only a bit older, knows Robert the Bruce's military exploits down to the last skirmish. Dalhousie has no brothers. Ergo, Tamerlane was educated as befit a spare. He'd know his Punic Wars, even if he can no longer recall how to form the passive pluperfect subjunctive in Latin."

"If I had ever been permitted to forget the passive pluperfect subjunctive," Lady Ophelia said, "I would have been shamed past all bearing. Pour us a nightcap, Julian, seeing as we're eschewing tea. I have some history to impart, and my digestion wants settling."

If I had ever been permitted... I would have been shamed... The passive pluperfect subjunctive in a very few words. After a short hibernation over the holidays, Godmama was back in fighting form and letting me know it.

"Whose history?" Hyperia asked, toeing off her slippers and tucking her feet up. She arranged her hems over her stockings in a gesture of natural modesty I'd seen her perform a dozen times, and each time, I wanted to uncover the silk-clad toes she'd just hidden. I dearly hoped I suffered from the same yearning for the next fifty years.

"Lady Dalhousie," Godmama began, "born Lady Dahlia Ostertag, has a positive genius for creating enemies."

"Lady Albert calls the marchioness dreadful," I commented from the sideboard. I passed each of my companions a serving of brandy and resumed my place on the sofa. "Lady Albert claims Susanna does all the household management, but the servants resist Miss Morton's authority out of loyalty to the marchioness."

"Or fear of reprisal from the marchioness," Hyperia said, nosing her drink. "What has a lack of charm on the marchioness's part to do with the present problem?"

I liked watching Hyperia hide her toes. I liked watching her appreciate decent brandy. I loved watching her mind work.

"Old enemies are the worst enemies," Lady Ophelia said. "You will hear it put about that Lady Albert and her late lord were a love match. They were not, not at first. Lady Albert was, in fact, courted by Dalhousie's father. In the course of those encounters, the old marquess was introduced to Lady Albert's older cousin Dahlia. Not as dewy, but ten times more determined. Ruthlessly charming."

An oft-told tale by Mayfair standards. "Lady Dahlia stole a march on her cousin?"

"She stole a marquess. One week, we were hearing that discreet inquiries were being made by the marquess's solicitors regarding Lady Albert's settlements—she was plain Miss Cora MacAllister then, though the family was much respected—and the next, we're hearing that Lady Dahlia and the marquess had set a date to marry."

"By special license?" Hyperia asked, sipping delicately.

"Of course not. The banns were properly cried, but only just. And then the current Lord Dalhousie came squalling into the world six months later."

"Lord Albert was Cora's consolation prize?" I asked. "Not much of a consolation to see the titled fellow you were publicly fond of swanning about with your conniving cousin for the next thirty years." And Miss Morton had made it a point to inform me that her auntie had made a love match.

"The previous Lord Dalhousie did not enjoy thirty more years on earth," Lady Ophelia said. "He died of a sudden stomach ailment when his only son was about eighteen. Very sad."

"Very suspicious," I said. "Do you imply that poison is a woman's weapon, and Lady Albert waited all those years to have her revenge?"

"The first part of her revenge," Hyperia said. "The second part will be sending Dalhousie to his reward so Tam inherits. That would show a frightening degree of dedication to a deadly purpose, if Lady Albert is our culprit."

"The timing fits," I observed, wishing I could pull off my shoes, knowing Lady Ophelia would scold me for it. "As long as Dalhousie remains single, Tam stays next in line. The marquess's promise to marry this year upends that scheme."

"There's more," Lady Ophelia said, finishing her drink. "Lady Albert has a younger sister, Cressida. Cressy was rumored to have an understanding with an earl's heir, but was waiting for Cora to marry first. We honored the rule about sisters marrying in age order mostly in the breach back in the day, but some families did adhere to it. If Cora, despite being a plain miss, married a marquess, then Cressy might well expect to eventually marry an earl. Heiresses tend to come up in the world, after all."

"Cora married a courtesy lord," I said, wishing I had paper and pencil, "who was soon bumped out of line for the title by his darling little nephew. What became of Cressy?"

"Despite settlements that would make a banker pant and drool," Lady Ophelia said, "she married gentry. Wealthy, respected gentry that has been in Hampshire since before the Flood."

"But gentry nonetheless," Hyperia said, yawning behind her hand. "Dahlia's maneuvering destroyed the dreams of two women, at least, and possibly those of several men. I do hope she's happy with the results of her ambition."

"One son," I said. "No extant daughters, even. I suspect the marquess was neither a devoted nor an affectionate spouse." He might well have been furious to find himself entrapped, his intended fobbed off on his younger brother. Echoes of my own family history resonated unhappily with this tale, though the Caldicotts, let it be said, had made peace with the past before anybody had resorted to murder.

"Is it possible," Hyperia said slowly, "that Tam *is* the rightful heir? I mean, possible that Lady Dahlia got with child, not by the old marquess, but under circumstances where his lordship was the party most likely to be blamed? Then matters unfolded such that Lady Albert disports with the marquess, despite any vows spoken, Tam comes along, and here we are?"

"Convoluted but possible," Lady Ophelia said, staring hard at the middle distance. "It's also possible Dahlia disported with her spouse's brother, which might make Tam the heir with the closer blood tie to the previous marquess. I would have to consult a few contemporaries to see if *probable* might apply."

Exhausted was beginning to apply, to me at least. "Ladies, you are making a learned study of the matter of motive. Who is angry enough to not only wish Dalhousie dead, but also to twice make an attempt on his life? A worthy question, though I am concerned as well with means. Who knows Dalhousie loves his trifle enough to eat every bite even after a heavy meal? Who besides Tam and the marquess was on the Northbys' shoot?"

"But that's the point," Lady Ophelia said. "Cressida MacAllister married Hugo Northby, and they are both still extant. That shoot was mostly on their land, and they organized it."

"Yes," Hyperia said levelly, "a woman could aim a fowling piece with deadly intent, particularly a woman raised in the shires and married to a hounds and horses man. I could. Lady Ophelia could. I'm sure your sisters could as well, Jules."

"You left out Her Grace," I said. The typical double-barreled fowling piece was about four feet long and weighed perhaps ten pounds. My mother, who was no sylph, had doubtless managed its like easily. "Except a fowling piece is an unlikely murder weapon. They fire pellets and are smooth bore. Not intended to be all that accurate because of the scattering nature of the projectile."

But the target had not been birds on the wing, but rather, a sizable marquess...

"What are you thinking, Jules?" Hyperia asked, uncurling her legs and toeing her slippers on. "We cannot aid the direction of your thoughts if you keep them to yourself."

"If a shooter knows what he's about, he can wrap a piece of round shot in cloth—turn it into a patched ball, to use the infantry term—grease the whole business up, and fire that from even a fowling piece." The result would put a tidy hole in a hat.

Or a man.

"We have an abundance of suspects," Lady Ophelia said, rising and taking the two glasses to the sideboard. "Good work for a mere day. The means attempted so far don't rule any of them out. More to do, my dears, and we'll do it best if we're well rested."

"Lady Ophelia is right." Hyperia rose unassisted, collected her slippers with one hand and offered me the other. "Come along, Jules, and see me to my door."

Her door was right around the corner, as was mine. I pushed to my feet—fatigue was not my friend—and escorted Hyperia to her apartment. She bussed my cheek, pushed me across the corridor, and then disappeared into her parlor.

I waved at the closed door, let myself into my suite with a key, and had barely pulled off my shoes before I was asleep in the chair by the hearth, my evening finery still on my person. I dreamed of ladies dueling with flintlocks, lampshades on their heads, while Dalhousie and a giant mouse acted as seconds.

CHAPTER FIVE

"We do the shoot at the end of January," Hugo Northby said, striding along a frozen bridle path. "Been doin' it since the Flood. Tradition, hospitality, socializing in the winter doldrums. Bag enough to fill the village stewpots and so forth. Gives the ladies an excuse to wear their new habits before spring, catch up on all the gossip."

While the men stumbled half tipsy through the undergrowth and shot at hapless birds. "Do the women participate?"

"Some do." He paused at a cross-path though he wasn't remotely winded. "Cressy is a dead shot. Miss Susanna can give a good account of herself. Her ladyship—Lady Dal, not Lady Al—used to. Lady Albert tromps around with Cressy to be sociable but rarely takes a shot. Makes a racket, does Lady Al, no matter how many times you shush her. Cressy pities her, so we endure as best we can."

Northby was lean, gray, and vigorous. His looks had something in common with the land—rugged but comfortable. The acres left in woods were by his choice. The acres turned to pasture were by his design as well. The terrain was natural but not wild, and similarly, Northby was a domesticated man, but he'd never be a pet.

I found him instinctively trustworthy, which had probably been said of many a murderer and swindler. "What of beaters?" I asked. "Did you use them to drive the game into the guns?"

"A half dozen or so. I don't care for the practice myself. Hunting dogs are all well and good. They know what they're doing. A lot of undergardeners and village boys scaring up the grouse... One has to manage it carefully so the game is driven at an angle toward the guns, and the beaters know precisely where to stop and how to retreat and such. Otherwise..."

"Otherwise, a marquess gets a hole in his hat?"

Northby considered the diverging paths, which ran through his sodden, barren wood. Melting ice dripped from curving branches of bracken, and tree bark appeared black against the pervasive mist. The occasional rhododendron still bore shiny green foliage, as did the thorny holly bushes lurking beneath the oaks and maples, but spring was not yet even a whisper in the wood.

I would return to Dalhousie Manor with dampness penetrating every garment, but one could not say the morning was rainy.

Mizzling, more like, and yet, Northby had nearly leaped at an opportunity to show me where the marquess's mishap had occurred.

"I cannot understand how Dalhousie got into anybody's gun sights, my lord. He was on the end of the line of shooters—he prefers not to be in the center—and I was on the other end, where I could keep the entire company in sight. The game was on the wing from the eastern woods, and the shots were popping off as will happen. As is supposed to happen. When we finished that round, flasks out, dead birds being collected, Dalhousie came tramping along behind the firing line with his hat in his hands and thunder in his eyes."

Northby started off down the right-hand path. "I give him credit for not rousing the watch. He pulled me aside, shoved his hat at me, and said he'd be going in early. He accused nobody, and as I am the magistrate, I am the person to whom such complaints should have been made."

"Explain who was standing where, if you please."

"Just getting to that part, my lord." He stopped about twenty yards farther on.

The map in my head said Northby's manor and surrounding outbuildings were to our back. We'd walked along the crest of a shallow ridge, surrounded on both slopes by old forest that bordered a tamer home wood, open pastures, and on the eastern side, good old English heath. Pushing game from the heath-side into the guns first made sense, there likely being more fowl closer to the open spaces, waterways, and uncultivated ground.

"The shooters were along here," Northby said, using his arm to designate the firing line. "Ranged around the slight rise. Cressy and the ladies were in the middle, I was on this end, Dalhousie at the far end of the line near that big oak."

"Can you recall who else was shooting at that point?" The typical shoot was a tiresome affair, with much waiting around while game was driven forward, then some shooting, then more loitering about while the kill was collected, and yet still more chat and tipple while the beaters went around to a different patch of ground and so forth. A reliable folding stool and a full flask were usually of more use than an actual gun.

I found the whole process unsporting, even if the result was a winter feast in a hungry village. In medieval times, when the hunter's weapon had been a bow and arrow, the practice had some justification. Not so with modern weaponry ranged exclusively on the side of the hunter and heath disappearing apace beneath plows and behind enclosure walls.

"I looked down the guest list," Northby said. "Cressy and I noted who was shooting, and it was most of the party, because this was early in the outing. Some of the ladies present didn't bother taking a shot, of course, and some of the gents were too busy arguing over the race meets to bother. I bagged a few grouse and had the gamekeeper send them on to Vicar."

"Can you assure me that Tamerlane Dandridge was accounted for?"

Northby studied the distant oak, a towering, gnarled specimen that would have done Birnam forest and its weird sisters proud.

"Tam was on the line when I looked. Cressy says the same, and believe me, Mrs. Northby does not agree with me for the sake of my pride. She speaks her own mind."

Northby respected her for it, which suggested that perhaps Cressy hadn't been all that enamored of her lordly intended all those years ago.

"I'd like to meet Mrs. Northby."

"She was accounted for as well, my lord, if you don't mind some plain speaking. Lady Al along with her."

Very plain speaking. "Several parties who might wish Dalhousie ill are in a position to hire their mischief done, Northby. The guests we can account for are relieved of immediate guilt, but not of all suspicion."

Northby considered me down the length of an undainty nose. "It ain't Tam, I can tell you that. The mischief you refer to is attempted murder, my lord. He lacks the stomach for it. He's bone-lazy and not as smart as he thinks he is—Susanna Morton runs circles around him and makes him think he's in charge—but Tam is singularly deficient in ambition. He has adopted the role of tolerated and not-quite-poor relation, and it suits him."

Northby echoed Susanna's assessment of her cousin—simply not interested in the title—in gruffer terms.

"A rattlesnake can appear harmless when enjoying a nap in the sun." Why did I want so badly to blame Tamerlane?

Northby resumed walking, taking us back in the direction we'd come. "The boot is rather on the other foot, my lord. Tam is among those who would genuinely lament Dalhousie's death. They get on. They understand each other. Tam no more wants to be marquess than I want to wear one of Cressy's bonnets. They're very fetching—on her. On me... You take my point?"

"You're saying Dalhousie is not well-liked?"

Northby stopped where the paths intersected. "He's a charming devil, and mind you, we are family of a sort, not that he'd see it that way. I'm sure in his clubs, with his cronies in the Lords, bidding at Tatts, he's the soul of bonhomie. He's polite to all and remembers to grace the village fete and so forth. Rides in the first flight, sees to Vicar's salary. The locals have fond memories of him as a boy. He tends to all the usual obligations."

"But none of the warmth?" Arthur wasn't warm to appearances, but he cared deeply about his responsibilities and the people in his employ. Wages alone did not earn him the sort of loyalty Caldicott Hall enjoyed.

"Dalhousie was and is spoiled," Northby said, striking off in the direction of his tidy manor. "Only son, heir, strapping handsome lad. His mother spoiled him, his tutors, his governors... He's put an enclosure bill before Parliament, and by God, he will get what he wants in even that."

"How many acres?"

"Half the damned heath. The other part is mine, and I haven't the means or the mean-spiritedness to build a wall around it. Most of the village depends on the open land to run a few ewes and heifers. The other half scrape up a patch of potatoes or turn their pigs loose on the heath in autumn. They need those common acres to survive, my lord, and Dalhousie merely wants them for himself."

In the situation Northby described, the marquess owned the common land, while the *commoners* retained various rights in it. A commoner was often entitled to graze livestock on such ground, to gather up building or walling stones from its surface, traverse the land freely, harvest its peat or sod, and fish its waters. In most cases, the commoners could also collect gorse for under-thatching, dyes, or mattresses and, provided they moved their temporary gardens regularly, grow the occasional patch of potatoes or turnips without drawing any notice.

"Are you telling me the whole village has a motive to kill Dalhousie?" I asked as we tramped along.

"Tam wouldn't pursue enclosure. He sees the harm in it and,

more to the point, sees the effort and expense of building miles of wall just to make full coffers overflow. I've half a mind to oppose the whole project, but our MP is Dalhousie's man, and the courts take forever to waste a lot of money."

"You've let your views be known?" Northby certainly wasn't being coy with me.

"In no uncertain terms." Northby moved aside a heavy branch fallen across the path and resumed marching. "Dalhousie smiles at me patiently, says I must accustom myself to the notion of progress, and assures me he will employ many of the village lads as hod carriers when the wall goes up. Hod carriers. You cannot eat hod, my lord. You cannot spin wool from hod. You cannot make your roof snug and dry with it."

Vast disgust filled that recitation. A few years' work carrying bricks, mortar, and rocks for Dalhousie's masons would be no compensation for the destruction of a lifestyle that had served the local families for centuries.

Would *Northby* kill Dalhousie to stop the enclosure from happening? "If you took a notion to do Dalhousie a mortal injury, a local jury would acquit you, Northby, or at least see that you got transportation rather than the noose."

His smile was fierce and merry. "But then Cressy would be wroth with me, wouldn't she? You do not cross that woman lightly, my lord, and while she would hesitate to put a bullet through Dalhousie, she might take him on in court, or have me do it. She's biding her time and probably devising some whispering campaign that will attack Dalhousie's vanity."

I was getting winded, so brisk was Northby's pace. "I trust finding a bride will keep Dalhousie occupied for the immediate future?"

"Oh, probably, and pity the poor lady who speaks her vows with him. Spoiled, I tell you, and spoiled brats do not make good husbands, according to the leading authority on the matter."

His own dear Cressy, no doubt. I liked her sight unseen. "Do you still have Dalhousie's ruined hat?"

Northby's rambling slowed as we topped the rise that gave us a view of his lovely home. North Abbey was fashioned of mellow gray granite with plenty of white shutters and trim and a bright red double door. The day itself was dreary, while Northby's dwelling looked like the snug refuge he likely found it.

"I kept the hat," he said. "Possible evidence, and also... I like looking at it. Somebody was inches from doing us all a favor, and yes, my soul is eternally damned for uttering such sentiments. As if Dalhousie will go straight to heaven for putting Tom Davey's eleven children on the parish when that wretched wall goes up."

I wished desperately that Arthur had been available to consult. The whole business of an enclosure was politically fraught, extremely expensive, and complicated. Dalhousie's project might not have a prayer of parliamentary support, or it might be mere weeks from gaining final approval. Arthur would know, and he'd have the particulars.

"Half the heath is still a lot of open land," I said. "Dalhousie might be amenable to compromise."

"Why?" Northby stomped off across the cold, wet ground. "Why would a marquess compromise when he technically owns half the common ground as well as the land under every building in the village?"

"He might modify his enclosure ambitions to save his own life."

Northby kept walking. "The idea bears consideration, my lord. You raise a good point. I will have to take this up with Cressy to see what she thinks. I've a Baker rifle, you know. Damned thing can shoot the halo off an angel at six hundred yards, when I'm feeling accurate."

"I will pray your accuracy deserts you, should we ever disagree on a significant matter."

We made the rest of the journey to the house in silence, and when Northby showed me the hat—a fashionably tall exponent of the species—I came to two conclusions. First, the firearm involved had been a pistol, not a rifle. The bore of the shot was too small for a long-barreled weapon.

Pistols were easier to hide than fowling pieces, drat the luck.

Second, the marquess had been damned lucky. Even assuming he'd cocked his hat far to the side to facilitate aiming his own weapon, a bullet that passed through only his hat brim was traveling at a very odd angle. The ball had likely ricocheted off a rock or grazed a tree limb. Pistols had to be fired at close range to ensure any sort of accuracy, but this shot had gone astray, and thank heavens for that.

The marquess had missed an appointment with Saint Peter by mere inches.

"May I keep this?" I asked, examining the hat's interior for a label.

"I don't see the harm in letting you borrow it, but don't lose the evidence, my lord. Cressy says third time's the charm, and we've heard all about the poisoned trifle."

"I will take better care of this hat than your wife takes of you."

Northby laughed at that notion, and five minutes later, he bowed me genially on my way, hat in hand, so to speak. By the time I returned to Dalhousie Manor, I was cold, wet, tired, and also very, very perplexed.

Lunch was an improvement over previous meals. The marchioness, so unwelcoming to me at first, had subsided into chilly civility since Lady Ophelia's arrival. Lady Albert was her usual chattery self, and both Susanna and Tamerlane encouraged her.

Dalhousie presided over the meal with the occasional gentle tease in Susanna's direction or quasi-flirtation aimed at Hyperia or Godmama. They reciprocated in good humor, and somewhere between the chowder and the hot apple dumplings, I realized how socially backward I had become.

Once upon a time, I'd been able to hold my own in the gallant-

banter department. My grasp of chivalry had included small courte-
sies in addition to risking my neck in the line of duty. Now, I was like
the oaks wintering in Northby's woods. Still standing, but unadorned
by the vitality of social badinage, my capabilities as a cheerful
companion withering even while I held imposing social status.

Hyperia was looking at me as I roused myself from that brown
study. Her eyes held not concern, but rather, curiosity.

"Lord Julian has grown contemplative on us," Tamerlane
remarked. "I grant you, old Northby is not the most stimulating
company, but he's a good egg. He settles many a local squabble with a
private chat over the brandy. A soul with less wisdom would escalate
a lot of that nonsense into legal wrangling."

"We do like Hugo," Lady Albert added. "Cressy is more than
passing fond of him, and that speaks well for anybody."

"Uncle Hugo is sensible," Miss Morton observed, "and devoted to
Aunt Cressy. I don't suppose I might have another half serving of
dumpling?"

"I'll share with you," Dalhousie said from the end of the table.
"On a day like this, apple dumplings in cinnamon sauce are inspired.
My compliments to the kitchen."

Miss Morton would doubtless ensure that Cook heard the acco-
lade. Dalhousie made a silly game out of giving Miss Morton a much
larger share of the divided dumpling. She predictably demurred, then
refused the smaller half, while the whole table smiled patiently.

Tamerlane was deficient in ambition, according to the squire.

I was deficient in... nonsense. The same shortcoming had set me
apart at university, where wagering, inebriation, and composing dog-
Latin sonnets to barmaids had figured heavily on the curriculum. *My
puella loves another fella...*

I'd suffered more than one prank from my brother officers as well
—tent flaps sewn shut when I'd been napping, boots rendered filthy
on the morning of a dress inspection—but I'd never bothered to
retaliate.

I'd instead ridden into the countryside and attached myself to the nearest available troupe of bandits, considering the company an improvement. Bandits were seldom idle for long, and they took their banditry seriously enough that sewing a man's tent flaps closed didn't figure on their agendas.

"I applaud sense in anybody," I said, trying to find a toehold in the conversation, "but kindness and a bit of jollity matter too." I had just described my brother Arthur, whom I much admired. Harry had been short on sense sometimes, but gifted in terms of strategy and charm.

"I agree," Miss Morton said, saluting me with a spoonful of dumpling. "We need sweetness to go with the sense."

"And in you, dear cousin," the marquess said, "the two could not be more agreeably blended."

Gallant of him, to acknowledge what was more a courtesy connection than true cousinship.

"Hear, hear." Tam raised his wineglass. "A toast to dear Suze, the best of us."

Even the marchioness condescended to sip her wine, though she also was the first to leave the table.

"You have reached the pondering phase of the inquiry," Hyperia said, taking my arm as the gathering broke up. "Anything in particular on your mind?"

Too much, of course, and I would have gone cogitating on my way without Hyperia's patient prompting.

"Let's collect Godmama, and I'll report to both of my resident generals at once." We moved down the corridor past lit sconces. Even the middle of the day was that gloomy, and the meal had left me physically lethargic. Mentally, Hyperia had the right of it. I was ruminating, which was not always a productive use of my mind.

We stopped at the foot of the steps that led up to the guest wing, and Hyperia nodded in the direction of an alcove several yards farther on.

Dalhousie shared the space with Miss Morton, and they were in close conversation. I could not make out the words, but clearly,

Susanna was worried, and Dalhousie was offering reassurance. She wrapped her arms around him. He hugged her back, patted her shoulder, then kissed her forehead and resumed his soothing patter.

Hyperia and I retreated up the steps silently—thank heavens for thick carpets—and kept moving until we reached Lady Ophelia's sitting room.

"What do you suppose that was about?" Hyperia asked, going to the window.

"Susanna, along with half the shire apparently, is concerned that Tamerlane will be blamed for Dalhousie's difficulties, and their worries have some basis in fact." I poked up the fire and added another square of peat to the flames. Apologies to the maids, footmen, and Atticus for my presumption.

"Tam would benefit from Dalhousie's, demise" Hyperia said. "That solution seems much too easy."

I admired the picture she made by the window, self-contained, mentally absorbed. "And yet, sometimes the French are truly retreating because they've been given a sound drubbing, and defeat is their only real option."

"You think Tam did it?"

"I resent Tam," I said slowly. "He's the heir, and the expectation sits so lightly on him, he probably forgets it himself from time to time."

Hyperia offered me the slightest smile. "Ah, jealousy is a cruel master. Everything sits lightly with Mr. Tamerlane Dandridge. If not for his pretensions to scholarship, he might just float away."

"You don't care for him?" Must I sound so pleased?

"I don't trust him. I like Dalhousie, and I wish I didn't."

"Because?"

"You mustn't start muttering, Jules. My dealings with the marquess are very old, boring business."

My meal abruptly sat uneasily. "I promise not to mutter, curse, fume, or sigh. Well, I might curse quietly. Was he your lover?" Her handsome, wealthy, titled, robust, mentally sound, ambitious, self-confident...

Heaven defend me. I made myself wait for her reply.

Hyperia and I had agreed to a certain protocol when it came to the past. We would inquire directly of each other if a matter had stirred our curiosity. The answering party could put forth facts or keep particulars private, as they so chose. All very direct and abysmally sensible.

Hyperia had discreetly sampled the wares of enough willing partners that the questions thus far had been mine to ask and the answers hers to give. I did not see that pattern changing. I hadn't been a monk, precisely, but I'd dallied rarely and never let a liaison turn into an affair.

"We were not lovers," she said. "Not even close. You were off in Spain, I was getting comfortably ensconced on the shelf, and Dalhousie decided I'd make a suitable bodyguard for about a month one spring. We were assumed to be in the pre-courtship phase of the dance. I suspect he started the rumors in the clubs, or allowed them to start, but they didn't reach my ears until after his lordship had moved on to another spinster-in-waiting."

A gratifying hint of disgust laced her words. "You were tempted?"

She shook her head. "I was certain of his objectives from the start, and I think that's why he preferred to escort the noncombatants. A plain miss, no matter her fortune, does not set her cap for a marquess in his prime. Lord Westhaven and I embarked on the same sort of campaign, but as a pleasant, expressly agreed upon undertaking from the start."

"Whereas Dalhousie thought he could dazzle you for a few weeks while the matchmakers looked on in puzzlement and then leave you to sigh over fond memories?"

"Something like that. Five minutes in the ladies' retiring room would have brought him down a peg. He'd used the same tactic so often that his eventual abandonment of me should have been the subject of wagers. And mind you, he was careful. He never led me to think we were courting in truth, and I would have warned him off if he'd put even a toe over that line."

Because of me, I hoped.

I ought to have resented Dalhousie's bumbling. He'd used—that was the word, *used*—the kind offices of unattached women to guard his bachelorhood. The arrogance of it, the if-I-shut-my-eyes-nobody-can-see-me reasoning limned his almighty consequence in human fallibility.

Spoiled he might be, but brilliance eluded him just as it eluded most of us. "Are you still angry with him?"

"I try to be, but I can also see that his dilemma is real to him. He did not want to marry. Society and the marchioness want him to marry above all else. He's haunted and doomed and struggling against a fate he cannot control."

"So he controls the fates of others, manipulating them as a consolation for his own titled, wealthy, vigorous powerlessness. What a coil."

"What others?"

"He's put an enclosure bill before—"

Lady Ophelia did not tap on the door before joining us—why should she?—but Hyperia and I were hardly in a torrid embrace when she interrupted us. That said a lot about the way we cared for each other and pleased me in the face of Godmama's obvious disappointment.

"You two are supposed to be engaged," she snapped. "I find you in a perfectly private situation, behind a solidly closed door, and one of you is staring out the window, the other frowning at the carpet. Must I draw you pictures?"

"Jules was about to report on his morning expedition to North Abbey," Hyperia said, smiling blandly. "I'm interested in what he has to say."

"Hugo Northby is nobody's fool." Lady Ophelia settled herself into a wing chair before the fire like a queen assuming her throne.

"Cressida MacAllister was an heiress, just as her sister was. That's why Tamerlane and Susanna are reasonably well-fixed. Those women were well set up. I'm not sure Dahlia could say the same, but she got her title, so perhaps her attractions lay in another quarter. Julian, stop looming. You'll give me a crick in my swanlike neck."

I handed Hyperia onto the sofa and remained on my feet. "Dalhousie is intent on enclosing half the heath. The village hates him. Northby and his dear Cressida joke about the third time being a charm, and I doubt even the local vicar will offer more than platitudes in Dalhousie's favor."

"Enclosure." Lady Ophelia spat the word. "Plundering by any other name."

"Progress," Hyperia countered. "Papa enclosed about twenty acres at the family seat. Turned it into a market garden, and that produce makes a very pretty penny when sold in London. Healy is paying the commoners a sort of annual rent in exchange for their rights, or forgiving the rent they owe him. By agreement, he will never enclose another parcel of common land, and every person working the market garden must be a commoner."

"Legal plundering," Lady Ophelia retorted, "is the worst plundering of all."

Or plundering was in the eye of the rights holder, depending on the financial arrangements. "Who thought up that scheme?"

"My mother, apparently. She said we all cooperated at haying, planting, and harvest. Why not cooperate when it came to gardening?"

"You should suggest that scheme to Dalhousie." I leaned an elbow on the mantel. "You might save his life." I went on to explain that he'd been shot at from behind, probably at close range, and almost certainly using a pistol. "Luck alone has preserved his life."

"And you don't share the general disdain for him?" Hyperia asked.

I thought of Harry, so glib and socially agile, but also so frustratingly self-absorbed. Or Arthur, the kindest of men, laced up in the most uncompromising dignity. Me, preferring the company of serious bandits to that of officers needing a bit of a lark.

"He's doing the best he can," I said. "He's patient and kind with his family, and they would vex a saint. He holds his cousins in genuine affection. Northby says that Tam and Dalhousie get on, that they understand each other. We saw him reassuring Miss Morton at some length, and a less decent man would not have bothered. His mother is hardly a comfort and Lady Albert even worse. If Dalhousie is reluctant to bring a bride and children into this milieu, one cannot entirely blame him."

My words surprised even me. My sympathy for Dalhousie had to do with Northby *joking* about the marquess's chances of survival. I was also unable to look past the matchmakers turning Dalhousie's evasive maneuvers into grist for amused female gossip.

Dalhousie would hate to be laughed at. He'd hate to think that his funeral would be an occasion for jocular gloating.

"The man needs allies, and he hasn't the knack of making them," I said. "Just the opposite."

"Gets it from his mother," Lady Ophelia replied. "Though, in her, the gift is more for making enemies. I have a few more letters to write, by the by."

A subtle hint to take our leave. I assisted Hyperia to her feet and parted from her outside her door.

"You have allies, Jules," she said when I would have gone in search of the marquess. "We aren't the usual glittering exponents of St. James's clubs or Mayfair's ballrooms, but you can count on us."

What had prompted her to issue that reminder? "Thank you for that from the bottom of my heart. Dalhousie was a fool for letting you slip through his fingers. My very luckiest of days when he did. I shall tell him that." I kissed her cheek and departed, happy to note that I had both pleased and puzzled her.

CHAPTER SIX

"What do you make of this?" Dalhousie thrust a single sheet of foolscap at me.

I'd found him at his desk in his private study. At Caldicott Hall, I'd learned to my dismay that a conscientious peer was in the ordinary course held hostage by mountains of correspondence. I'd taken months to develop a system for dealing with Arthur's vast piles of mail, and only a battalion of well-trained clerks made my absence from the Hall possible at all.

A single sentence in tidy black script adorned the page: *Hampshire's woods might be dangerous, but for you, London's streets shall be deadly.*

"Do you recognize the handwriting?" I asked, holding the paper up to the window.

"No, I do not. Looks like schoolboy penmanship to me. Tidy, unembellished, no flourishes. And before you ask, Tam scrawls. I'd expect that sort of precision from Northby or any clerk. I employ at least a dozen."

The marquess remained seated at his desk, and adherence to strictest decorum dictated that I should not sit until he'd given me permission to do so. I took the wing chair opposite the desk anyhow. My presence at Dalhousie Manor hadn't deterred the marquess's detractor one bit, and that was both alarming and satisfying.

"Do you buy all of your paper from Reading Stationers?" The watermark was clear and simple, the paper pristine. New, in other words. Not a specimen that had been moldering in some traveling desk for years.

"For the London residence, I buy from a shop in Bloomsbury. For the Manor, Reading is cheaper and more convenient."

I considered the precise, legible script. "Does everybody in this shire patronize the Reading shops?"

Dalhousie lounged back behind a desk that was built in proportion to the marquess himself and doubtless six times his age. "What are you getting at?"

"Who wrote this note?" I set the page on the desk blotter. "Somebody dwelling at the Manor, or somebody who does not dwell at the Manor? If the Manor alone uses the Reading stationer, then we are more likely dealing with somebody who dwells at the Manor."

"Not definitely?"

I leaned forward and tapped the paper safe sitting on the corner of the desk. "Not definitely. How many callers have you had in the past two weeks? Any one of them could have ducked in here and helped themselves to some of that paper. Was the note mailed?"

Dalhousie shook his head. "Stashed in with the usual lot. We pick it up from the posting inn before noon each day. Anybody could have dropped this into the innkeeper's mailbag. By courtesy, he'll handle mail locally without bothering to see to the postage."

Well, no. Postage was usually paid by the receiving party, but Dalhousie, as a peer, had the privilege of franking mail with a simple signature in lieu of paying postage. He ought to reserve that privilege for official parliamentary mail, but most peers extended franking to any correspondence passing through their households.

The innkeeper's system wasn't courteous so much as it acknowledged the practical realities. Northby was doubtless charged for even local mail. Dalhousie could not be—reason number three hundred and seventeen for the locals to resent him.

"This note should reassure you," I said, wondering how soon I could show it to Hyperia. "You are instructed to avoid London. The implication is that you are safer in Hampshire."

Dalhousie rose, and because he was superior to me in rank, I should have been on my feet as well. I remained seated, and he didn't seem to mind.

"The reality is that I came close to death twice in Hampshire. I might well be easier to kill here at the Manor, and I can't very well court the proper heiresses if I'm cowering behind the hedges in Hampshire."

"Are you doomed to court an heiress?" Most peers were.

"Not doomed, but Mama favors unions that blend affection with practicality."

Meaning the previous marquess had not married money—had, in fact, stepped off that path after a willing and well-heeled bride had been found in Lady Albert, lest Dahlia create a gargantuan scandal. The present marquess was apparently solvent, but if he married a woman of modest settlements, his son might be forced to take a more mercenary path to the altar.

Assuming Dalhousie lived long enough to marry and have a son. "Have you made those lists I requested? Liaisons, social enemies, debtors?"

He opened a drawer and thrust another sheet of paper at me. "I had the same mistress in Town for eight years. Paid her off in the autumn, and we parted friends. She should be in a position to become one of the grander ladies in her home village, given the terms of parting."

A common enough arrangement. The paper bore fewer than a dozen names, half of them women.

"Explain the ladies to me."

Dalhousie found it necessary to straighten up the perfectly aligned decanters on his sideboard. "I can't call them broken hearts, but those are women who might have developed hopes in my direction. I played the gallant to each of them for a handful of weeks here or there, but only that. Most women grasp that an escort is merely a friendly companion for an outing, but a few... I took a while to learn which women were reconciled to the realities and which were more fanciful."

The fanciful ones skewed toward ladies, meaning the daughters of earls, marquesses, and dukes, or widows of peers. Dalhousie had also chosen women of noted beauty, and not a one qualified as an heiress. Hyperia's name was not on the list. Was that tact on the marquess's part, arrogance, or a simple oversight?

"Ladies," I said gently, "tend to expect marriage from lords, Dalhousie." I debated telling him that he'd become a laughingstock in the women's retiring room, but why add to the man's misery? "What about these men?"

Dalhousie's relief at the change of subject was sad to behold. "I dueled with Lord Stanbridge. He said I'd toyed with his sister's affections. I deloped, he missed, and that can leave a man resentful. He snubs me in public, not a cut direct, just moves away when I approach. Silly business. His sister is happily married to some earl. They have two sons."

And Dalhousie had a raging case of envy toward the earl over the sons if not the countess. Live and learn. "Clarence Tenneby?"

"I still hold vowels he signed two years ago. Made a thousand-pound bet on the St. Leger, and his horse barely made it around the course. He claims the colt was somehow interfered with, but has no proof. The beast hadn't been properly trained for flat racing. Plenty of speed, no stamina. A common error when an owner won't listen to his horse trainer."

We went on down the list, Dalhousie pacing while I made notes. The exercise was depressing—why did people cling so tenaciously to slights and hurts?—and enlightening. In each case, Dalhousie had tried to mend the breach. With the ladies, he'd made it a point to congratulate them on subsequent unions. With the men, he'd trotted out the put-the-past-behind-us speech and had thought it effective in about half the cases.

"This gets us nowhere," he said, resuming his seat. "Fallow ground. Somebody is trying to kill me, but most of that lot haven't motive anymore, or they bide in the shires at this time of year, or they lack the sort of bitterness that turns deadly."

I put down my pencil. "You have a lot of experience with deadly bitterness?"

Dalhousie offered me a lopsided smile. "Lady Albert is bitter, though she hides it behind fluttery airs and eccentric behavior. Cousin Cressy isn't bitter. She simply regards my mother as lower than vermin, and local opinion tacitly did not disagree with Cousin Cressy. My younger cousins are fortunately less interested in old feuds."

"Tell me about the enclosure project."

The smile winked out. "Northby's been nattering on, hasn't he? Let's go for a hack. I'll show you the land in question, and you can make up your own mind about my plans."

"You've just been given a written reminder that the out of doors is dangerous for you, Dalhousie. Northby told me himself that he counts a Baker rifle in his arsenal, and those are deadly over a very great distance."

"Now you imply that I should remove to London on the instant. Make up your mind, my lord."

What decided me was the rising wind. The morning had been still. As the afternoon had progressed, the clouds had broken up, and damp sunshine was now accompanied by a chilly breeze. Over any distance, that breeze would affect the trajectory of a bullet, even one dispatched by an expert marksman.

"I'll introduce you to my horse," I said. "Don't bother trying to buy him from me. Atlas saved my life more than once, and he will live to a contented old age in my care."

Dalhousie all but galloped for the stable, and that more than anything told me the marquess was feeling the strain of the day's developments. A stray shot in the woods and a passing stomach ailment had innocent explanations, however improbable.

A note delivered to a man's own home was a different order of threat and, in its way, more unsettling. I accompanied Dalhousie from the house, more than a little unsettled myself, and the day was far from over.

∾

"So this is the famous Atlas," Dalhousie said, visually caressing my horse's shoulders and chest. "He's in the betting books, you know."

"My *horse* is in the betting books? I haven't raced him, not since we mustered out."

A groom led Atlas to the stable yard, where another groom was already preparing Dalhousie's majestic bay gelding for our outing. The bay had pronounced withers, which put him an inch or so taller than Atlas, with the neck set on higher, which also resulted in a taller presence.

"Your Atlas isn't the subject of racing wagers." Dalhousie watched the undulating muscles of Atlas's quarters and the perfect motion of his gait at the walk. "One wager says he'll outlive you. Another says you'll provide for him specifically in your will."

I had, of course. Arthur was to inherit Atlas, just as I was to inherit Beowulf, Arthur's personal mount. Though why tell me this?

Not exactly kind, to bet that a man not yet thirty years old would be lucky to make it to forty.

Dalhousie ambled down the barn aisle, away from the grooms in the yard. His stable was the same blend of repose and industry that characterized any well-run equine establishment. Horses munched piles of hay or dozed contentedly while a lanky youth raked the dirt floor. Another junior groom had collected a half-dozen wooden buckets and was scrubbing them out at the pump in the yard.

The place smelled clean—for a stable. Of horses, manure, hay, grain, and straw rather than musty damp, rotten bedding, or mold.

This wing included a dozen loose-boxes, with what I presumed were mounts for Tam, Miss Morton, Lady Dalhousie, guests, possibly Lady Albert, and the grooms when ferrying messages about the neighborhood. A chubby pony likely pulled the market cart for the cook, and a couple of gray-muzzled pensioners suggested a sentimental attachment on Dalhousie's part to equine retirees.

A more compact version of the bay—still grand, though going swaybacked—whuffled as we approached.

"This was my father's last mount," Dalhousie said, "though Papa seldom took him far. Blenny expects his tithes." The marquess withdrew an apple quarter from the pocket of his riding jacket. "Proper name Blenheim. Papa won him from Marlborough in a card game. I poach on Blenny's behalf from Cook's larders almost every morning."

Marlborough, as in the Duke of, whose ancestral seat was Blenheim Palace. The horse crunched the apple into oblivion and would not be satisfied until he'd eaten all four quarters. Only then did he return to his pile of hay.

Dalhousie's gaze became wistful. "Papa told me to take good care of the beast in the same breath that he admonished me to be patient with my mother and cousins."

"And for the most part," I said, "the horse is better company."

Somebody was angry enough at Dalhousie to kill him, and yet, the more time I spent with the marquess, the more I could see him in a positive light. He was a decent sort, if inclined to think well of himself. Not exactly humble, but dutiful, generous with family, and pleasant company.

"Tell me about the enclosure," I said as we returned to weak sunshine and dripping eaves. The marquess had avoided the question previously, and that made me more determined to have an answer from him.

The groom at the water trough gave me a dirty look, collected all six buckets, and marched off.

"That's the usual reaction," Dalhousie said, running a hand down

Atlas's glossy neck. "Unfortunate and understandable. How is your steed over fences?"

"Honest to a fault, powerful. Unbelievable stamina, in part because he doesn't waste energy on nervous fidgets. He'll overjump rather than risk misjudging an obstacle. He takes care of his rider, but you must do your part, or he grows rambunctious."

"Rambunctious." Dalhousie sent me a sideways glance. "One barely recalls the concept. This horse looks as nimble as he is fit. I don't know when I've seen a more handsome specimen."

"Would you like to try his paces?" I was protective of Atlas generally. I also knew he was capable of looking out for himself. If Dalhousie and I switched mounts, even a marksman at closer range would have difficult discerning that the tall bay carried me instead of the marquess.

"I would like to ride him," Dalhousie said, thumping Atlas on the shoulder. "I most assuredly would. Very kind of you. You'll find my Dover is a perfect gentleman on a grand scale."

I was being pragmatic rather than kind. If Northby, for example, took a notion to attempt some target practice while Dalhousie and I trotted along the bridle paths, Altas could be counted on to get the marquess to safety.

We chatted about bloodlines and equine personalities as we rode from the stable yard at the walk. For all his height, I found that Dover had comfortable gaits. Atlas was on his best behavior with the marquess, and the marquess was acquitting himself well.

When we no longer had an audience, I circled back to the possible source of the enmity Dalhousie faced.

"The enclosure bill," the marquess said, on the same sort of sigh reserved for mischievous children and dotty aunts. "It's not even a bill yet, but I intend to see it pass. Our common land is mostly fen, my lord, and fen is worthless."

"Fen as in peat bogs and marshes?"

"Exactly. Sodden most of the year. Fit only for birds and briars.

Drain soil like that, and you have excellent farmland. Leave it wild, and it yields an occasional trapped ewe and a fine crop of bugs."

We debated as we rode the perimeter of the marshy ground. I pointed out that waterfowl made good eating, peat made for free heat, reeds were good thatch, and blackberry briars grew bountiful harvests of fruit. Dalhousie countered that land under cultivation could produce more than an occasional bucket of berries and that draining land and enclosing it would provide many jobs. With coin in hand, the commoner could buy all the berries and reeds and coal he pleased.

"You'll pay generous wages, then?" I asked, even knowing that most of the jobs Dalhousie offered would be temporary and unskilled.

"Good wages," he replied, frowning. "The village is not a charity to be supported by generosity alone. If I'm to install steam pumps instead of windmills—"

"Steam pumps! Great heavens, Dalhousie, you blaspheme."

He grinned. "That's what Northby says. He has no vision whatsoever. I've been to the true fenland east of Cambridge, my lord. The modest little project I envision here is nothing compared to what's been accomplished there. London would starve without all that acreage under cultivation."

"And you clearly judge London to be a public good." Arthur would enjoy this discussion, which balanced conserving the old with taking advantage of the new. The topic made me uncomfortable.

The Creator had fashioned man a little lower than the angels, according to man's account of his own rank, and the same hand had made the briars and birds. Who was the Marquess of Dalhousie to displace those residents from their God-given patch of earth?

The whole business left me with a sense of foreboding. "Talk to Miss West," I said as we turned onto a bridle path bordering some mature woods. "Her father managed an enclosure without too much resistance from the commoners. He developed a scheme whereby he essentially pays rent to them for obliterating their rights in the land. I don't believe drainage was involved, but the same principles apply."

Dalhousie patted Atlas's neck. "You and she are engaged to be married?"

"We are."

"Congratulations. She's a fine woman."

Did a hint of regret lace that observation? A hint of missed opportunity? More than a hint?

Well, it should, and yet, Hyperia would want me to be gracious. "Miss West speaks highly of you as well, my lord. Shall we let the horses stretch their legs?" Atlas was being a pattern card of equine deportment, and the marquess's bay was a polite soul as well, but both horses were keen to run.

So was I. Too much chat, too few answers.

"If you'd like to hop a stile or two, this path leads to the village, and then another will take us back to the Manor."

"Lead on, and please recall that Atlas can overjump if he's feeling mischievous." My boy was capable of great leaps that could heave an unsuspecting rider right up out of the saddle.

"Dover doesn't have to overjump, as tall as he is." Dalhousie tugged down his hat brim, touched a heel to Atlas's side, and cantered off.

I held Dover back enough to ensure we followed at a safe distance and prepared to enjoy the first decent riding I'd had in days. The bay tended to sprawl onto his forehand, but he was fit and took direction willingly enough. We were soon organized into a canter that covered ground like an equine version of the seven-league boots.

Up ahead, Dalhousie yelled, "Ware, stile!" just as Atlas gathered himself for a mighty bound over a weathered stile. His landing was foot perfect, and away he went, truly enjoying himself.

Dover knew the path well and came straight at the stile in excellent form. As he, too, soared over the obstacle, I heard a muted sound like a book smacking into a pillow. The horse landed well, then swerved hard to the right. The popping sound had become an erratic jingling, and my seat confirmed what my ears were telling me.

The girth had sprung loose on the offside, the double buckles dangling around Dover's hooves.

"Dover, halt," I said, hauling back stoutly on the reins and minding my balance as if my life depended on it. "For the love of God, boy, *stand*."

We came to an awkward, sidling stop, every iota of my equestrian ability challenged by the process. The horse was unhappy to be parted from his trail mate, while the rider was considerably unnerved.

I hopped to the ground as Atlas's hoofbeats faded to silence. "If you were not so well trained," I muttered, patting Dover's neck. "If I had not lived in the saddle for several years in Spain..." Dover and I were both breathing heavily, the horse still discontent to be denied his gallop home.

I unbuckled the nearside of the girth, draped it over the saddle, studied the saddle in some detail, and led the horse back to the bridle path along the trees. I could make my way to the Manor through the woods, but I had no guarantee that I'd find gates to lead Dover through along that path. Stiles did the work of gates, for two-legged traffic anyway, and I was unwilling to leave the saddle in the woods and do the riding bareback.

Dalhousie eventually found us when we were within a quarter mile of the lane leading to the stable.

"Atlas is absolutely splendid. We were a good mile on before I realized you'd gone missing. Did you take a tumble?"

"Nearly, but Dover's good manners got us through what could have been a bad moment. The girth came undone."

Dalhousie swung down. "Undone? The buckles somehow came *undone*? That makes no sense. Do you mean the girth wasn't tight enough and the saddle slipped to the side? I suppose that can happen, but you checked the snugness before you mounted."

The marquess had completed his hearty gallop, Atlas had made the experience delightful, and his lordship's mind was free of worries. I hesitated to end his respite from anxiety, but the obvious had to be stated.

"Dalhousie, Dover is your personal mount. Who else rides him?"

The marquess walked along beside me, Atlas and Dover following us on loose reins. "Nobody else rides him. There's been no need. I'm here. I hack out regularly. The grooms could, I suppose, and in the past, they have if I'm from home for any length of time, but in this season of the year... oh rubbishing hell."

Too rubbishing right. "The damage was done to the saddle," I said. "The girth itself is fine, the buckles all securely stitched to the leather. The billets the buckles fasten to on the saddle all look fine as well, but high up under the skirt, near the tree, somebody worked at the stitching."

"Somebody wanted me dead. Again."

Northby's profane humor—*third time's the charm*—came to mind. Had he known a third attempt was in the offing? Had Northby arranged it?

"Somebody wanted you to take a fall, in any case." From a very tall horse. "The billets held as long as we were toddling around, but as soon as Dover began to breathe deeply and move more quickly, the stitching was stressed enough to give. This little mishap tells us your detractor is a knowledgeable equestrian."

"How do you figure that? Anybody can take a knife to leather stitching."

A few years spent in the intermittent company of cavalry officers —to a man, experts on all matters equine—had taught me a thing or two.

"What was wanted was the right degree of stress on the stitching," I said. "A horse's lungs are huge, capable of holding roughly ten times the amount of air a man's lungs can hold. When working hard —galloping over a distance, for example—the horse can take in as much as ten times the amount of air he'll use at rest. He can also breathe much faster during exertion than we can if we take a notion to sprint. Somebody had to know how forcefully Dover's barrel would expand and contract, how hard and how often, when he was given his head and put to the jumps."

"He likes to jump," Dalhousie murmured. "He's good at it, being so tall. How the hell did you stay on?"

"Blind luck." For years in Spain, I'd all but lived in the saddle. Those years had turned a competent equestrian into a horseman. I was nowhere near as fit as I'd been then, but the reflexes remained, thank the heavenly powers. "His high withers helped. Hard to get a saddle off conformation like his if the rider stays centered."

"Bloody hell." Dalhousie stopped as we came within sight of the stable. "The grooms might well be scheming to end my life. I've known those men since I bounced around on my first pony. I knew their fathers and uncles. The head lad scolds me if I neglect to poach Blenny's apple of a morning. They hate the enclosure idea, but their jobs aren't jeopardized by it. I don't know what to say."

He scrubbed a hand over his face. The next part was too hard to put into words: Dalhousie also *did not know what to do*. For a man of Dalhousie's standing, that admission was too difficult to even think.

"Mishaps occur." I walked on, Dover in step with me. "We look after saddles and bridles because we know mishaps occur, despite our every effort to prevent them. No harm done."

Dalhousie got moving and swung his gaze from the handsome stable to me. "No harm done? You could have been killed."

"Not likely. The ground is soft with incessant dampness, the bridle paths free of rocks and boulders. If this is the part where you nobly send me home in an effort to keep the noncombatants safe, might I remind you that I wore a uniform for years and was often at large behind enemy lines while wearing civilian attire, a far more dangerous state of affairs for a British officer. The French did get hold of me. The torments of the damned did befall me. Whatever my shortcomings, and they are legion, I am hard to kill. A little tumble from the saddle would not have signified."

I half expected the hand of God to come down from the winter sky and spank my lordly bum for those lofty pronouncements, but I also spoke the truth. Spend enough hours on enough horses, particularly traveling at speed over rough terrain, and one made an unscheduled departure from the saddle sooner or later.

Usually without lasting ill effects. Usually.

"A mishap," Dalhousie muttered, trudging onward. "Very well, a mishap. A shooting accident, a stomach ailment, a nasty note, and now a mishap. At this rate, I should qualify for honorary cat status, assuming I survive the next few months. I will name my firstborn son Leo." He babbled on, half to himself, while I considered the day's events.

Dalhousie's enemy knew horses, had access to firearms, had access to the very food in Dalhousie's dining room—unless the stomach ailment had truly been a stomach ailment—and knew that Dover was an avid jumper.

That all sounded like Tam Dandridge to me, but then, perhaps it was supposed to.

I had handed Dover off to the groom and was accompanying Dalhousie back to the Manor when his lordship put another question to me.

"Do I make plans to remove to deadly London, my lord, or prepare for more dangerous mishaps here at home?"

"That is up to you. We simply take different precautions depending on where you bide."

He looked puzzled, so I spelled it out for him. "Who knows your personal mount and knows that he's a keen jumper? Who knows your favorite dessert? Who knows *which saddle* goes on your personal mount, of the dozen or so I saw in the stable? Who can tell which shooter you are from the back, out of a line of gentry all similarly attired and similarly engaged?"

Even applying himself to the riddle, the marquess still needed a moment to admit where the evidence led. "It's not Northby, is it? Somebody in my family wishes me dead."

"Not quite. Somebody in your *household* wishes you dead. Could be the head footman, the gardener, or Lady Albert. The point is, your enemy might well be among those who will remove to London with you."

We made the rest of the journey to the Manor in silence, and when I had changed out of riding attire, I crossed directly to Hyperia's apartment and rapped stoutly on her door.

CHAPTER SEVEN

"You came off of *Dover*?" Hyperia said, frowning at me. "He's the tallest of the riding stock. Named for the towering cliffs. It's a long way down from his back."

I'd put Dover at about the same weight as Atlas, but because Dover had mountainous withers, he seemed the larger horse. Then too, his posture was upright, and he wasn't as short-coupled as Atlas.

"I did not quite come off."

"But it was a near thing. I don't like this." Hyperia and Lady Ophelia exchanged a glance that spoke of conversations I'd not been privy to. We enjoyed the seclusion of Hyperia's sitting room, a less formal space than Lady Ophelia had been assigned. The floral-patterned rug was a trifle faded, the curtains plain burgundy velvet. Not as many pillows on the sofa, and the hassock had been beaten into slouching comfortableness by the passage of time and a number of tired feet.

Lady Ophelia moved stitches about on her knitting needles. Her yarn was a periwinkle blue that went with her eyes. Hyperia's embroidery sat neglected on the mantel, her sewing box adjacent to the hassock.

Her ladyship resumed knitting. "I've known more than one skilled rider who came to grief in the course of a routine hack, young man. Perhaps you should consider retreat or hiring Dalhousie some bodyguards."

Dalhousie had been on the point of suggesting I quit the premises. I'd felt that wrongheaded notion germinating in the vicinity of his pride and hoped I'd ripped it out root and branch.

I lounged into the comfort of the wing chair angled to catch the heat from the hearth. "That feeling you have now, my lady, of unease, of anxiety, of a malevolent intent stalking unseen behind the hedges, that's what Dalhousie has been living with for weeks. He doesn't feel safe, and with good reason."

"And thus you cannot abandon him," Hyperia said. "*We* cannot abandon him." Her tone invited Godmama to challenge that conclusion. Godmama started a new row and held her peace.

"How is it you've made Dover's acquaintance?" I asked.

"Tam and Miss Morton gave me a tour. Miss Morton claims that if she doesn't get Tam out of doors regularly, he will spend days reading in the library or scribbling letters to other classical scholars. He's working on some sort of rebuttal for Mr. Gibbon's explanation for the fall of Rome."

The History of the Decline and Fall of the Roman Empire had made for interesting reading. "Gibbon blamed Christianity, if I recall correctly. He claimed the church sucked up enormous resources that had been available to the state previously and turned the aristocracy into spineless monks and nuns where before they'd been devoted citizens of Rome."

"What of the Huns and Goths and Scythians?" Lady Ophelia muttered. "Mustn't forget them."

"Odoacer was a Christian," Hyperia countered, "if you're referring to the events of 476 AD. He was a German chieftain and a Christian."

Which rather put Gibbon's theory on the hind foot. "What is Tamerlane's brilliant addition to this riveting topic?"

"He claims that Rome disintegrated in part because emperors had too much latitude in the matter of succession. If an emperor had no heir of the body, he simply adopted some promising young sycophant, or his sister's latest husband, or a general who claimed to be loyal. Tam thinks the whole business would have been stabilized by stricter rules of inheritance. Less infighting, more preparing the heir for the job of ruling."

"Said the man whom strict rules have currently put in line for a marquessate." The same strict rules resulted in about one out of three peerages going extinct in the first three generations and the title and its holdings reverting right back to the crown. That—interestingly—did keep the crown in better fettle than if that same wealth had trickled away into the hands of the deceased peer's family, or—echoes of the Black Death whispered—into the hands of a rapacious church.

"What does any of this ancient history have to do with Julian nearly bashing his head in?" Lady Ophelia asked, needles clicking steadily.

"I was nowhere near bashing my head in," I said. "I didn't even come off. One can ride without a girth securing the saddle to the horse's back. A lot of military academies use that very exercise to teach balance and control." Also how to safely fall. "It's a matter of keeping your head and attending to matters in the proper sequence."

Hyperia looked inordinately interested. "You've ridden without a girth?"

"Practiced it a few times. One very quickly learns that the first order of business if in danger of falling is to get both feet out of the stirrups. The second priority is to protect your head." The third was to pray for soft ground and a horse nimble enough to avoid stepping on the fallen rider. "Why are you both looking at me as if I've announced a notion to take up the bagpipes?"

"Please, not the bagpipes," Lady Ophelia said, coming to the end of her row. "Hyperia and I have noticed another sequence of activities that might interest you."

I waved a hand amid more exchanged glances. The decision was tacitly made that Hyperia would do the enlightening.

"At meals, Jules, when it comes to desserts, the footman places trays of individual servings on the sideboard and then hands them around one by one."

I recalled this little ritual. The desserts were brought in with something of a flourish, the first serving set before Lady Dalhousie, the second before the ranking lady guest, down the honor roll until the host was served... last.

"Dalhousie gets the final serving," I said slowly. "Anybody who had observed a few dinners at the Manor might have picked up on that." Though I had not.

"There's more to it," Lady Ophelia said. "In a household of this caliber, the cook will be aware that Lady Dalhousie avoids salt, that Tamerlane is partial to ginger, while Miss Morton dislikes it, and so forth. For a family meal, the serving order would be both simple and predictable. The footman can look at a tray of nearly identical compotes, for example, and be sure to give Lady Dalhousie the one without brandy in the sauce and Tamerlane the one with extra honey."

"All the footman has to do," Hyperia said, "is serve in the same order every time, and Cook places the individual dishes on the tray in accordance with that order."

"Do all kitchens use such a system?"

"Or something like it," Hyperia replied. "A cook tires of hearing that her soup was too salty for this one, not salty enough for the other. She can only make one pot of soup at a time, so individualizing servings makes for fewer critics."

"Many footmen cannot read," Lady Ophelia added. "They thus enjoy the prodigious memories of the unlettered. Seating arrangements are fairly standard, and standardizing the arrangements of servings on a tray would make sense to any fellow who'd watched a few formal meals."

This all amounted to more evidence that Dalhousie sheltered a traitor within the Manor itself.

"Henceforth," I said, "we will direct the cook to place two extra servings on every tray and tell no one of the change."

"I can do that," Lady Ophelia said. "Harmless, eccentric old thing that I am, though anybody with brains enough to run a marquess's kitchen will grasp the sense in your suggestion, Julian. Dalhousie should have thought of it himself."

"Dalhousie has a lot on his mind, Godmama. Recall, too, that he's anticipating bringing a bride home in a very few months." Assuming he lived to speak his vows.

"What if people want seconds?" Hyperia asked, and we spent a few moments puzzling over how to prevent the most-easily-poisoned servings from being consumed in the future. Vigilance seemed to be the only real course open to us, assuming Dalhousie's foe would resort to the same tactic twice.

"If somebody asks for seconds," Lady Ophelia mused, "and only one serving remains on the tray, is that person exonerated from attempting to poison the marquess?"

"No," I said, having already parsed this puzzle. "That person might well be the only one at the table who knows for a certainty that the last serving is safe to consume on that occasion. That said, I doubt our enemy will attempt poison again."

"It nearly worked the first time," Hyperia said. "Miss Morton told me the marquess was deathly ill, though he recovered fairly quickly. She's the head nurse in addition to her other duties."

"A thankless task," Lady Ophelia observed, "and often unpleasant. If she married a man appropriate to her station, she would be spared such drudgery. Miss Morton has the blunt to attract respectable offers. She's pretty enough, sensible, not that old... Some women simply don't feel the need, though."

I thought back to Miss Morton's comments about marriage. "She claims to honor the institution, but said she'd rather drudge for the devils she knows."

"Marriage for her should not be drudgery," Hyperia said. "Lady Ophelia is right, though. According to Tam, both he and Susanna are comfortably fixed. Their respective mothers' settlements were set up to ensure that all children of the union were well provided for."

"And all turned out to be a mere one apiece," Godmama observed, finishing another row. "Why is that the way when a substantial fortune is involved, but royal dukes and princesses burden the nation's paltry exchequer by the dozen?"

I was glad to know that Tam and Miss Morton were financially secure. They had options, in other words, and chose to stay at the Manor with their cousin, which spoke well for Dalhousie and the family as a whole.

"I'm off to inspect the pantries," Lady Ophelia said, tucking her knitting into a workbasket more ornate than Hyperia's simple quilted box. "I'd best inspect the cellars while I'm being eccentric. They often tell an interesting tale."

I rose and offered her a hand. "You like impersonating an eccentric."

"I do. One has so many examples of the genuine article in polite society. That Dalhousie hesitates to choose a bride from among them is understandable."

She wafted off and left me behind a closed door with dear Perry. I took the place beside my intended on the sofa.

"What is it?" she asked, lacing her arm through mine. "You have turned up positively brooding, Jules, and that worries me."

"Nothing in particular. I would simply rather sit beside you." Would rather be touching her. "I missed that bit about the serving order. Seems obvious when you point it out."

"Obvious in hindsight. Something troubles you, Jules."

I explained about the note Dalhousie had received, written on the most common sort of paper in the shire, in a hand without distinguishing features, and delivered among a heap of correspondence with no sign of a sending address.

"Was the page clean?" Hyperia asked.

"Very."

"Then the note was likely sent after your arrival, Jules. Mail doesn't sit about for long in a mailbag or behind the bar of a posting inn and remain pristine."

"In the alternative, the note was written here at the Manor and slipped into the morning stack by somebody who dwells here. You're right, though. That note was definitely delivered after I arrived and probably written after I arrived as well. Our opponent is determined."

Hyperia took my hand. "Our opponent is continuing his campaign even after Dalhousie has summoned reinforcements. That suggests recklessness, Jules."

We fell silent, both no doubt musing on the mixed blessing of having a desperate and determined foe. On the one hand, such a person was more likely to make a revealing error. On the other, they would not stop until they succeeded, a troubling thought indeed.

Nothing less than an innocent life in danger would have motivated me to take on the task I faced, but Dalhousie was clearly in peril. With that thought in mind, I rapped on the door of the marchioness's sitting room.

"Enter."

I found her ladyship working at her embroidery, the pattern stretched on her hoop a tidy repetition of pink rosebuds on pristine pink linen. The project appeared to be a pillowcase and of a piece with the soft hues and understated grace of the sitting room as a whole.

Where would the nation be without the labor of the ladies with their needles? Naked and unembellished with flowers, at least.

Her ladyship's wallpaper might once have been a commanding Prussian blue, but had faded to the color of summer skies. Her mahogany escritoire was a tribute to delicate inlays and piecrust edging set atop ball-and-claw feet on elegantly carved legs.

Lace curtains, even at this chilly time of year, admitted what sunlight was available. Touches of brightness came from candelabra, gilt picture frames, and a cheval mirror set opposite the windows. The floor was pale oak parquet polished to a gleaming shine, and the whole room bore the soothing fragrance of orange blossoms.

The marchioness glanced up from her perch on a tufted pink sofa and went right back to her needlework. "Is my lord lost?"

I bowed. "I am where I intended to be in the company I sought to find here. Might I sit?"

"Why? I have nothing to say to you. You are held in contempt by most of Society, and what Dalhousie expects you to do here, I cannot imagine."

When we had no audience, she was consistent in her antipathy. "What I hope to do is prevent your son from being murdered." I wandered about the room, indulging the habit of reconnaissance.

The music box on the mantel played the lilting opening theme to Mozart's "Ave Verum Corpus." The violin on the wall was ever so slightly dusty. A bouquet of daffodils on the reading table by the window blended their unique fragrance with the warmer citrus scent pervading the air.

The fire in the grate was wood, to my surprise, an extravagance that also kept the stink and nuisance of coal dust from befouling the room.

No newspapers, pamphlets, fashion magazines, or books cluttered any surface, and the escritoire was similarly ruthlessly organized. Three quill pens in the stand were set at exact angles from one another, ink bottles lined up as neatly as toy soldiers. The same tidiness was evident on the sideboard, where three decanters sparkled in the precise middle of the surface, brass trays flanking them in exact symmetry.

"When you finish snooping, my lord, you may leave."

"You aren't in any hurry to throw me out," I said, taking the wing chair closest to the sofa. "You like this room and want me to appreciate it." I liked it too. The space was peaceful, pretty, and pleasing to the nose. The ample cushions were pleasing to the body, and the light and fragrance soothed the heart.

"I should like this room," her ladyship said. "I directed its appointments. I do not like you, though I assure you my antipathy is impersonal. One must be discerning about the company one keeps." She drew her needle through the fabric in a relaxed rhythm, finishing one prosaic little bloom and moving on to the next.

"You need not hide from Lady Ophelia," I said. "She lost two children earlier in life. She will not strike at you when you have reason to fear for your only son's life. She joined me at the Manor because Miss West could not travel out from Town without a chaperone."

The needle hesitated, then resumed its work. "Her ladyship will not strike at me now, perhaps, but one avoids Ophelia Oliphant if one wants the past to remain out of sight."

"Godmama has a prodigious memory." A tremendous asset when attempting to unravel polite society's arcane riddles. "She is not your enemy."

"Perhaps I am hers."

"Are you your son's enemy?" I rose and tugged the bell-pull twice. "Somebody wants him dead, and I don't see you taking any steps to preserve his life."

She was accounted a good shot "back in the day" by Squire Northby. She certainly had command of the serving habits in the dining room and would know her son's preference for sweets. She was a needlewoman and probably a seamstress, meaning she could have worked at the stitching holding the girth billets to Dover's saddle.

Means and opportunity were hers to command, though what her motive might be—other than discrediting Tam—eluded me. Though discrediting Tam mattered to her.

The needle paused again, and this time, the marchioness lowered the embroidery hoop to her lap. "Why on earth would I threaten my only son's life?"

"*Appear* to threaten him." I resumed my seat. "You could scare the Dandridge cousins off to some other venue with repeated attacks on Dalhousie—or the appearance thereof. Tam is the logical suspect if Dalhousie comes to harm, and the best way for him to avoid suspicion is to quit the scene and remain out of pocket until the culprit has been caught."

"Tamerlane is too lazy." She stared hard at the painting over the mantel, Dalhousie Manor in high summer. All sunshine and potted geraniums, stately oaks in full leaf, and deer grazing at the edges of the park. "Tam is occasionally decorative and nobody's fool. Witness, his step-cousin dotes on him as if he were three years old. Tam has merely to sigh, and he finds a tea tray has arrived without him lifting so much as a manly finger."

His step-cousin, not Miss Morton or Susanna, and certainly not Suze. A theory I'd tossed onto the table mostly to annoy the marchioness into conversation took on new possibilities. Perhaps her ladyship wanted Miss Morton, usurper of the role of chatelaine, off the premises? Wither Tam goest, Susanna would likely follow.

"If you do not suspect Tam, then who is our culprit?" I rose at a tap on the door and took the tray from a startled footman. I closed the door with my foot and set the tray before her ladyship. "I can pour out if you're still enjoying your tantrum."

"Sit down, my lord, and stop baiting me."

She was inviting me to sit. I took that as progress and forbade myself to gloat. "I prefer mine plain, unless you're serving jasmine gunpowder, in which case a dollop of honey suits."

Her ladyship took the lid off the pot and sniffed delicately. "China black. We'll let it steep."

I helped myself to a petit four draped in cinnamon icing. "Who wants Dalhousie dead?"

"You were accusing me a moment ago. Most insulting."

"I was positing a hypothetical. If you were bent on murder, you would not bungle, much less three times in succession, and I agree that you lack a motive to kill your son. Just the opposite. If he dies without an heir of the body, you lose your place in Society to Lady Albert. I cannot envision you embracing that change enthusiastically."

"Then why aren't you questioning Lady Albert?" She peered into the teapot again, though she'd clearly enjoyed firing off that broadside.

"I'm saving that delight for later in the day, but be assured that her ladyship will be interrogated, as will Cressida Northby, the innkeeper in charge of the post, the grooms, and Tamerlane. He was in the stable earlier today and had plenty of time to tamper with Dover's saddle."

"*Miss West* was in the stable earlier today, and tampering with a saddle isn't so easy, young man. The place is awash in grooms and stable boys. The home farm lads come and go from the stable. Even the footmen bring messages there to order the carriage and so forth. Sawing away at stitching takes time, even with a sharp knife."

This little lecture told me three things. First, her ladyship had a keen appreciation for the stable as a place with little privacy. She'd observed the foot traffic closely, though for what purpose? Second, she was already apprised of the smallest details of the day's mischief. Third, she was mentally absorbed with the threats to her son's life, and yet, she had not named a suspect when asked.

What was she hiding? As she passed me a cup of steaming tea and put two petits fours on a serving plate, I inventoried what I knew of her thus far.

She was organized to a fault—as most successful criminals tended to be—and indulged herself regarding the comforts of her station. She had no friends. She might intimidate servants fearing to get the sack, but she had no true loyalty from anybody save her son.

"I ask myself," I said as her ladyship poured her own cup of tea, "why now? Why come after Dalhousie at this moment rather than when he was larking around London in the spring, or overseeing harvest in autumn? Why not plague him when he was in Paris over the winter and far from familiar surrounds? Why is he in danger at this moment?"

She stirred honey into her cup. "And what answer does the oracular Lord Julian provide?"

"Somebody is trying to keep his lordship from going to Town, but is he to bide in the country to make a murderer's job easier, or were the earlier attacks intended to scare him off of a trip to London?" That question had been vexing me since Dalhousie had shown me the threatening note.

Her ladyship looked up from her tea cup, a hint of real worry lurking in her gaze. "Keep him from going to Town? He must go to Town. What are you talking about?"

Her dismay appeared genuine, but then, her ladyship excelled at displays of dismay. I had made the tactical decision to share news of the note with her mostly to spare Dalhousie from the same chore. Also because I wanted to gauge her reaction for myself.

"His lordship received a note on plain paper, no postage marks, clerically impersonal penmanship: 'Hampshire's woods might be dangerous, but for you, London's streets shall be deadly.' He received it just before we went riding. He offered to show me the parcel of land he'd like to enclose, and I agreed to the outing."

She set down her tea cup silently. "He receives a threat like that, and you parade him around the countryside for any fool to use for target practice? If that is your idea of protecting another man's life, the French must have been delighted to have you in a British uniform."

Had she been male, that remark should have seen her called out. She was not a man. She was a mother sorely vexed and trying to hide her upset from even herself.

"Over any distance, my lady, the day's fresh breeze would have foiled even an expert marksman. Then too, I'd rather have Dalhousie trotting about with my escort than alone, and at the last minute, I had us switch horses, which should have made his lordship safer still."

While putting me in danger, a detail I chose not to mention.

"The marquess must go to London," her ladyship said. "He must. If I could summon all the heiresses on offer here for his inspection, I would. Dalhousie would never put innocent lives in danger like that, but, my lord, he must marry and soon."

One hoped Dalhousie would not conduct his courting like a horse auction. "He has been warned to stay home, though, of course, that could be for the murderer's convenience." If we *were* dealing with a murderer. I was beginning to have my doubts. "Why can't he take a bride next year?"

She took up her embroidery. "He has had nearly fifteen years to kick up his heels, indulge his manly humors, and disappoint the matchmakers. Dandridge men do not enjoy long lives, my lord. They seldom live to see fifty, and if Dalhousie were to become a father today, he'd be unlikely to live long enough to see his son's majority. I will not tolerate... That is, a boy needs his father, especially a boy upon whom a great deal of responsibility will rest."

A great deal of responsibility—and wealth.

"You dread the estate falling into the hands of solicitors, guardians, and trustees." She herself could live to see that grim day. She'd be north of her three score and ten before her grandson came of age, and she'd have little ability to legally safeguard the family's interests. "Surely, Tam would prevent the worst disasters."

"Tam is a Dandridge too, my lord. Who is to say that he won't also succumb to a stomach ailment, as my husband did? A peer yet in his minority is a goose to be plucked, and Dalhousie has finally promised to do his duty. Not a day too soon, for me. If I could deposit him in wedding finery on the steps of St. George's tomorrow, I'd do it."

I wanted to dismiss her fears as fanciful, but she was expressing concerns that ought to press upon Dalhousie sorely.

Arthur and I were both abundantly aware that the Waltham dukedom could revert to the crown on our collective watch. Arthur had moved the family wealth where royal paws could not touch it, but that still left the Hall itself and a significant trove of funds, goods, and revenue for plundering.

Lady Dalhousie was trying to protect her husband's legacy, and what widow could be faulted for that?

"Given recent developments," I said slowly, "would you advise your son to bide here or journey to London?"

She stabbed the needle through the linen. "I'd advise that man to marry, my lord. To marry by special license and secure the succession with all due speed. The sooner he marries and has a child, the sooner killing him will do nothing to further Lady Albert's schemes. Even a daughter would safeguard the earldom—it's Scottish—but better still if Dalhousie has a son."

Better a Scottish earldom than a family who'd lost their title altogether.

I snatched up the two petits fours I hadn't yet eaten and rose. "On that dire note, I am off to see Lady Albert. I have left to Dalhousie the decision to bide here or travel to Town. I conclude that his enemy is either a family member or a member of the household. Changing venues might result in no increase in his lordship's safety. I'm inclined to think the issue is the enclosure, though, and not Lady Albert's old grudges."

"You don't know her, my lord. She strikes you as a bit of aging fluff, going from harebrained to dotty, but she is more calculating than you can possibly believe. The late marquess had well and truly decided not to marry her—he didn't need her funds, and she was too silly much of the time. For thirty-five years, Lady Albert has ensured that polite society's hostesses are as rude to me as they dare to be, and that is not the work of a frivolous woman."

"She wants Tam to inherit?"

"She is desperate for Tam to inherit. Depend upon that, if you believe nothing else I've said."

I took my leave of the marchioness, the interview having given me much to think about. Shooting at a man in Dalhousie's situation might send him pelting to the altar, but by his own admission, he would not bring a bride into a perilous situation.

The effect of Lady Albert's campaign—if it was hers—was to ensure that Dalhousie avoided marriage so long as he believed himself to be stalked by danger. A note warning him to stay away from Town also seemed designed to keep him from marrying rather than to prevent him from enclosing half the heath.

Too many suspects, and now, too many motives. I turned my steps in the direction of Lady Albert's sitting room, prepared to be chatted half out of my wits.

CHAPTER EIGHT

Lady Albert welcomed me with a wave of her pencil. "I am busy, my lord, but never too busy to pass the time with a charming fellow. Ring for a tray, if you please, and then sit where you won't interfere with my light."

She faced the window, a pot of forced violets on the table before her, and a sketchbook braced against the table edge. I dealt with the bell-pull then peered at her work.

The image was botanically precise and perfectly shaded, right down to the pattern of the lace table runner.

"You're talented."

"And you, dear sir, are peeking. Have you come to drag me away in chains?"

I made a show of patting my pockets. "I knew I forgot something. Left all my chains down in the dungeon. How desperate are you to see Tamerlane inherit the title?"

She kept right on sketching, adding a suggestion of the velvet curtains folded back to admit the weak sunshine.

"Desperate? My lord, I haven't been desperate since Lord Albert fell ill, and the doctor was off tending some farmwife birthing twins.

Most disobliging of her, but then, the physician would have seen poor Albert bled again, and that would have hastened his death, in my opinion."

She sat back and surveyed her sketch. "Flowers want oils, I tell you. The hues are so vivid, and the little dears love the light. Pastels for some, but for such bold specimens as these violets, I fear I must resort to oils."

Lady dabblers—society's term for talented female artists—usually avoided oils, though my sisters assured me that watercolors were the more complicated medium.

I took the seat at her ladyship's elbow. "Let me rephrase the question, which I will continue to do no matter how artfully you evade me: Have you attempted to kill Dalhousie?"

I did not expect honesty, of course, but like a beater flailing at the underbrush, I hoped something interesting would burst from the hedges if I smacked enough bushes hard enough.

"I have wished to kill Dalhousie many times. His stupid enclosure bill will set the whole shire against us, take years to show any return, and ruin some perfectly lovely landscapes. If the Almighty were to see fit to call Dalhousie to his reward, I would honestly be relieved. Do I act on my wishes? Of course not. I do hope you rang for a tray. I am positively peckish."

"I used the bell-pull. If you are blameless, who is your pick for the role of villain?"

She peered at me over her sketchbook. "Dalhousie is not as well-liked as he once was. I do like him, more's the pity, and he's beyond decent to Tam and Susanna, but the marquess made a habit of toying with the affections of proper ladies, and the hostesses and match-makers disapprove of such behavior, especially from a peer. The village despises this enclosure nonsense, and Tam tells me that in the clubs, Dalhousie doesn't know when to talk politics and when to play cards. A bit of a bumbler, in other words."

But did the fine denizens of St. James's clubs place bets involving Dalhousie's horse? "For a bumbler, his acres are in good repair—what

I saw of them. His house is well managed, and his finances appear to be thriving." To say nothing of the forgiving nature of the match-makers when a titled bachelor made plain his intention to take a bride.

Lady Albert bent closer to her paper and added some fine lines around the base of the flowerpot, perfecting a shadow.

"If you talk to the marchioness, she will tell you that I have poisoned every well in Mayfair against her and her son. I haven't the time or inclination to take on such a thankless task. Her own high-handed behavior and Dalhousie's genteel roguery have painted the family in a very unflattering light. You might wonder—any man with blood in his veins would—why my dear Susanna has not married. I place the blame at Dahlia's slippered feet. Susanna is well dowered, sensible, and comely. If anybody has been poisoning wells, it's the marchioness."

"All the more reason for you to see Tam inherit Dalhousie's title."

She set her sketchbook aside and looked past the violets to the damp, chilly day beyond. The sun was making an effort, but the effect was still wintry rather than springlike. Light without heat, gratuitous brightness, and my weak eyes did not care for it at all.

"I love my son, my lord, but I also see Tamerlane clearly. He doesn't want the title. He wants precisely what he has—a life of ease and plenty, a devoted mama and cousin, enough social standing to be invited anywhere, not enough to attract the matchmakers' notice. He's happy. I'm not sure anybody else in this household can say the same."

For all her ladyship's rousing diatribes and stirring speeches, she wasn't telling me much. "Who wishes Dalhousie ill to the point of attempting to take his life?"

"Why ask me?"

"Because you seem to fit the description. You are accounted capable with a gun, and you were present at the shoot. You have access to the stable. You certainly have access to the kitchen, and while Tam might be unhappy to inherit the title, the marchioness would be miserable to see that happen."

Lady Albert smiled brilliantly. "So she would, and I would gloat endlessly, after I mourned Dalhousie properly, of course. I nonetheless tell you this in all honesty, my lord: If I sought to end Dalhousie's life, I would have tended to the matter years ago and not waited until he's mere weeks away from taking a bride. Why would I spend all these *decades* putting up with Dahlia's spite when I could instead have been mother to the peer? Doesn't make any sense, does it? And you do strike me as a sensible fellow. Where is that tray? Did you pull the sash twice?"

"I assuredly did." And I was being chattered in circles.

The simplest way for Lady Albert to deal with my suspicions would be to provide an alibi for the shooting incident. If Lady Albert had been in sight of Cressida or some handy neighbors when Dalhousie's hat had been ventilated, she would have moved several steps away from clear culpability.

She failed to exonerate herself to even that extent, and yet, I could not truly see her aiming at the back of a man's head and pulling the trigger. Murder, as every soldier soon learned, was harder to commit than most people realized, even on the battlefield.

The tray arrived, and I declined refreshment, lest I wash away on a tide of tea. "I suppose I will have to reserve my chains for Tamerlane, then."

Her ladyship paused with her hand halfway to the teapot. "I beg your pardon."

"He has no alibi for any relevant occasion. He is handy with firearms—the whole family apparently is—and has access to the stable. He was present when Dalhousie was poisoned. He benefits the most from Dalhousie's death. Therefore, he must be considered a suspect."

She regarded me, then poured herself a cup of tea. "Susanna said this would happen. You would blame Tam, and he is very blamable.

Dahlia is probably in alt to think of my son charged with attempted murder of a peer. She's like that. Always keeping score."

They were both like that, apparently, and how tedious for the rest of the household.

"For Tam to be convicted," I said, marshaling my patience, "somebody would have to lay information, Northby would have to find the charges credible, and the judges presiding at the assizes would have to find Tam guilty. I cannot see Dalhousie allowing a scandal of that magnitude to becloud his bride hunt."

She stirred both milk and honey into her tea. "But the decision will not be Dalhousie's. Dahlia will stick her oar in and maunder on about justice, duty, standards, and whatnot, and my son—the most harmless fribble ever to tie a *trone d'amour*—will be consigned to the Antipodes for life."

"If you fear that result badly enough, you will allow suspicion to hang above your own head as a counterargument to his guilt, won't you?"

The woman who returned my stare was neither jolly nor shallow. Lady Albert fixed such a look of distaste on me that I was reminded of the marchioness's warning, that Lady Albert was more calculating than I could possibly believe.

"If you cast undue suspicion on Tamerlane, my lord, my wrath will make the rage of angels look timid, and all of it will be directed at you. You may show yourself out."

Plain speech from the confirmed chatterer at last. I withdrew on a nod and considered what, if anything, I had learned.

Both Lady Albert and the marchioness were concerned for their sons, and neither one was dealing with me honestly. Lady Albert had means, motive, and opportunity to harm Dalhousie, and the marchioness had ample motive to see Tamerlane cast in the role of villain.

Dear, dear, dear. Time to consult with my own oracles and see what they made of the day's developments.

"I support a remove to Town," Lady Ophelia said, pausing to pinch a dead bloom from a camellia. The pink petals disintegrated in her hand and fell to the bricks lining the conservatory's main walkway. "I'd have to send for my carriage, which might mean another two days' delay. Dalhousie isn't safe on his own property. Witness, your mishap earlier today, Julian."

"The marquess has been warned to avoid Town," Hyperia pointed out.

"If I wanted to put period to the man's existence," Lady Ophelia countered, "I'd keep him where I could fire at him from a distance, where I knew the whole setting and the entire cast, where his habits and routines are well established. Why are conservatories so gloomy?"

"Because," I said as we shuffled along between potted lemons and potted oranges, "we tend to frequent them at gloomy times of the year. We take ourselves out of doors in more temperate months." Then too, a conservatory in winter smelled more rotting than fresh, more moldy than fertile. The damp added to the unpleasantness of the air, but I'd needed to move rather than sit before yet another tea tray.

"I vote we stay," Hyperia said. "In Town, Julian will have no excuse to bide under the same roof as Dalhousie, and neither will we. We'll be the ones put at a distance, and such inroads as we've made with the staff will have to begin anew with the Town employees. Dalhousie will be expected to attend every possible function, and we can't follow him about like footmen."

"Julian, what say you?" Lady Ophelia sank onto a wooden bench.

"We debate particulars all we please," I replied, handing Hyperia onto the same bench, "but Dalhousie must make the decision himself, and I suspect he's at best torn regarding a remove to London."

"Why?" Ophelia snapped. "Town is the epicenter and apex of all culture, the best gossip, and the premier matchmaking possibilities. If Dalhousie is serious about taking a bride, he must go to Town."

On that, she and Lady Dalhousie agreed.

"I suggest," Hyperia said, "if he's serious about remaining alive, he must bide at the Manor, and sort out his difficulties, with our assistance."

For myself, either choice—city or shire—had both advantages and disadvantages. "We'd know better how to advise Dalhousie if we knew why he's being threatened."

Lady Ophelia harrumphed. "We'd know *best* how to advise him if we knew who was doing the threatening."

"Are we bickering?" I asked, taking up a lean against a potting table. "I do believe we are, which is pointless. The decision is not ours to make. Dalhousie probably views trotting off to Town now as running from danger. Having already swallowed his pride to the extent necessary to recruit our good offices, I can't see him tucking tail and heading for London or Paris. He's said as much, in fact, though I know his dear mama's opinion on the matter carries a great deal of weight with him."

Poor fellow.

"Heading to Paris is never a matter of tucking tail," Lady Ophelia shot back. "If you'd simply..."

I regarded her levelly. "Yes?" My aversion to French soil was deep and abiding.

"Never mind."

Godmama in retreat was a rare and, in this case, welcome sight. "We have avenues yet to explore," I said. "I was hoping you'd both come with me when I call on Cressida Northby. My lady, what do you know of her?"

Godmama studied the shriveled pink petals on the bricks. "Little of her recent habits. Cressida was said to be in consideration for the Pelham heir, years ago. Nice boy, and he's a nice man. On his second wife now and up to a dozen children. In any case, when Cora—that's Lady Albert now—lost the race for Dalhousie's coronet and ended up with Lord Albert, Cressida accepted Northby's suit, and that was that. She comes up to Town for fittings occasionally, but mostly bides in the country. We see more of Lady Albert in Mayfair's ballrooms and entirely too much of Lady Dalhousie."

"You truly dislike her?" Hyperia asked.

"Dahlia broke the rules by snatching a cousin's beau, and now she pretends to be a high stickler. Hypocrisy is unattractive. One does not envy the bride Dalhousie will eventually bring home, not with the marchioness having a perfect excuse to avoid the dower house."

I hadn't thought of that. Lady Albert's presence in the dower house ensured the marchioness could continue in her role as queen of the manor.

"A bride might banish the marchioness," I said.

Both ladies looked at me with tolerant amusement.

"If not the bride," I retorted, "then Dalhousie himself might banish the marchioness. He is the head of the family, after all."

Amusement became grins. So much for my lordly perspective on *that* topic. "Very well, having made a complete cake of myself, I suggest we change into such attire as will make a proper but not ostentatious impression on Mrs. Northby and treat ourselves to her perspective on Dalhousie's difficulties."

"Lady Albert won't give up the dower house," Hyperia said, rising without assistance. "She reigns supreme there, as is a widow's right. Lady Dalhousie, by contrast, is subject to her son's wishes at the Manor, insofar as appearances go. Behind a closed door, she clearly keeps the marquess on a short leash."

What would Dalhousie give to be left alone, free of family intrigues, done with humoring Tam and mediating feuds between the elders? No wonder he'd been reluctant to bring a bride home to the Manor.

I offered my hand to Godmama, who rose somewhat less than gracefully.

"I will leave Cressida Northby to you young people," she said. "I was never particularly acquainted with her, and I have correspondence to tend to. Lovely to have Dalhousie on hand to frank the mail, I must say."

She left us at the door to Hyperia's suite, bustling off with her usual vigor.

"Winter takes a toll on her ladyship," Hyperia said. "She does so enjoy the social whirl, and I am not much for whirling myself. I suspect your riding mishap has also unnerved her. Are we going on horseback over to North Abbey or taking a coach?"

My mishap had unnerved me, though every rider risked a tumble on even the quietest hack.

"We'll take a coach, and not because I fear my saddle has been tampered with. The weather is changeable and chilly. We'll be more comfortable in a coach." And because Hyperia and I were engaged, we were permitted to share that coach over a short distance without a chaperone.

Happy, happy thought, despite the frustrations Dalhousie's situation engendered.

"Carriage dress, then," Hyperia said. "Give me twenty minutes. I'll meet you out front." She kissed my cheek and ducked through the doorway.

I stood where I was for a full minute, basking in the glorious joy of a man affianced to the love of his life. Poor Dalhousie, off to make an expedient, cordial match—assuming he lived to take a bride— when he might instead marry a woman whom he loved passionately.

He would likely pity me, though, did he know the extent of my masculine dysfunction.

I pondered his situation as I tidied up and came back again to the issue of motive. Who would want him dead? What sort of would-be murderer then turned around and sent along helpful, if menacing, notes purporting to address the victim's safety?

That behavior made no sense. I was halfway down the main staircase before it occurred to me to again question whether the motive for Dalhousie's misfortunes was, in fact, murder.

Hyperia awaited me at the front door, looking luscious in an ensemble of chocolate velvet trimmed in red, a wool cloak the color of gingerbread over her arm.

"Allow me." I settled the cloak about her, smoothing the fabric gently over her shoulders. "I like these colors on you. They put me in mind of rich, warm desserts and cozy evenings."

She patted my lapel. "Such an imagination you have. Who am I to be with Mrs. Northby? Am I the featherbrained intended? The penance you are resigned to marrying? A bluestocking whom you esteem as a genuine friend?"

I was unprepared for the question, but then, I was besotted, which could leave a fellow muddled.

"You are my dearest beloved, and it is my privilege to have your support and insight in these investigations."

She gazed up at me with touching solemnity. "You mean that, about the support and insight."

"About the dearest beloved part too, you goose. Also about the insights. The complexities of Lady Albert's and Lady Dalhousie's grudges and feints and stratagems... I would never grasp those, and they might well be relevant to Dalhousie's problems."

Those cherished resentments might well be at the heart of the problem, though the enclosure project deserved serious examination as well.

"How is dessert served at the Hall, Jules?"

"The whole dish is brought in by the footmen and served individually from the sideboard in whatever rank order applies. One can ask for a greater or lesser portion or decline a portion altogether that way, and Mrs. Gwinnett says we have less waste as a result." As a youth, I'd often watched hungrily through the whole little ritual as each sister was served before me, then my older brothers.

"You do pay attention, Jules. You would have picked up on the stratagems and subtleties eventually. Feuding ladies aren't that unusual in polite society."

"They are in my family. They seem to be the norm in Dalhousie's." Even Susanna was caught up in the crossfire.

"God pity the man," Hyperia muttered, going to the window. "Where do you suppose the coach is? They've had more than enough time to put a team in the traces."

Horses could be fractious, grooms slow to act. "Hyperia, what if nobody is trying to kill Dalhousie? What if the objective is simply to harass him, to frighten him, to make him doubt himself? To reduce his desirability as a husband?"

She opened the door and stepped onto the terrace. "Firing a bullet at a man's hat comes perilously close to murder rather than harassment."

Well, yes, but the bullet had missed, as it might well have been intended to, and there was something else about the incident that bothered me. Something a soldier ought to notice...

But what?

I accompanied Hyperia into the inhospitable elements and closed the door behind us. "I grant you, a bullet is serious business, but depending on the poison used, giving somebody a bellyache need not risk death at all. Tampering with a saddle isn't likely to result in an experienced equestrian's demise either." Though it could, and poisons were notoriously hard to dose correctly. "If we're having trouble discerning the proper motive, maybe that's because the goal isn't murder after all."

"We have plenty of motives," Hyperia said. "Perhaps we should ride over to the Abbey. I'd have to change into a habit, but..."

The young groom who'd been scrubbing buckets jogged around the side of the house and stopped at the foot of the steps, his breath puffing white in the chilly air.

"Milord, miss." He dragged off his cap. "Won't be no coach coming around. Apologies from John Coachman."

"No coach?" Hyperia said. "Is the coachman ill? We can drive ourselves if you have a phaeton or dog cart."

The groom shook his head. "Best not, miss. Vehicle might be unsafe. Milord, you'd better come have a look. We've sent the stablemaster to fetch the marquess."

"Miss West, shall you accompany us to the stable?"

Hyperia took me by the arm and all but hauled me down the steps. "Of course, and we will postpone our call on Mrs. Northby. Lead on, my good fellow, but at a walk. You will catch a lung fever charging about in this cold air."

The groom slapped his cap back on his head and set off for the stable quick time, but without breaking into a run.

CHAPTER NINE

"Whoever tampered with the coaches did not account for spare cotter pins," I said as Atlas shuffled through the dead leaves carpeting the path between the Manor and North Abbey.

"They pulled out all four, Jules," Hyperia replied, her borrowed mare mincing along at Atlas's side. "Does your coachman carry four spares?"

"No, but most coaching inns and smithies will have pins for sale. The smashed wheels on Dalhousie's traveling coach bother me more." Fortunately, Godmama's traveling coach had been sent into Reading to spare the marquess having to feed four extra horses.

As for my own traveling coach, the cotter pins had been removed from all four wheels.

Dalhousie's conveyance had suffered more violent damage. Somebody had taken a sledgehammer to all four wheels on his crested monstrosity, as well as two wheels on his heaviest baggage coach. His phaeton had suffered one smashed wheel. The dog cart and farm wagons appeared unscathed—so far.

"Somebody," Hyperia said, "grasped that it's not enough to have four wheels of equal diameter." She steered her mare around a puddle. "The wheels must fit the vehicle, else we could pop the farm wagon wheels onto the carriage. Dalhousie seemed oddly resigned to being hobbled."

The marquess's reaction had struck me as more pensive than resigned. He'd surveyed the damage with us, the head lad, stablemaster, and coachman silently standing by. His lordship's sole reaction had been to order the village wainwright onto the scene to make repairs in due course.

The woods around us were damp and barren, which suited my mood. As a sleuth, I was failing Dalhousie spectacularly, and the destruction in the coach house had me frankly flummoxed—more flummoxed.

"Dalhousie is ashamed, Hyperia." From flummoxed to ashamed was only a short step, for me as well. "The enemy has stolen another march on him. Told him not to go to Town, then when he made no plans to decamp, spiked his guns. Unless he wants to borrow a neighbor's coach and announce to all and sundry that his castle wall has been breached, he will miss the first few weeks of the Season."

"The marquess could have the phaeton fixed first, Jules, and brave the elements. He could take a post-chaise or go to London on horseback."

I had not realized how desserts were served at the Manor, but in other regards, my perception was better informed than Hyperia's.

"You'd have the marquess arrive in Town without his mama as a hostess in the one year when he truly needs her good offices. He would have to explain to the neighbors why he's borrowing a plain coach, despite being the one fellow in this shire to whom anybody can turn in emergencies for support and generosity.

"His unorthodox arrival in Town would be remarked," I went on, "particularly when he's known to be embarking on a search for the next marchioness. Whatever his faults, Dalhousie has a natural aversion to being the subject of talk."

Hyperia maintained a silence that I took for diplomacy on her part.

I offered one more point for consideration. "Dalhousie might also have told the wainwright to make repairs 'in due course' because planting approaches, and the farm wagons, harrows, and plows all merit the highest priority for the coming weeks. He's mindful of the appearances, and in his position, most men would be. Then too, he's not about to leave the ladies to fend for themselves when violent mischief is afoot."

The timing of the vandalism had been excellent from the standpoint of causing maximum bother, in other words, provided one knew Dalhousie well and could play on his pride and consequence.

"He will not abandon his mama," Hyperia said after her mare had sniffed at a dangling branch of rhododendron. "On that we are agreed. The destruction in the coach house speaks of significant malice."

Enough malice to get the perpetrator hanged, and the miscreant had to know as much.

"The coach house put me in mind of a battlefield, Perry. An hour after the last shot is fired, the air clears, the birds sing, the sun shines, and yet, if you look at the ground—gore, tragedy, suffering, and such pure *wrongness*..."

Dalhousie's elegant traveling coach, a pleasure dome on wheels with a diameter nearly as tall as I stood, had been canted at an angle. In the next bay, the phaeton had nearly toppled to its side, like a pair of drunks leaning on each other to remain upright. The damage had been done mostly to the spokes of the wheels—easy to smash—while my own coach had looked deceptively seaworthy. Broken bits of wood had littered the coach house's dirt floor, and the coach door had swung silently on an invisible breeze.

"A woman could have wrecked those wheels," Hyperia said slowly. "A very angry, determined woman. I lifted the hammer, Jules. The weight was stout, but not prohibitively so."

We emerged from the trees, North Abbey rising up before us a hundred yards on. I drew Atlas to a halt, and the mare stopped as well.

"A woman?"

Hyperia adjusted her reins. "Isn't poison traditionally a woman's weapon? The ladies would know how the desserts were served, too, and many a stylish lady carries a peashooter when she goes traveling."

Great Jehovah's flaming arrows. "I cannot see Lady Dalhousie swinging even that smallish sledgehammer." She was more likely to fire verbal darts, though her ladyship was in resolute good health... My reservations were based not on lack of ability, but lack of motive. "She above all people wants Dalhousie doing the rounds in Town."

"Lady Albert is quite robust," Hyperia said. "She could come and go from the carriage house or stable without anybody remarking upon her presence. She doubtless has the ability to loosen stitching. She was present at the shoot. She has motive, Jules. For that matter, Tam could have made that mess in the carriage house."

Hyperia urged the mare forward, and Altas moved off as well.

"We're forgetting somebody," I said.

"Susanna. I don't want her to be the villain, Jules. She's the voice of reason amid the Dandridge eccentrics."

"She is barely related to the Dandridge eccentrics, but she's quite close to her step-cousin Tam."

We edged onto the drive that circled before North Abbey's granite façade.

"I still can't see Susanna being so beastly," Hyperia said. "You'd have me believe she has brought all this mayhem down on Dalhousie, perhaps to kill him, perhaps to keep him away from Mayfair, while she waits for dear Tam to take a bride, have a son, and eventually inherit?"

"What if she hopes to be dear Tam's bride?"

Hyperia wrinkled her nose. "If so, she's an actress of more talent than Mrs. Siddons herself. Susanna dotes on Tam, but with a generous leavening of exasperation. Marriages have been built on less, of course, but the theory doesn't convince me."

"Nor me, though neither can I rule her out. She has the relevant access to the marquess and his property and possesses the means necessary to trouble him."

"But no credible motive," Hyperia said as we clip-clopped up the drive. "Do you suppose the damage to your coach was limited to mere missing cotter pins so as to encourage our departure?"

"Possibly. I'm not blowing retreat, Hyperia."

"Neither am I, Julian."

Her tone was merely pleasant, as mine had been, though in my heart of hearts, the impulse to keep Hyperia safe, to ensure hostilities never endangered her, battled for expression. She would be deeply annoyed at my chivalry.

"We shouldn't stay long at the Abbey," Hyperia said. "Darkness still comes early."

"The requisite two cups will do," I said, hoping to escape even that penance, "and I see well in the dark." Harry had envied me that skill.

"Good," Hyperia said as a fellow in humble attire emerged from the side of the house and approached the mounting block. "I would not want to be lost after sunset on Dalhousie land when a hammer-wielding, poisoning, saddle-tampering, pistol-wielding maniac is on the loose."

Not a maniac, but certainly a person whose mental peregrinations had yet to form into any pattern I could discern. Hyperia's observation, that a woman's hand might be directly evident in Dalhousie's troubles, bothered me.

We had considered both Lady Albert and Lady Dalhousie as suspects in theory. To see firsthand the results of malicious mischief that could be attributed to either of them was unnerving, like hearing shots fired and realizing the guns were aimed in one's own direction.

"I want Tam to be guilty," I said, sounding forlorn to my own ears. "Disgruntled staff would do. Unhappy neighbors would suit my purposes as well, but please not the ladies and especially not sensible, gracious Susanna."

"You are old-fashioned, Jules. For the most part, I like that about you."

"Who is your current favorite for Dalhousie Manor's criminal-at-large?"

Hyperia considered the stolid, tidy façade before us. "Jules, I have not the faintest inkling. The evidence confuses, the witnesses condemn one another, and here we are at the home of the magistrate, who does nothing. I am utterly confounded."

"Which makes two of us."

The groom took our horses with promises to loosen girths only and offer hay and water.

I raised my hand to rap the owl-shaped knocker on the right side of the Abbey's double, red front door, but the owl swung away before I achieved my objective.

"You are Miss West," an aging blond Valkyrie said, "and you would be Lord Julian Caldicott. I know your godmother. I'm Cressy Northby. Your brother has been derelict in his duty to the ducal succession. One cannot approve, however much one admires independence of spirit. I suppose you want some tea. Squire won't be joining us. Do come along."

Hyperia swept into the house, and I followed more tentatively. I'd been expecting Cressida Northby to convey substance and sense with her presence, and she'd certainly achieved that much.

The rest of my impression surprised me: This was a woman who'd wield a hammer easily, even gleefully, and she was doubtless a dead shot as well.

I leaped to that conclusion without a moment's hesitation. So much for my old-fashioned notions of chivalry.

❧

"No tea?" Cressida said, gesturing with a full silver teapot. "One heard your lordship was eccentric, but perhaps you have a point. Brandy goes better with chocolate, if you ask me, particularly on a chilly afternoon. Miss West, mustn't let good China black go to waste."

Mrs. Northby did not speak so much as she declaimed, boomed, and orated. Hers was a large, self-assured presence, though she carried less in the way of extra flesh than her sister, Lady Albert. She was Junoesque in the flattering sense. Her features included a nose any patrician Roman matron would have been pleased to point into the air and blue eyes shining with both interest and intelligence.

She could have done it. She could have done all of it.

Cressida poured out with the same air of brisk efficiency that seemed to emanate from her organically. The resemblance to Lady Albert was present about the chin and mouth and also in a sense of watchfulness lurking beneath purposeful distractions.

"Will your lordship deign to sample a biscuit?" she asked, thrusting a plate of cinnamon biscuits at me.

"Go ahead," Hyperia said. "Good sweets are best appreciated when fresh." She plucked one of the three from the plate, and I accepted the other two.

"You are an engaged pair," Mrs. Northby said. "Such a relief, to finally bag a mate. One can stop all the posturing and games and get on with life. Squire would agree."

Squire doubtless agreed frequently. "Northby suggested we discuss with you the particulars of the recent shoot," I said. "Dalhousie's hat came to grief, and that incident has been followed by other troubling developments."

"A bout of the grippe would trouble anybody, but young men make the worst patients. Miss West would agree with me, I'm sure."

"Young men also, oddly enough, make our best soldiers," Hyperia mused, munching on a biscuit. "All very perplexing."

Cressida sent her a keen look. "You have brains. A mixed blessing for a young lady, but more useful than burdensome by my lights. Somebody did put a hole in Dalhousie's hat. He's lucky that shot wasn't three inches lower. Would have been an inquest, suspicions, fingers pointed. Scandal and talk, and the squire would have been in the center of it. He's getting on, you know. Still spry, still sharp, but death by misadventure is a bad business, and I'm glad my old boy didn't have to deal with it."

"The verdict could not have been murder by person or persons unknown?" I asked. The biscuits were fresh, rich, and sweet. Hyperia was eyeing the only one remaining on my plate, so—old-fashioned gudgeon that I am—I offered it to her.

She took it.

"Murder sounds exciting," Cressida said. "Makes for great talk on darts night and at the hunt meets, but Dalhousie is a marquess. Putting out his lights wouldn't be a matter for seven years transportation. Somebody would swing for that, if convicted. We aren't exactly timid souls hereabouts, but we're sensible. Send Dalhousie to his reward, and then Tam steps into his boots."

Hyperia broke the biscuit into two equal halves and gave me back one of them. To refuse her generosity would have been churlish, and yet, I felt I was conceding some philosophical point when I accepted the offering.

"Tam is well-liked," Hyperia said. "Or am I mistaken?"

"One suspects you are seldom mistaken, Miss West. Tam is well-liked, but he can afford to be. He doesn't sit on the commission for the peace. He doesn't hold the living for three parish churches. He doesn't control tens of thousands of acres or decide who can rent them on what terms."

She paused to sip her tea with curious delicacy. "Tamerlane Dandridge has a pretty little estate five miles to the east," she went on. "He lets it out to some banker's son and visits only quarterly. He fribbles away his days and drinks and sports away his nights because he has sufficient income to do so. The least such a decorative creature can do is be agreeable.

"Hand him a title, though," she went on, "and he will either soon take on some of Dalhousie's less charming characteristics, or he'll erode the family's wealth and standing with his self-indulgence. Spares can't help themselves. Give them the title, and they must out-peer the peer."

"And yet," I said, "somebody fired a bullet through Dalhousie's hat, and Tam would benefit greatly if the aim had been lower. Who was present at the shoot?"

She rattled off a list that matched the information provided by the squire.

"What his lordship means," Hyperia said, "is were any of the attending guests missing from the firing line. We are interested in both the ladies and the gentlemen."

Blue eyes narrowed shrewdly. "We ladies are kept in the middle of the line, like biddy hens penned into our roost. Mind you, we are experienced with firearms, more sober than the men, and most of us as accurate as the men as well, but we are considered a hazard to be guarded against."

When had women become so averse to personal safety? I did not dare ask the question, because I had the sense even my query was somehow missing the mark.

"So there you were," I said, "in the middle of the line with the other ladies, enjoying an excellent vantage point for keeping an eye on the whole lot. Did you see any of the men step back to load a fresh fowling piece or find a handy log to sit on?"

"The beaters were getting closer, so the men weren't about to leave their posts. Squire is very strict about no firing early, because that scares the game off in the wrong direction. Cora—Lady Albert, rather—doesn't care for the noise when the whole line starts shooting at once, so she did step back a bit, and Susanna went with her, which I took for... Well, the best time for a lady to step behind a handy tree is when all the men are keen to fire."

"Lady Albert and Miss Susanna both took a break from the shoot-ing?" Hyperia asked.

"They did. I got off a few shots. Heaven knows we've grouse enough to spare, and this is a hungry time of year for the lesser folk. You needn't bother accusing either Susanna or Cora of attempted murder, though."

"Was I about to? From what I understand, nobody has laid information, and nobody intends to."

Cressida gave me a thorough perusal over her tea cup. "You say that now, and one can rely on Dahlia's aversion to scandal up to a point, but she would see Tam whipped at the cart's tail, hanged, drawn, and quartered rather than let him have the title."

"Why do you exonerate Lady Albert and Miss Susanna?" I asked. Cressida Northby would have reasons, well-thought-out, sensible reasons for the opinions she held.

"I heard no pistol shot during their absence. All sorts of fowling pieces booming up and down the line, but a pistol has a very different voice. More of a crack or a pop than a proper weapon firing."

"Why a pistol?" I asked, because her usual confidence imbued her latest recitation.

"The size of the hole in the hat for one thing, and birdshot leaves a very different pattern, as my lord doubtless knows. A pistol fits the bill as well because it's easily hidden in the folds of a shooting jacket or cloak."

Points the magistrate himself had not passed along, but then, I hadn't needed him to. "Is it possible," I said slowly, "that the pistol shot was drowned out by the fowling pieces?"

"Possible, but bass voices don't drown out the sopranos, do they, my lord? And my hearing is excellent."

Her self-assurance was in equally good repair, but I took seriously the evidence she presented. An experienced artillery sergeant could listen to cannon fire and know exactly how far away the enemy's pieces were as well as the type of shot fired—until the constant noise took the inevitable toll on his faculties. Even going deaf, some of them could gather the same information from the feel of the thud in the chest caused by the reverberation of the cannon fire.

Hyperia held out the empty biscuit plate. "Lady Albert would seem to be as devoted to furthering Tam's prospects as Lady Dalhousie is to limiting them."

"The pair of them deserve each other," Cressida observed, putting four more biscuits on the plate. "The boys have made their peace with one another, which is fortunate. I pity Susanna, though, having to mediate between Cora and Dalhia, cosset Tam, and keep the household running without tromping on Dahlia's dainty toes. One must enjoy a challenge to thrive in such a situation, and Susanna does."

"Would Susanna be happier here with you?" Hyperia asked, accepting the biscuits.

"Yes and no. She is welcome. She is always welcome, but the squire and I are set in our ways, purely gentry, and happy to be so. At the Manor, Susanna isn't as socially isolated—they do entertain quite a bit over there—and she is fond of both Tam and Dalhousie. Obscurity is an acquired taste for some of us and better served later in life."

"She would be wasted here," I suggested.

"Very much so, though we'd love to have her. Tam would miss her, and Dahlia would soon learn how much the staff relies on Susanna. Dahlia was so determined to become Lady Dalhousie. I suspect even Cora is beginning to wish her ladyship the joy of her prize."

These observations had little to do with who had fired a bullet at Dalhousie, and yet, Cressida's perspective merited attention.

"The marchioness seems quite well suited to her station," Hyperia said, taking a biscuit and offering me the plate.

"She is now. She was an awkward fit originally. Obviously with child almost upon the church steps, clearly not a love match despite that evidence. There was talk—isn't there always?—and she had no allies. Just deserts, I say, and yet, Dahlia failed to anticipate the reception she'd earn for her obvious conniving. Mayfair has an infernally long memory when it comes to scandal."

Said with some satisfaction.

"And then Cora married Lord Albert." I yielded to temptation and ate another biscuit. "Was that to spite Lady Dalhousie?"

Cressida topped up Hyperia's cup and poured herself more tea. "I daresay, but Cora and Albert surprised everybody by rubbing along quite well. Tam has his father's charm and his mama's talent with the arts. If he ever grows up, he'll make a passable husband and a wonderful father."

Would he and his wife bide at that estate five miles to the east, or would his bride become another pawn in the family feud at the Manor?

"Can you tell us anything more about the day of the shoot?" Hyperia asked. "Somebody fired a bullet at the marquess's back. Such a creature lacks honor and must be held accountable."

An inspired angle, given Cressida's forthright nature.

"The squire and I have discussed this at length, and we honestly cannot settle on a preferred villain. Cora and Susanna stepped back for only a few moments, and neither one of them wishes Dalhousie harm. I can tell you this, though." She took another placid sip of her tea. "Dahlia did not participate in the shoot."

Never let it be said that Cressida Northby lacked thespian inclinations. "Northby said she no longer cared for shooting, but she's a competent shot."

"She was a dead shot, back in the day. She's the lady of the manor now. After the decimation of the wildfowl, the lot of us were to enjoy a buffet at the Manor. Dahlia as hostess should have been annoying the staff with last-minute orders to do what had already long since been done and so forth. I popped over on horseback as Squire was assembling the shooting party here and offered the use of my maids and footmen."

"And her ladyship was out?" Hyperia asked, dipping a biscuit in her tea.

"Truly *out*. The Dalhousie butler is cousin to my housekeeper, and when he means 'not receiving' rather than 'out,' he lowers his voice as if imparting a confidence. He meant her ladyship was away from the premises just before the shoot. I have no idea when she returned, or if she'd been doing a bit of target practice while away from her duties."

"What woman," I said, genuinely horrified, "what parent, could aim a bullet at their own offspring? What you suggest is heinous, and I can think of no motive that would justify filicide."

Cressida set down her tea cup. "Is there a bullet hole in the brim of your hat, my lord?"

I thought for a moment. "I would say not, but you are correct: I donned my hat without examining the brim. Why would Lady Dalhousie put a bullet hole in her son's...?"

While the ladies regarded me patiently, I worked out the answer to the hypothetical for myself: abuse his lordship's hat, send him into the woods to the shoot, then fire a pistol at the ground in proximity to him. He whirls about, finds his hat has been potted, and assumes he's been targeted. Suspicions swirl, Tam is accused. The marchioness is happy.

"Far-fetched," I said. "Too Byzantine." By comparison, smashing the coach wheels was a direct means of ensuring the marquess remained at the Manor.

And yet, Cressida's scenario explained the odd angle of the shot, didn't it?

Cressida took one of the two uneaten biscuits. "A woman of wealthy antecedents who will get with child to ensnare the peer courting her cousin is a woman who is comfortable with complication, my lord. She wants Tam disgraced and Dalhousie safely filling the nursery. Depend upon that."

We left a short time later and made our way on horseback through woods going prematurely dark.

"What are you thinking, Jules?"

Hyperia seemed to ask me that rather a lot. "I'm thinking about crossfire, Perry, and complications. One party might be trying to discredit Tam, and they are doing a lively job of it. Another party might be harassing Dalhousie and preventing him from going to London. That team has scored runs aplenty too. The war in Spain became similarly complicated." I patted Atlas absently, my sole companion for some of that war.

"I thought the Peninsular campaign was a simple matter of driving the French back over the mountains?"

Simple. Ye thundering angels of understatement. "In one sense, you are right, but some of the Spanish supported the French, some did not. Some of the Spanish who opposed the French were equally opposed to the British or the Portuguese. Some of the French generals could be relied on to aid the others. Some were too invested in looting their Spanish fiefdoms before retreating to the comforts of Paris to bother with fighting the British and so on. One tread carefully."

"But you stayed there, even when you could have come home on winter leave." A thread of bewilderment ran through her words.

A thread of hurt.

"I was better at my job if I kept my instincts honed, Perry. War can make a certain twisted sense when it's your daily reality. When you reach that point, ballrooms and tailors' fittings become irrational distractions. Days at sea to resume playing cards at the clubs for a few weeks or hacking out despite a sore head... I saw no point in it when I could have been forming alliances among shepherds or learning exactly how to pass safely through a particular mountain range."

"You were safer if you didn't look away."

So safe, I'd ended up chained to the wall of a French dungeon. "Something like that. I don't miss it." And I did not enjoy the topic, particularly when aired with Hyperia.

Her mare stepped daintily over a fallen branch. "You miss something about it. You would have told Dalhousie to hire himself bodyguards otherwise."

I had tried. "He was in mortal peril, or so I believed." I wasn't as sure now. Peril, yes, but was his life at stake?

"You could not rescue Harry, so you will rescue Dalhousie."

Hyperia aired a theory more than she made an accusation, and yet, her words stung.

"Must we discuss this?"

"Yes," she said gently. "A little bit at a time, when we have the privacy and fortitude to do so, we must. I missed you, Jules. I prayed for you. I wrote you letter after letter that I tossed into the flames. Those morning hacks and card parties you disdained were unavoidable for me, and I would have given anything to be with you in those mountains."

My proud, brave beloved was sharing with me a piece of her heart I did not deserve. I wanted to change the subject, to canter off down the path and claim Atlas had taken a fright.

Atlas was plodding along beside the mare, not a care in his horsey world.

I mustered all of my courage and followed Hyperia's inspiration.

"I would have given anything to have had you with me, Perry, and I am for damned sure grateful to have you with me now."

I had written her letters, too, but in the normal course, a gentleman did not correspond with a member of the opposite sex to whom he was neither engaged nor related. In the freezing snows, I had pictured her by the hour enjoying the social whirl, turning down the room with this handsome heir or that charming younger son. By dark of night, I had prayed for her safety and happiness, and when I'd been chained to that wall, I'd kept the memory of her in my heart, a beacon of hope and determination.

Someday, I would tell her all of that, truly I would. She was right, though. Baring the soul was best done slowly, in small steps, in the exclusive company of one's beloved.

I offered up a truth I could share joyfully, one I'd conveyed previously to happy effect. "I am utterly besotted with you, Perry West, and that I merit even your passing consideration continually astounds me."

She smiled. "Good, and that's enough flummery for now. We

have another family dinner at the Manor to endure, and we haven't had a report from Atticus the livelong day."

Subject changed, though I would ponder the hurt I'd done my darling at length, and if a man in love could make amends for past wrongs to his lady, I would find a way to do exactly that.

CHAPTER TEN

"Bad business," Atticus said, tromping from the stables with me and Hyperia. "Very bad business, going after the coaches like that. The grooms are all off in corners whispering by twos and threes. The gardeners are keeping to themselves. The footmen aren't hanging about the harness room like they sometimes do."

"Any theories?" I asked as we ambled along.

"When was those coach wheels smashed?" Atticus replied. "When *were* they, I mean. Bashing about like that makes noise. The carriage house is some distance from the stable, but still... If the lads were in the yard watering the horses, bringing in stock from the pastures, dumping the muck carts into the pit around back... Somebody shoulda heard something."

This detail, like Cressida Northby's comment about not having heard a pistol fired among the fowling pieces, caught me up short.

"Excellent point, Atticus. When do the lads take their nooning?"

"Early. They are up at the crack o' doom, so they eat before the family at midday. They eat supper same time as family, finish up at the stable, and seek their beds."

"At noon," Hyperia said, her arm linked through mine, "the stable and carriage house are empty?"

Atticus peered up at her. "Should be. If a man were in a fury, he'd need only ten minutes or so to wreck those coaches. The carriage house isn't locked, and that sledgehammer is kept in the carriage house for bangin' on this and that. The farrier says it's not one o' his."

"That suggests a spontaneous bout of destruction," Hyperia observed as we emerged into the dreary shadows of the formal garden. "Use what's to hand, lay about when nobody's around, decamp unseen."

"Or," I said, "it suggests familiarity with the carriage house appointments, right down to the tools hanging on the wall." Those walls were also adorned with harnesses, every equipage being care-fully fitted to the vehicle and the horses for which it was used and the whole being draped on custom pegs and racks in the precise order in which it was put on the horse.

The sledgehammer, pliers, hasp, and so forth hanging on nails in the corner were not the first thing the eye would notice.

"What else are you hearing, Atticus?" I paused by the empty fountain. I could see the boy's features only indistinctly, the twilight shadows having deepened to the point that from inside the house, one would believe darkness had fallen. Out in the elements, the sky to the west was yet streaked with gray.

An hour for trysting, spying, and being spied upon.

"Not much bein' said." Atticus shuffled his boots among the dry leaves accumulated beside the fountain. "It's unnervin' when the lads and footmen stop their chatting. Seems like talk is how they get through the day. Gossiping about the maids, complaining about the work, joking about nothing, and longing for a beef roast. They're lively, usually. They aren't lively now."

"Who goes on as if nothing is afoot?" Hyperia asked. "Who pretends he has nothing to fret over?"

Atticus aimed a stare in the direction of the stable, the rooftop of which was visible against the darkening sky through the bare hedgerow.

"The head lad is all business," he said. "Back to work, quit yer lollygaggin', that sort of thing. He had the grooms tidy up the carriage house right smartly, all the broken bits swept into a pile for the wainwright to salvage what he can. Nobody is pretending nothin', miss. We know trouble when it smashes a marquess's coach wheels."

Atticus's voice told me what I might have seen in better light: The boy was afraid. He was acutely sensitive to the moods of the adults around him, and those adults were afraid as well. For their jobs, very likely, also for their physical safety.

"Take yourself to the kitchen," I said. "Linger in the servants' hall, pine for home, doze off in the corner by the fire. Keep your ears open. You've given us an insightful report, and I thank you for it."

"Aye, guv. Miss." He vanished up the walkway, his steps pattering into the darkness.

"You are pondering," Hyperia said, making no move to follow the boy into the house.

I cast caution to the wind—we were engaged—and brought her into an embrace. "Why not wreck the coaches properly, Perry? If you were the guilty party, you'd be furious enough to wreak havoc. You have a stout hammer in your hand. The stable and carriage house are downwind of the Manor by design. Sound won't travel to the Manor, and the lads and gardeners are all off, wolfing down a midday meal. You have the extra five minutes to destroy the vehicles themselves, but you stop after whacking the daylights out of a few wheels. Who are you, and what is your goal that you limited the damage like that?"

"Perhaps," she said, bundling close, "you are a woman or a youth and not truly strong enough to destroy the vehicles. Perhaps you are of a calculating nature and enjoy the notion of causing the marquess a fortnight's delay, during which you will devise another means of annoying and harassing him."

Daunting thought. "I want to find this fiend, Hyperia, and shake answers out of them. I cannot see a pattern, and that in itself suggests we are dealing with either an unhinged mind or diabolical cleverness."

She stepped back and took my hand. "Or we are dealing with the chaos of war, as you noted earlier. One faction poisons the marquess's trifle. The other faction whacks at the carriage wheels. If this is what you dealt with in Spain, Julian, it's no wonder you came back to us slightly the worse for wear."

My French captors had had something to do with my shoddy condition, but I wasn't about to bring up that topic again.

We parted in the Manor's chilly atrium, Hyperia to change for dinner, me to find the marquess. Atticus was afraid, Hyperia was likening the situation to a war, and they were both prudent, canny individuals, whom I wanted to keep safe above all else.

I made the appropriate inquiries of a footman, then rapped on the door of Dalhousie's study. I did not yet have the pleasure of shaking answers from the perpetrator of the day's mischief, but I could question mine host, at length and in detail, and caution him regarding the need for extensive preventive measures.

"My lord." Susanna seemed surprised to find me requesting entry to Dalhousie's sanctum sanctorum, but she quickly recovered. "I was just leaving. Mind you two aren't late for dinner." She sidled around me with a smile and bustled off.

"Come in," Dalhousie said, rising from behind his desk. "Susanna was just reviewing the household books with me, the appointed day and hour for that exercise having arrived. I daresay I was not very attentive to the ledgers. Brandy?"

"Brandy would suit." Dalhousie was trying for the persona of the gracious host, but his gaze was wary, and two brandy glasses had already been used and returned to the sideboard. If the intention had been to steady his nerves, the project was still a work in progress.

"I brought this home from Paris," he said, pouring two more servings into clean glasses. "To your health and to... spring."

I sipped, finding the vintage agreeably fragrant—oak, apples, a hint of cinnamon—and blessed with the smooth fire that soothes even as it warms the gullet.

"What did Cressida have to add to the day's mayhem?" Dalhousie asked, gesturing to the wing chairs before the fire.

I took a seat, finding the cushions warm and comfy, the fire nicely blazing. "She did not hear a pistol fired on the occasion when your hat came to grief," I said, setting my brandy on the side table. "She noted that detail very clearly and admitted as well that both Lady Albert and Susanna took a brief respite from the firing line at a moment when such a pistol shot might have been fired."

Dalhousie sank into the second chair with the sigh of a man carrying heavy burdens. "Do you believe her?"

"She strikes me as being more disinterested than either the marchioness or Lady Albert, and her first loyalty would be to the squire. He's the magistrate, and if a crime has been committed on his watch, and he's failed to investigate, then he's derelict in his duty. She would guard his flank before involving herself in the intrigues and foolishness here."

"He would not be derelict," Dalhousie said tiredly. "He'd be discreet. I am not about to make wild claims about bandits lurking in Northby's very woods, and because he was present on the scene in the capacity of landowner and organizer of the shoot, some other authority would likely have to be brought in, and Mama..." He sipped again. "The marchioness does not want to foment ill will with the neighbors."

I was fast losing patience with the marchioness. "Bit late for her to turn up diplomatic and delicate, Dalhousie. For that matter, your enclosure scheme has already set the entire shire against you, and you haven't yet drafted the parliamentary particulars. The marchioness at her sweetest would need generations to overcome the malice your enclosure scheme has already earned you."

"Tam says the same." Another listless sip. "He says I can look forward to salted wells, pasture gates left open, haystacks mysteriously catching fire... The talk has grown ugly, and all because I want to bring a bit of progress to my corner of the realm."

That sounded exactly like the sort of unhelpful, generally threatening observation Tam would make before nattering on about Cato the Elder on the topic of warfare.

Bellum se ipse alet. The quote popped into my head as I nosed my drink a second time, a reference made by Cato himself to his brutal, lightning campaign to conquer and subdue Hispania Citerior.

"What are you muttering about?" Dalhousie asked, finishing his drink.

"'The war feeds itself,' meaning that once mayhem and violence pass a certain point, the destruction itself tends to engender yet more chaos and horror. Loyalties evaporate in the face of suspicion. Imagined slights escalate into vendettas. Looting has no consequences..." Horrible images from Spain—Badajoz and Ciudad Rodrigo in particular—tried to crowd into my head.

This was what came of allowing Hyperia to peek at my wartime memories.

"You refer to my smashed coaches," Dalhousie said. "Disturbing, I grant you, but we can walk to divine services if the weather is fair, and the farrier says he can fashion cotter pins to make your vehicle serviceable by noon tomorrow."

Divine services were not on my mind. Divine retribution, on the other hand... "You must post guards, Dalhousie. Plowing and planting have not yet begun. Recruit from the yeomanry and the tenants you trust, choose only the stoutly loyal and reliably alert."

"You said it yourself, my lord. I have sown rancor with my neighbors over the enclosure scheme. They will eagerly take my coin in exchange for extra duties, then look the other way when my livestock is spirited away."

"Then post your footmen and gardeners to keep watch on the outbuildings. Close the estate's main gates and insist your gatekeeper remain sober during daylight hours. Roust the gamekeeper to make regular patrols of the footpaths most commonly used by the villagers and tenants."

Fortify the camp, for pity's sake. Post the sentries, dispatch the scouting patrols, secure the ammunition under lock and key.

Dalhousie rose to pour himself another brandy, his third, at least. "I haven't regiments and battalions to command, my lord. The footmen and gardeners have regular duties, and my mother does not believe in hiring excessive staff. She will notice that her evening posset takes longer to come up from the kitchen, and she will take umbrage at a lack of fresh flowers on the breakfast table."

Wellington, notably gallant toward the ladies, would not have spared the marchioness five minutes beneath the chandeliers at Almack's.

"What does your dear mother make of the havoc in your carriage house?"

Dalhousie fiddled with the decanters at the sideboard, examined his drink closely, and acquired the truculent air of the unrepentant schoolboy, all without saying a word.

"Dalhousie, I despair of you. You have not told the marchioness we'll be walking to divine services."

He resumed his seat, tossing the drink back at one go. "You don't know my mother, my lord. She nearly flayed me alive for attending the shoot on the anniversary of my father's passing. He's been gone for nearly two decades. I was away at school when he died, and yet, I am to remark the day and the hour and spend them in contemplation of a father I recall as self-absorbed and at best benignly negligent regarding his heir."

"If your mother was so wroth with you, why did she host a buffet for the shooting party on the same occasion?"

"To punish me, of course. To throw in my face that not only did I fail to honor my father, I had also expected my mother to ignore the occasion of her bereavement. She could have reminded me of the date. She could have mentioned something to Suze, who surely would have warned me, but that's not how Mama works. She excels at ambushing others with guilt."

Did she excel at more deadly ambushes? "A martyr to misery and determined to ensure everybody else suffers the same fate."

"Not misery. Duty, propriety, consequence... I have not told her about the coaches. I was hoping you might broach the topic with her."

"Of course." Her reaction to the news would be interesting, though by now, her spies could well have made their reports. "Cressida says your mother went absent without leave during the shoot."

"Mama wasn't with us. She remained here, preparing for the buffet."

"No, she did not, and nobody seems to know where she got off to. I'll ask her." I rose, ready to make haste where Dalhousie was dithering and wallowing. "The situation is escalating, Dalhousie, from threats to your person to wanton destruction of your property. Time is of the essence, and if I were you, I'd jettison any notion of enclosing that heath."

He nodded, which I took as acknowledgment of a sensible suggestion rather than assent. He was unfailingly resolute about his enclosure and an absolute invertebrate when it came to managing the marchioness.

How hard could it be to have some frank words with one's own mother?

I was halfway to her ladyship's suite before I could admit even to myself that such discussions could be very difficult. I knew from experience how trying those honest, painful conversations could be and knew as well that my own dear and occasionally exasperating mother would agree with me.

"My errand is brief," I said, strolling past a lady's maid intent on repelling boarders. "One must not make the marchioness late for supper, after all."

Lady Dalhousie occupied a settee facing the hearth of her sitting room, her workbasket at her feet. Compared to Hyperia's rather plain kit, this basket was rife with the regalia of feminine productivity—pins; a darning egg; an abundance of pointed knitting needles; and no less than three pairs of gleaming, razor-sharp scissors in different sizes.

Her ladyship spared me not so much as a glance. "You have a positive gift for rudeness, my lord. Hames, you will return in a quarter hour."

"Yes, my lady." Hames curtseyed, glowered meaningfully at the clock, and decamped, closing the door silently in her wake.

I seated myself on a fussy little blue and gilt Queen Anne chair. "If it's courtesy you want, I will do you the very great honor of not wasting your time. Where were you on the day of the shoot, Lady Dalhousie?"

Her needle moved in a slow, steady rhythm. "Here, of course. Where else would I be in the middle of a winter's day?"

"You were not at the Manor when Cressida Northby came over to offer you the loan of some staff. You were out."

"I was merely too busy to put up with Mrs. Northby's nosiness. She doubtless intruded to try to winkle the menu from the staff and otherwise find grounds to fault the Manor's hospitality."

A thief attributed larceny to his every acquaintance. "She is your cousin, and yet, you refer to her formally even as you attribute base motives to her. Do you accuse Mrs. Northby of the destruction in the carriage house?"

The needle paused. "What destruction?"

"The family conveyances have all been violently hobbled. Wheels smashed to kindling and left in bits on the floor. My own coach saw the removal of every cotter pin holding the wheels to the axle, which in some ways is the more dangerous mischief. I might well have sent Miss West to Town in that vehicle, only to have it come to grief a mile from your gateposts."

Her ladyship slapped her needlework atop the open workbasket.

"The traveling coach must be repaired at once, and Dalhousie must go to Town. Easter is but a fortnight away, and he should already be in evidence at the clubs and shops."

"Don't expect me to lend him my coach," I said. "I might well need a means to flee the battlefield, or at least send my ladies to safety." I silently apologized to those ladies for hiding figuratively behind their skirts.

In point of fact, Dalhousie hadn't *asked* me to loan him my coach, which I would have cheerfully consented to do, provided that I, two armed guards, and the ladies traveled with us.

"You are not known for fleeing from battles," Lady Dalhousie said, folding her arms. "Getting yourself captured, yes, and committing treason, possibly, and even the next thing to fratricide, but nobody has accused you of lacking courage."

The barb stung, as it was intended to. "You have misled me regarding your whereabouts on the day of the shoot. You left the Manor premises for some time. You may cast all the insults upon my honor you please—more bad form, alas, and me a lowly invited guest —and I will still demand to know where you were and why you dissembled."

She closed the lid of her workbasket with an audible snap. "By what right do you demand anything of me?"

"Your son has been shot at, poisoned, threatened, his saddle tampered with, and now his property has been viciously destroyed. Somebody is willing to risk a hanging to wreak havoc on his lordship's person. The marquess has charged me with finding the perpetrator. If you thwart me, you abet a criminal intent on tormenting your son." I picked a piece of lint from my sleeve and flicked it to the carpet in the tradition of the best arrogant boors.

"But then," I went on, "you delight in tormenting Dalhousie."

My aim had been true as well, though the business of verbal skirmishing with the marchioness wearied and disgusted me. I understood her. She was driven by pride and haunted by regrets, though she would never admit to either.

I did not like her, and yet, I had to respect her ruthlessness.

"I love my son." Never had those same words carried such a load of venom.

"You do not even know your son. You love some paragon of filial devotion who exists only in your imagination and to whom you constantly compare the very good and decent man Dalhousie has become. Where were you on the day of the shoot?"

"You think I would aim a gun at my only offspring?"

"No, actually, but if you were abroad in the general vicinity of the woods, you might have seen something of note, might have crossed paths with the steward or undergardener or head lad, who should have been walking in the direction of the assembling beaters, but was instead headed elsewhere."

She frankly stared at me.

"You might have seen a footman scurrying off to the bridle paths rather than making haste for the kitchen gardens. Need I go on?"

Some of the righteousness left her bearing. "I went to the family plot. I crossed paths with nobody. I did not return to the Manor until I heard the guns start up."

Credible, given Dalhousie's earlier remarks, but not quite convincing. "Why not tell me that sooner?"

"Grief is private, as you would know if...."

I'd lost a brother, a father, and countless comrades, along with half my wits, the majority of my dignity, and the better part of my reputation. "You were saying?"

"My grief is private. If my lord has accomplished his errand, he will please leave."

"Your grief is private, but you feel free to instruct Dalhousie on the metes and bounds of his mourning for his father, to let him accept a neighbor's invitation and even offer the hospitality of the Manor on the anniversary of your bereavement, and then castigate him for his supposed thoughtlessness." I rose, only too happy to quit present company.

"You should rejoice that your son is not a hostage to grief," I said.

"You should give thanks that he can look to the future rather than make a graven idol of the past. You should thank the heavenly powers that Dalhousie cares enough for his own welfare to call in reinforcements when trouble is afoot. Instead, you hector and belittle him over trivialities. My lady, I bid you good day and thank you for your honesty, however belated."

"I left flowers," she said, rising. "I left nineteen roses on my husband's grave. All the roses we had, but it was enough. One for each year."

Not an apology, but a plea of some sort. Very well, I'd offer her a report. "The vandalism in the carriage house today likely took place at noon, when the whole of the stable staff would have been in the servants' hall at the midday meal. A short sledgehammer was on hand to effect the destruction, and Dalhousie has summoned the wainwright to do the repairs."

"Dalhousie said nothing to me. Do the others know?"

Others meaning Lady Albert, Tam, and Susanna, I supposed. "They do, and now you are informed as well."

"Why wouldn't he tell me himself?"

I might have heard some genuine bewilderment in that question, along with the predictable complement of indignation.

"If ever you find the courage to query your son on that point, please *listen* to his answer. Don't interrupt, don't accuse, don't lecture. *Listen*."

My exhortation was met with silence, so I bowed and withdrew, wishing more than anything that I could avoid the ordeal of supper. Alas for me, I was never one to run from a battlefield, even in Lady Dalhousie's grudging estimation.

CHAPTER ELEVEN

Supper was a subdued affair, carried mostly by Lady Ophelia's humorous recollections of Mad George's royal court, seconded by Susanna's recountings of the local assemblies, and Tam's flirtation and flattery. Lady Dalhousie sent her son brooding looks, the marquess maintained a host's polite interest in the conversation, and I nearly fell asleep over the crème brûlée.

Hyperia declared a need to retire early, and I claimed the honor of lighting her up to her room.

"The marchioness was surprised to learn of the mischief in the carriage house," I said as we trudged up the steps. "I'd bet Atticus's boots on that."

"Such an odd sort of vandalism," Hyperia said. "Why not steal the silver, slash the portraits, cut down the rhododendrons?"

"The house is never entirely empty, and hacking down rhododendrons takes time and makes a ruckus."

"I was thinking out loud, Jules, not asking for an analysis. You should dodge off after a single glass of port. You are tired."

"I am, and I miss the Hall." Until the words were out of my mouth, I hadn't known my own sentiments. A soldier learned to merely nod at homesickness in passing, lest it deliver blows to the spirit that felled him as effectively as bullets to the heart.

In that chilly, shadowed corridor, I longed as ardently for my home as I did for answers to Dalhousie's problems. Caldicott Hall was safety and repose, welcome and peace. The one place on earth where I had always been welcome.

The goodwives and yeomanry in the local surrounds might be equally attached to the thorny expanse of heath where their children played and their goats grazed—a sobering thought.

Hyperia stopped outside her sitting room door. "You miss the Hall. I worry about Healy. He's at the family seat, ostensibly putting the finishing touches on his second play." She slipped her arms around me and leaned against my chest. "Tell me my brother is not becoming a sot, Jules. Tell me his playwriting isn't just an excuse to hide from his creditors and from me."

"You are a devoted sister, and Healy is not a complete gudgeon. His first play was good, the second will be better, and having two on offer rather than a single debut effort is shrewd of him." The first play was humorous, sly, and a bit ribald, but not overly so. "We can look in on him when our business here is concluded."

"When will that be, Jules?" She straightened to peer at me by the light of the corridor sconces.

I kissed her nose. "Feeling restless and preoccupied? Frustrated perhaps because you cannot already see patterns of cause and effect in the evidence we have thus far? Wondering if there are patterns, but fearing you lack the acumen to see them?"

"More or less. The restlessness is the worst. I feel as if I ought to be doing something, peering into cupboards, lurking at keyholes. How do you bear the impatience?"

I drew her back into my arms and thought of months spent wandering the Spanish countryside, impatience my constant companion. Was the drunk snoring in the corner of the cantina a spy, and if so, for how many factions? Should I follow him into the night or pretend to doze in my own corner?

After a few near disasters, I'd learned the value of waiting and watching and waiting some more. Observing, listening, and lengthy bouts of cogitation and rumination had been the most valuable tools of my trade, and I hoped they were sufficient for present purposes.

"I persist," I said quietly. "I do the tasks likely to yield information, and when I've done them, I regroup and try again. Rest is important too, Hyperia. You said that yourself. Give your mind time to consider what you know, to sleep on the questions and riddles. If you asked Susanna to introduce you to a few neighbors, you'd likely learn things about Dalhousie's enclosure scheme that he isn't telling me."

"Such as?"

"Are the ladies as opposed to it as the men? Dalhousie will need an army of masons to build his walls and an army of gardeners to get any produce off the acreage. He'll need a fleet of wagons to move the goods to Town or to the ports, and that means a herd of mules or draft horses to pull the wagons."

"It means," Hyperia said slowly, "an ocean of laundry, another ocean of ale, cottages to be built, farriery for the hoofed stock... more apprentices for the cobbler, more candles bought from the chandler. Not only progress, but prosperity—perhaps."

"Perhaps, and perhaps the ladies view the matter in that light. I'd best rejoin Dalhousie and Tam and raise this very topic over the port. I plan to call on the innkeeper tomorrow, chat up the head lad, let Northby know of today's developments, and—"

"Why bring Northby into it?"

I opened her sitting room door, and a gust of warm air greeted us. "Let's finish the discussion before the fire, shall we?" Rather than in a corridor where any footmen could be lurking in the nearest alcove.

Hyperia scooted through the doorway. I followed, and we gained both warmth and privacy. I took advantage of the latter to kiss my beloved properly—also a bit improperly—and then she was once again cuddled in my embrace and radiating far less frustration.

"Northby is the magistrate," I said when my mind was again able to connect words into sentences. "Dalhousie's pride is one thing,

Lady Dalhousie's horror of gossip is another, but the king's peace is Northby's responsibility. He should be kept informed as a courtesy."

"Dalhousie should inform him, then."

"Dalhousie is not comfortable confronting his elders, much less taking them to task. Then too, Northby, as host of the shoot, might well suggest calling in another magistrate to investigate, and Dalhousie dislikes that notion." Dalhousie disliked even more the prospect of explaining such an eventuality to his mama.

"Better to call in you?"

"Us. Will you visit the vicarage with me tomorrow?"

"Yes, but why?"

"Because we conduct our investigations as reconnaissance missions. We do not posit a theory—Tam is to blame—and then see only the evidence that condemns him. We collect as much relevant information as we can and follow where the facts lead."

"I'd rather blame Lady Dalhousie."

"Tempting, I agree. She has much to answer for, but she did not aim a gun at her son or wield that sledgehammer." I was nearly certain of my conclusion. "I asked Susanna for her ladyship's whereabouts at midday, and the marchioness was said to be inventorying the linen closets at tedious length."

"Where was Tam?"

"I hope to find that out in the next half hour. Dream of me, my darling, and know that I will dream of you."

We engaged in another spate of kissing, but of the subdued variety necessary when a man must return to polite company with his wits about him, drat the ruddy luck.

"Be careful, Jules," Hyperia said, seeing me to the door. "You've been lucky thus far, but please... be careful."

"You too, Hyperia, and we must both exhort Lady Ophelia to exercise caution as well."

I left, despite a towering impulse to linger, and Hyperia let me go. I was right in one sense—we had work to do, days of it at least—but Hyperia's frustration was understandable too. Matters were growing more dangerous, and the author of Dalhousie's trouble grew bolder with time.

For the sake of all concerned, we needed to catch our culprit, the sooner the better.

Tam had been in the library from breakfast until the nooning bell had rung, observed by any number of footmen, Lady Albert—the light in the library was the best for close work—and the butler. He thus provided an alibi for his mother and produced one for himself, at least as regarded the vehicular destruction.

As the investigation moved into the second week, I settled in as if for a siege. The innkeeper knew nothing about any unfranked notes being delivered to the Manor. The vicar had little to say regarding the enclosure scheme or anything of merit, but then, Dalhousie held the local living, and the vicar's opinions were perforce tempered by prudence.

Hyperia dutifully embarked on a round of social calls with Susanna, swilling tea by the gallon and gathering only a vague sense that the ladies were as opposed to enclosure as their sons and husbands were. Even the local stonemason, fearing that all his custom would be stolen by crews brought in from Cornwall, wanted nothing to do with any enclosure walls.

"We feel becalmed in our inquiries," I said to Northby as he and I walked along on opposite sides of a drystone wall along the border of the Abbey and the Manor. We paused occasionally to heave a tumbled rock back into place among its brethren, or to assess a patch of greater damage wrought by the past year's frost heave.

On Northby's side of the wall, a pair of aging hounds gamboled about, sniffing the base of the wall here, anointing it in the time-honored fashion of canines there. The breeze held a hint of mildness by early spring standards, though on my side of the wall, patches of snow lingered from an overnight dusting.

"You wait for the hounds to pick up the scent," Northby said, gaze on his companions, "but no matter how you cast them, Reynard has left no trace of his passing." He put a sizable rock atop the wall, filling a gap made by nature. "Dalhousie should have raised the alarm sooner if he wanted the matter investigated. Any tracks in the woods are long gone by now. Alibis are in place, silences secured."

I had looked for those tracks anyway, and the squire was right. Rain, wind, the passage of time, and the denizens of the wood had obliterated any useful signs.

I wedged a flat rock into a gap on my side of the wall. "I've questioned the entire household about the hour when the coaches could have been tampered with. Everybody from the boot-boy to the pensioners can account for their whereabouts. This time of year, the noon meal is conscientiously well attended."

The marquess had been inspecting some fallow ground with the steward, which had spared me the chore of interrogating a senior and much-respected employee regarding his movements.

"You are left with two possibilities, my lord. Dalhousie's enemy in this case might not bide under his roof, which is easily possible. In the alternative…"

The hounds gazed intently in the direction of the village, then looked to the squire.

"Somebody is lying," I said, hefting another rock on my side of the wall. "The Dandridges are good liars, the marquess in particular."

"You insult the man, my lord. I don't care for Dalhousie's enclosure ambitions in the least, but he's honest. Even foolishly honest."

"He dissembles daily and to good effect. His whole family thinks he's a bit spoiled, not overly bright, something of a poseur, but generally well intended. He smiles, he quips, he hugs the ladies and goes about his business, and not one of them realizes how hard he's working or how much he has to manage."

My respect for Dalhousie had grown as I'd watched him at close range. He had my brother Arthur's ability to accomplish a great deal without ever resorting to hurry or ill humor. Perhaps a successful peerage depended on that talent, and in Dalhousie's case, an agreeable demeanor meant his industry was even less obvious to the casual observer.

He made time to take meals with family in the usual course. He teased the ladies and was friends with Tam. He shielded his dear mama from *any* confrontations and kept a roof over family members who ought by rights to be housed in humbler circumstances.

"Dalhousie isn't a liar in the insulting sense," I said. "I stand corrected, but he's an accomplished actor."

"Needs must, given his station, I suppose."

We came to a patch of wall half disintegrated by the elements. The component parts lay in disarray on muddy ground, and the tracks of hoofed stock and large fowl led in all directions.

"They leap upon the wall over and over," Northby said, "the sheep, the deer, the errant bullock, or ambitious heifer, and the wall weakens. The water gets in, the freezing and thawing take a toll, and without anybody intending any destruction, a wall guaranteed for a hundred years yields at last. Mind you don't put all the heaviest specimens on the bottom. That's not how a stout wall works. The top must secure the bottom as the bottom supports the top."

We toiled in pleasant silence, the activity sending me back to boyhood, when Harry and I had tagged along after the dikers who'd kept the miles of stone wall at the Hall in trim. The crews who mended walls for us were a peripatetic lot, but every spring they showed up, quiet, thickly muscled, and as steady in their labor as the sun moving inexorably in the sky.

While I put the finishing touches on my side, the squire took a pull on his flask. "Dalhousie has company."

A lone rider on a lathered bay galloped up the long curving driveway to the Manor. Because the wind blew from the south, the tableau took place in silence rather than accompanied by a tattoo of hoofbeats. The dogs watched the horse intently, but remained on their haunches two yards from the squire.

"Not company," I said as the horse barreled right past the front steps and around to the porte cochere. "News. News from Town, I'd say. That's a messenger, given the state of his attire, not a caller, and that horse was chosen for stamina and speed rather than elegance or the comfort of his gaits."

Northby capped his flask. "Bad news, then, in all likelihood. Your lordship had best go pour oil on troubled waters, or whatever it is you're about these days. If you're ever in want of work, you can mend wall for me. Somebody taught you properly."

"I'll bear your offer in mind. Northby, where were you at noon on Friday?"

He decided to be amused rather than affronted. "At my midday meal, with my wife, where I always am at noon, lest I be lectured endlessly about domestic bliss resting on a solid foundation of domestic routines, et cetera and so forth. When we refer to domestic bliss, we don't mention whose bliss, do we?"

He sent the Manor an unreadable glance and ambled off along his side of the wall, the dogs trotting at his heels.

I made my way across the park and told myself that asking the squire to account for himself was simply being thorough, but, in fact, I was grasping at straws. My coach had been restored to seaworthiness, as had the marquess's phaeton, and the wainwright promised a functional traveling coach in time for divine services—Palm Sunday, as it happened.

I'd told the squire we were becalmed, but a more accurate description was that we were awaiting the next calamity. If some local malefactor wanted to prevent Dalhousie from journeying to London with his enclosure bill ready for submission before Parliament, only another calamity would suffice to thwart that aim.

Atticus met me in front of the porte cochere. "Messenger from Town, guv. Nothin' good ever comes from Town on a fast horse." He was walking that fast horse, the beast's sides still heaving with exertion.

"Give that one a sip of water, Atticus, then keep him walking for at least the next thirty minutes. A sip of water every five minutes, his tack off after three sips, then back to walking. A light sheet on him after the next sip—he's to be uncovered for no more than five minutes. Hay, water, or such grass as you can find for the next three hours, but no grain. When he's dry, curry him to within an inch of his horsey life. He's not to be kept in a stall overnight, lest he stiffen up."

Atticus until recently had been entirely illiterate, resulting in a prodigiously fine memory. "Aye, guv. You'd best get inside. This fine weather won't last. Come along, horse. You've earned your keep this day."

The gelding trudged after him, head low, steps plodding. I watched them depart for the stable yard, the horse in particular. A well-made specimen in good flesh, despite the time of year. Not a livery stable hack or a coach horse subjected to the indignity of work under saddle.

The news from Town had arrived on a Dalhousie mount, stabled along the route for Dalhousie purposes and likely ridden by a Dalhousie groom.

More bad news, indeed.

~

I let myself into the Manor by the side door and was met by Susanna.

"Dalhousie received the messenger in the study," she said. "I've warned the kitchen that a hungry rider needs immediate sustenance, and we'll find a place to house him overnight. I've seldom seen so haggard a countenance."

"Where is the rest of the family?"

"Their ladyships are resting at this hour. Tam is playing billiards."

"Say nothing to anybody, Miss Susanna, but please fetch Miss West and Lady Ophelia for me. I will join the marquess in his study."

"Lady Ophelia is in the village looking over the shops. I'll find Miss West."

Lady Ophelia was on reconnaissance, then. "My thanks."

She bustled off, apparently agreeing with me that the older ladies were best left to their embroidery and tea trays for the nonce.

I rapped on the study door and admitted myself before permission could be granted. Dalhousie stood by the window, a study in pensive, gentlemanly contemplation. A dusty, lanky man of indeterminate years waited by the hearth, a glass of what appeared to be spirits in a gnarled hand. His age could have been anywhere from thirty to fifty, but having seen him on horseback, I knew him to have been to the saddle born. Former steeplechase jockey would be my first guess.

"Lord Julian Caldicott," Dalhousie said without turning away from the window, "may I make known to you Richard Franklin, who has the honor to be my London stablemaster. Dicky began as a groom under my grandfather. I trust him without limit. Dicky, Lord Julian is equally in my confidence. Tell him what you told me."

Dicky took a swig of fine spirits and sized me up with a gimlet glance. "We've had a fire in the Dalhousie town house." This dire news was imparted with the incongruously musical lilt of the native Welshman. "Started in his lordship's apartment. The staff caught it early, and the damage is mostly to his lordship's quarters. We're dealing with the stink and mess now—the housekeeper has been nigh moved to profanity, and her a God-fearing woman—but the structure remains sound."

Fire, the godmother of all calamities. "When was this?"

"Last night. The place has been all astir in anticipation of the family arriving. Airing this, beating that, dusting the other. Flues should have been clean in the family rooms because they haven't been used all winter, but something went amiss. Bad business, my lords."

Dicky was given to understatement. "You've kept it quiet?"

"Aye. Fire in London is grounds for riot and panic. The staff will keep mum if they value their jobs."

No, they wouldn't. For a time, shock and loyalty would ensure nothing was said, but some junior footman, three pints down, would let slip a grumbling comment about having to strip the paper from the walls of the marquess's sitting room. An exhausted chambermaid would complain to the coalman about all the carpets having to be taken up because they had been ruined.

Word would get out, meaning the time to investigate was *now*.

"We can take my coach," I said to Dalhousie's three-quarter profile, "though you will please ask the wainwright to complete repairs on your own conveyance as quickly as possible for the sake of the ladies. If we leave in the next hour, we might make London by midnight."

If Dicky had set out at dawn, he'd covered fifty miles, give or take, in less than eight hours on roads alternately muddy and frozen. Dispatch riders had been capable of such feats, and once upon a time, I had been, too, given enough sound horses.

"I'd wait, my lord," Dicky said. "We're into that season where the top half inch of ground thaws by midmorning, and that same half inch won't freeze again until after sundown. Deadly perilous going for even a surefooted team. I have the messenger mounts shod with studded shoes this time of year for that reason. The coach teams haven't any studs."

Studs, small metal protrusions that gave a horseshoe purchase on wet grass or slick footing, were another dispatch riders' trick.

"Get you to the kitchen, Dicky," Dalhousie said, turning at last. "My thanks for your haste. You were right to bring the news directly to me. Your discretion belowstairs would be appreciated as well."

Dicky grinned, teeth showing white against a dusty, lined countenance. "I'm too knackered to gossip, milord. I'll be asleep before I've done justice to my first pint."

"The horse is in good hands," I said as Dicky moved toward the door at a slightly uneven gait. "He'll be walked, watered, rugged up, fed, and fussed over until he's turned out for the night."

Dicky nodded. "Could not ask for better. If you do decide to make for Town, I'd appreciate a seat on the box. Don't like to leave my post for any longer than I have to."

Dalhousie nodded. "Understood, and again, my thanks."

The door closed behind a man prepared to travel one hundred miles in a day to be home with his horses. "He should have been a dispatch rider."

"He lost two brothers that way and a cousin. One of the brothers left a young wife and son behind."

"You provide for them." Why else would Dalhousie keep track of such a detail?

"Of course. I suppose I should offer you a drink."

"Dalhousie, you've had a shock. Sit down and stop trying to be the gracious host."

"I am a gracious host." Even the marquess apparently grasped the inanity of his reply. He took a wing chair by a fire that had nearly gone out. "Fire in London. To risk that... My God, Caldicott. I'm dealing with a lunatic."

I poured a stout tot of brandy and brought it to Dalhousie. "Medicinal. Drink it, if you please." My next task was to build up the fire. People enduring a shock were often menaced by unaccountable shivers and trembling. Warmth was in order.

"The town house blaze was contained," I said. "Your staff was alert and took prompt action. I am mindful that Dicky speaks as an expert when he says we ought not to leave now, but if we travel on horseback, we'll be less at risk. Any attempt to clean up the scene of the crime could destroy evidence."

Dalhousie sipped his drink with elegant restraint. "I want this to be a mishap. Somebody overlooked one of the chimneys at the last cleaning. Birds nested, the usual chimney fire that's mostly smoke and soot. Birds don't nest in winter, do they?"

His mind was unequal to the enormity of the latest disaster. He'd need time to absorb the facts and more time to make any worthwhile decisions regarding next steps—time we did not have.

"I have pigeons." I set the fireplace poker back on its stand. "I can get word to your London staff to cease any cleaning or restoration efforts immediately. I can be in Town by midnight."

"Pigeons don't nest in winter either—oh. Those sorts of pigeons." He sipped again, nosed his drink, and set the glass aside. "I should go with you."

He was trying to think, bless him. "You should bide here with the ladies." I took the second wing chair and did some thinking myself. "I'll take Tam."

"Tam?"

"If anything else should go amiss here, Tam can't be immediately implicated when he's in Town with me." Tam fifty miles distant from Dalhousie would also be less able to *make* anything go amiss. "You have a stout reinforcement in Susanna, and you should mention this development to Northby as well."

"Susanna should be told. She worries about everybody, and she will want to know why Tam was dragooned off to Town."

That was more of Dalhousie the old-fashioned paterfamilias surfacing, which was probably an encouraging sign.

"Will Susanna respect your confidences?"

His smile was wan. "She even respects me, I think. Sometimes. Who would risk fire in London, my lord? Damnable business. Desperate. I wasn't even in Town, and anybody could have ascertained that fact simply by peering into the mews or dropping 'round the nearest pub."

Or reading the newspapers, or inquiring of the family's London gardener. "You make an interesting point, but try not to trouble yourself overly with speculation. Carry on here, keep up the rounds with the steward, inspect every piece of fallow ground, admire the mares in foal, carry the baritone part at divine services."

He picked up his drink again. "Fallow ground doesn't need inspecting, though I grant you, the mares in foal are a lovely sight. I'm more of a tenor than a baritone." He sipped with every appearance of contentment. "I don't know how much more of this I can take."

"Another calamity arrived, right on schedule. I find that encouraging, Dalhousie, not daunting. Before you remove permanently to Lisbon, let me poke around the scene of the fire. Good decisions are made based on good information, and I might bring exactly that back from London."

He finished his drink. "The fire is blazing, and yet, I'm cold. I don't envy you a ride to Town, my lord. I should go with you."

"You will defend the castle. I will take Tam. I'm off to send a pigeon and to let Miss West know what's afoot. You may trust her and Lady Ophelia with your life."

Dalhousie saluted with his empty glass. "Pray heaven, I am not doing just that. Safe journey, my lord, and good hunting. See that you return in one piece."

CHAPTER TWELVE

Tragedy, in my experience, invariably inflicted a stink along with upheaval and sorrow. The cloying stench of lilies at a funeral, the acrid aroma of gun smoke above a battlefield, the symbolic odor of false pity surrounding a scandal of any size.

The marquess's London sitting room reeked of both damp and sulfur, with notes of scorched wool adding a bitter tang.

"Devil take it," Tam said, flourishing an embroidered handkerchief and covering his nose. "Rotten affair, literally rotten." He stood surrounded by destruction in the middle of the sitting room. "Could have been worse, I suppose. We might have already removed to Town, along with the rest of polite society."

He used the toe of his boot to flip aside a burned length of carpet. "Grandmama decorated this room before I was born. Gordie wasn't willing to see it changed. Said that was for his bride to do."

Gordie...? Then I recalled that Dalhousie's given name was Gordon.

"Try not to move anything else," I said, remaining in the doorway to the corridor. "We are exceptionally fortunate that the housekeeper decided to allow the rooms to dry before cleaning them." The windows were open to the raw early morning air, Tam and I having arrived a mere three hours earlier. By agreement with Dalhousie, we bided at the Caldicott London residence rather than under a roof that had survived a bout of possible arson.

Arthur's pigeons had done a yeoman effort, alerting the Caldicott staff to my itinerary and, through the good offices of the ducal butler, warning Dalhousie's staff away from the crime scene.

"What can you possibly tell from this mess?" Tam asked, turning a circle, "other than that somebody tried to burn us out."

I'd already reviewed with Dalhousie's butler the schedule followed by the chimney sweeps. Those dubious fellows had sworn on the souls of their sainted grannies that every single chimney on the premises had been duly cleaned in early January. London laws were strict and unforgiving on the topic of dirty chimneys, and if a sweep were to cut corners, he'd do so somewhere other than a marquess's household.

"The fire started on that hearth." I took a few gingerly steps across the room. "Observe the pattern of smoke stains on the wallpaper. The bedroom suffered much less damage and little on the inside wall."

"Meaning?"

"The prevailing breeze in London is from the west, for all but a few weeks here and there. In mid-April, it often comes from the north, though only temporarily. To ensure the flue draws, most footmen will crack a window, even in cold weather, when the fire is first started."

Tam's gaze went to windows thrust open as high as the sashes allowed. "Therefore...?"

"The greatest portion of smoke is accumulated on the eastern-most wall." I gestured to a smoke-blackened landscape of Dalhousie Manor hanging above a sideboard. "The window was opened, the mess in the hearth did not draw, and thus you see the smoke billowed nearly to the ceiling."

"But the rug isn't completely charred," Tam said.

"A passing footman smelled the smoke, and because his errand had been carrying washing water from the laundry to the dormitory on the next floor up, he heaved a lucky few gallons right onto the heart of the fire." Or so a teary housekeeper had informed me.

I would talk to the footman who'd been in such an opportune place at such a fortunate time. All of London smelled of coal smoke. What had alerted this fellow to inchoate tragedy?

I sniffed around in the bedroom, which had been damaged as much by water as by smoke, despite there being little evidence of an extinguished fire.

"An abundance of caution," I muttered. "At least they spared the bed hangings."

"But not the carpet." Tam seemed genuinely unhappy at the state of his grandmama's rugs. "This one can be saved, don't you think?"

"The wool will dry, but getting the stink out will take some effort. Lend me that walking stick."

He passed over an unprepossessing wooden affair that would barely qualify as an accessory in the better clubs. "I like that one. Susanna gave it to me, so please..."

I jabbed the hooked end of the walking stick up the flue of the sitting room chimney. A shower of soot, ashes, and charred rags came down onto the andirons. More hard poking dislodged a larger wad of what had likely been intended as tinder.

I bent down and sniffed, but could detect no odor of gunpowder or kerosene.

"A very odd sort of arson," I said, handing Tam back his walking stick.

He wiped the handle with his handkerchief and tossed the exquisitely embroidered square of linen onto the heap of detritus half burying the andirons.

"What is my lord wittering on about now?"

I picked up the handkerchief, both because it did not belong among the evidence and because some careful washing would restore it to usefulness. The stitchery had taken some lady—probably

Susanna—hours to complete, and Tam hadn't sense enough to value that labor.

"We can confirm that the fire was deliberately set," I said, dusting my hands and making for the door. Dalhousie would be displeased. When I'd left the marquess, he'd graduated to muttering about faulty flues, lazy chimneysweeps, and bad luck on top of worse.

"Well, I didn't set it," Tam said. "Neither did my mother or—one must admit the obvious—the marchioness. What does a lot of old rags stuffed up a chimney prove anyway?"

"In itself, nothing, except that Dalhousie's malefactor has had access to his town house in the past few weeks. That rules out practically every soul on the estate, as well as the family."

"But not Northby," Tam said, following me from the room. "He and Cressy come up to Town to see his brother after the holidays. He's dead set against the enclosure, and if Dalhousie can't come to Town, he can't introduce his bill before Parliament."

We moved down the corridor, the scent of smoke fading, though I knew it would linger in my clothes and hair until both were thoroughly washed. Artillery crews resigned themselves to reeking for days after a battle—provided they survived the hostilities—and some of the older sergeants lost their sense of smell as well as their hearing after years of campaigning.

Damn the Corsican for that, too, and damn whoever was plaguing Dalhousie.

"Why doesn't Dalhousie ask somebody else to introduce his bill?" I asked.

"Because he wouldn't," Tam said, accompanying me down the main staircase. "That would be... not exactly cowardly, but it would ask another man to take on one skirmish in Dalhousie's battles, and our Gordie is too honorable for that. Before all this upset, he might have relied on a crony or two to see to the formalities—he will be waltzed off his feet once he does come to Town—but not now."

"Waltzed off his feet by prospective marchionesses?"

We reached the frigid main foyer, a temple to white marble flooring, white gesso pilasters, robust ferns, and uninspired landscapes. The whole was illuminated by a skylight in addition to large windows facing the street and their mirror images facing a back garden sporting a few ambitious daffodils.

"This is the year Dalhousie must wed," Tam said. "Or that was the plan. I will miss him, and his defection from the ranks of bachelors might inspire me to take a bride myself. Of course, that would leave Suze to the tender mercies of the Dandridge dragons, and what sort of cousin would I be if I allowed that fate to befall her?"

Precisely the sort of cousin the world expected him to be? "You will leave the Manor if Dalhousie marries?"

"I might." He leaned conspiratorially nearer. "When a man of any standing marries, he tells himself little need change. A pleasant duty features on the end of some evenings, but other than that, his life will continue as he wishes it to. This is a lie perpetrated upon the unsuspecting by the majority of former bachelors. They prevaricate out of a combination of self-delusion and declining faculties. Marriage makes a fellow see things differently, and children... They are noisy and dear and nearly inevitable following the vows and sometimes even before them. One shudders."

No, one did not, but from Tam's perspective—an overgrown boy with the means to cherish his juvenile self-indulgence—the recitation was doubtless honest.

"Tamerlane, whom do you think set this fire?"

He glanced up the steps. "Devils. Playing with fire is for devils or the poor souls they torment. I'm off to the club for a decent beefsteak. Care to join me?"

"Thank you, no. I'd like to question the footman who found the fire and led the efforts to contain it. I will also speak with the sweeps who look after this house and do some further nosing around."

Tam retrieved his hat from a hook over the deal table beside the porter's nook. "You be careful, Caldicott. Potshots and poison are bad enough, but arson in London breaks all bounds. Dalhousie is a peer in his prime, and anybody who'd do him a mischief isn't right in the brainbox."

"Tamerlane, for the love of all that is discreet, you will not bruit it about that mischief of any sort has befallen your family. The sweeps missed one chimney, a bit of smoke and mess resulted, all's well, if you must mention the incident at all."

"Right." He tapped his hat down and tilted it a half inch to the right. "I can be discreet, but my warning stands. Be careful."

His admonition was offered with odd gravity, and then he was off down the steps, his walking stick propped jauntily over his shoulder.

I surprised myself by repeating Dicky's feat of stamina two days after having arrived in London. The Dalhousie mounts—kept in readiness for the marquess himself—were first-quality riding stock and up to my weight. The weather was chilly but reasonably obliging, meaning the roads were dryish.

Winter was on the run, though the farther I rode from London, the less evidence of spring I saw. In the shires, the occasional lambing snow might yet fall, but plowing had begun, and planting would soon follow.

Where was Arthur? Was he idling about on some Greek island, delighting in milder climes, or was he dreading the prospect of a return to the Hall?

"You're back," Atticus said, taking the reins of my tired chestnut gelding when he came to a halt in the stable yard. "Miss West said you wouldn't tarry in Town."

The boy had fretted that I would abandon him, of course. Only time and unfailing reliability on my part would ease that anxiety.

"I am back. Tamerlane will follow at a more leisurely pace, just as soon as he's tithed to his bootmaker, tailor, glovemaker, half the clubs in St. James's, and a few addresses a gentleman doesn't name in mixed company. Atlas is well?"

Atticus patted the chestnut's neck. "That Dicky fellow said Atlas were a fine specimen in fine condition. He left yesterday. Showed me how to pull a horseshoe so I don't tear off any hoof."

"A vital skill, and not enough grooms take the time to learn it. What of Shakespeare, my boy?"

Atticus busied himself loosening the horse's girth. "Why does everybody say he writes comedies? What he thinks is funny is mostly people insulting each other. Poor people making fun of rich people, men making fun of women, smart people putting down the simpler folk. The simple folk putting down the queen. I don't care for it."

"His audiences weren't allowed to put down much of anybody, so they enjoyed his humor, but you make an interesting point. Anything else to report?"

"All quiet. Too quiet. Everybody knows Dicky came out from Town hotfoot. Then you and Tam tore into Town hotfoot, while the marquess swans about like the King of Palmyra, not a care in the world."

"Beginning to wish you'd stayed at the Hall?" I could certainly admit to that sentiment.

"Not on your life, guv. I wrote to Leander and Her Grace. Miss West checked my spelling."

I was overdue to report to the duchess, and she would certainly get word that I'd been spotted in Town.

"Keep your ears open, Atticus. The problem in London was arson, a fire set deliberately in the marquess's very apartment."

"That's serious, that is. Londoners hate fires."

"With good reason. Somebody willing to go to such lengths is not to be underestimated." In its way, arson was worse than firing a bullet at a human target. The bullet might kill the man, but fire—fire in Town—could rage for days, end countless lives, and destroy structures that would take years to replace. The Great Fire had changed London forever and left an indelible stamp on Londoners too.

"Julian."

At the edge of the stable yard, Hyperia stood swathed in a plain brown cloak and simple straw hat, looking like an unprepossessing gentry miss out for a bit of sketching. She preferred subdued colors—they drew less notice—though I was becoming aware of how subtly she managed Society's impression of her.

"Dearest lady." I bowed. "I have a report, and the news is interesting. Atticus, I'll see you after supper. Don't wait up for me if I'm late."

He waved and led the horse away, and abruptly, I felt every mile of the journey I'd made.

"You've overtaxed yourself, haven't you?" Hyperia slipped her arm through mine and gently marched me to a bench bathed in the weak afternoon sunshine. "Rode out from Town in a single day. Julian, you know better."

"Fatigue makes me irritable. I know. I will nap before supper." I handed her onto the bench and came down beside her, the wood surprisingly warm against my backside. "Arson, Perry. Arson plain as day and in the marquess's private sitting room. Somebody stuffed the chimney full of tinder, and the first time a fire was lit in the hearth, disaster came calling, or nearly so."

"A stuffed chimney doesn't draw, does it?"

Straight to the heart of the riddle, of course. "I interrogated the head sweep on that very point, and he said it depends. If the packing is done just so, the chimney is essentially narrowed, the speed of the updraft is increased, and the packing is set ablaze faster and hotter."

"And yet, we are told a dirty flue won't draw as well."

"A chimney all but obstructed with dirt and ash won't draw, which is the other side of a coin. The head sweep's example was a bird's nest. Most chimneys are capped, but if the cap rusts or comes loose, and birds begin nesting, they can quickly accumulate several feet of thickly packed twigs, straw, and feathers at the top of the chimney. They keep adding to the pile until the chimney is so full, the nest is stable."

"And then, the chimney doesn't draw at all, or—depending—it can ignite with a spectacular explosion that spreads to the whole house, all because a pair of robins needed a home. Dalhousie was lucky, then. Very lucky."

"He was lucky in more ways than one, Perry." I wanted to take her hand, and it occurred to me *that I could*. We were engaged to be married. I slipped my fingers through hers, and she allowed it. "The footman who discovered the fire was fairly new to Town. He had both the country lad's keen nose and the terror of fire impressed upon all who go into service in London. He'd laid that fire himself and thus felt responsible for keeping an eye on it."

"Or a nose, but if the marquess wasn't expected in Town, why light that fire at all, Jules?"

"I needed a day's pondering before I put that question to Dalhousie's housekeeper. She said the marchioness had notified her to prepare the house for the family's arrival. The day and hour had not yet been chosen, but the fire was lit because an army of maids would be dusting and polishing the entire suite. Beeswax polish apparently works better when the chill is off the air."

"True enough. I wonder if Dalhousie knew of his mother's instructions."

Another excellent question. "How are they getting on?"

Hyperia withdrew her hand. "Have you noticed, Julian, that nobody in this family really talks to anybody else?"

Whatever was she getting at? "I haven't noticed any such thing, Perry, though I grant you, the lot of them avoid needlessly confronting the marchioness. At meals, the conversation flows easily. These people have the gift of chat, of pleasant conversation. I envy them that. They laugh together, tease one another, poke fun at the neighbors and the Regent and everybody in between. The marchioness tries to cast a pall over the meal, but seldom succeeds."

"Because she doesn't *chat*," Hyperia said, rising unassisted. "Let's get you to the house. You have to be famished and weary."

She was unhappy with me. What had I said or failed to say? I tried to mentally review our dialogue, but found to my horror that I was a bit unsteady on my pins.

Hyperia laced her arm through mine, her grip on me stout and supportive. "I will make your excuses at supper, Julian. You will rest. You will take a tray and eat every bite. If you'd like a bath, I can have one sent up as well, but you are not to fall asleep in the bathwater."

"A bath sounds divine." And having Hyperia fuss over me was divine as well, but the edge of annoyance in her tone troubled me. "I have time to bathe and nap before supper. How is Godmama managing?"

"You should ask her. She has bought out the village shops, she spent two hours wandering around the local market yesterday, and she is already on friendly terms with half the goodwives in the churchyard. Susanna took us to call on Cressy Northby, and an endless game of do-you-recall and whatever-became-of ensued."

"Sizing each other up?" When had the Manor moved five miles from the stable?

"Or genuinely enjoying their reminiscing. Susanna and I sipped tea and ate biscuits. Nobody is discussing the marquess's problems, and everybody is aware of them."

"Atticus said the same thing. Too quiet, belowstairs and in the stable." Life in a military camp had had some of the same quality. We might have been crossing half of Spain to confront the French army and face death itself, but we played cards, groused about rations, and traded newspapers weeks out of date, all without a word regarding what loomed ahead.

"What are you thinking, Jules?"

I had been thinking about campaigns that ended in death. "If the marquess had been asleep in his London bed, Perry, then the smoke itself might have overcome him without waking him. The sweep swore noxious gases claimed as many lives as flames when it came to house fires."

My observation was greeted with another fulminating silence from the lady on my arm. I was on the point of asking what *she* was thinking when a man's raised voice cut across the deserted back garden.

"That's Dalhousie," Hyperia said. "He never loses his temper."

"Somebody must be with him in the study." Somebody who had provoked him to shouting.

"... and that, madam, is my *final* word!"

"He's not chatting," Hyperia said, moving more quickly. "I suspect the marchioness is with him. Jules, do come along. They likely don't know you're back yet, and you have news to impart."

I'd sent an express to Dalhousie with only a few particulars. *Domicile secure, nuisance property damage only, more news to follow.* Messengers could have mishaps, and thus I'd avoided any mention of arson, mischief, personal animosity, or luck.

We slipped into the house through the door to the back terrace and headed for the marquess's study. Lady Dalhousie herself emerged, the study door closing stoutly behind her. She whisked past us, then stopped and turned.

"This is your fault, Lord Julian. I knew you were trouble, and now Dalhousie refuses to go to Town. I blame you, and I demand to know what you intend to do about it."

I bowed to the proper depth. "I intend to applaud the marquess's sound judgment. Had he been in London a week ago, he might well be dead by now. Good day."

Her eyebrows rose nearly to her hairline. "What on earth do you mean?"

"I report to your son, my lady, not to you. If Dalhousie wants you apprised of the latest threat to his life, he will do so himself."

"That wretched boy never tells me anything!"

He's not a boy. Fortunately for my self-respect, Hyperia's hand on my arm stayed me from flinging those words at the marchioness. How many years had my mother and I struggled to exchange anything other than civilities, and how painful had those years been for all concerned?

"Come with us," I said, extending a hand to her ladyship. "I must inform Dalhousie of the situation in London. He might be surprised to hear that you have ordered the town house put in readiness for the family's arrival. You can explain your reasoning to him in person."

"I do not explain myself to my own offspring."

The door to the study opened, and Dalhousie stepped into the corridor. "My lord, Miss West. Won't you join me?"

The look that passed between mother and son was arctic on both ends. Hyperia decided the moment by proceeding past the marquess and into his study. I bowed to the marchioness again, and Dalhousie did likewise.

After another fraught moment, the marquess closed the door not quite in his mother's face, but as near as made no difference.

CHAPTER THIRTEEN

"The marchioness gave orders more than a week ago that the town house was to be put in readiness." Dalhousie assumed his pensive-gentleman pose by the window, though even half turning his back to Hyperia was rude. "My own mother, letting the whole world know to expect me in Town. The repairs on the coaches are barely completed, and she's marching me down the pike to Mayfair."

Hyperia poured a tot of brandy and brought it to Dalhousie. "She meant no disrespect, my lord. She meant to do her duty as your hostess and the lady in charge of your households."

"I am in charge of my..." He looked at the brandy. "Thank you. I *should* be in charge of my households, but do you know, if it weren't for Susanna, I would not even have a say over the menus? French cuisine is all the rage—sauces smothering everything from our good English beef to that inedible atrocity known as asparagus. I am rambling."

The gift of chat running amok. I tried to steer us to the matter at hand. "The fire in your town house was deliberately set, but the arsonist's intentions are not as easy to read."

"Miss West, please do have a seat," Dalhousie said, gesturing to the wing chairs by the hearth. "My manners have gone begging. I apologize."

His wits were nearly absent without leave as well, poor man. "Let's all sit." I brought the chair behind the desk around to the fireplace and explained about the ambiguity of the fire-setting. Somebody of significant cunning had set out to create a filthy nuisance, or somebody of significant malevolence had set out to destroy a household.

"The evidence was inconclusive," I said, "but in either case, the risk to you might have been significant. Smoke can kill as effectively as fire."

"I suspected something like this." Dalhousie tapped a manicured fingernail on the arm of his reading chair. "By damn.... Pardon my language, Miss West. I told Mama we cannot possibly go to Town with all this trouble afoot. We settle the business here, on Dalhousie land, where my enclosure project will happen—*shall* happen. Mama has no idea of the sort of criminals who can be had for two-a-penny a stone's throw from Mayfair. Sabotaged carriages will be just the start, and all of Society will soon know that I'm unable to sort out my own affairs. Mama isn't thinking clearly."

He sipped his drink, and Hyperia raised the question I would have been loath to ask. "Your enemy clearly has the ability to make trouble for you both here and in Town," she said. "That speaks to some means, knowledge of how London works, and the ability to penetrate your domestic defenses in either location. Might you not let it be known that the enclosure scheme is looking more costly than you'd first thought?"

Dalhousie aimed a tired stare at her. "Hesitate? Appear to hesitate? You don't ascribe to Addison's maxim that the person who deliberates is lost, Miss West?"

"Mr. Addison's play, from which that line is taken, was a tragedy for the hero, who ended up falling on his sword rather than compromising his ideals. Since Lord Julian has arrived, you have suffered no

threats of deadly harm. Foul play certainly and destruction of property, too, but no more bullets or poison."

I saw where Hyperia's reasoning led—to a point obvious in hindsight, a point I'd entirely missed. "Miss West is suggesting, Dalhousie,
that your enemy grows desperate and is facing some limits. Setting
the fire in your sitting room took stealth and determination—and
probably the good offices of a second-story thief willing to stuff the
chimney nigh full from the top—but any housekeeper knows your
rooms would have been thoroughly warmed in anticipation of your
arrival."

The scheme had been doomed to failure, in other words, *if the
intention had been to murder Dalhousie.*

The marquess glowered mulishly at the hearth. "What a consolation, that my arsonist failed because he did not grasp the comforts
attendant to my station."

"You've been safe in the Manor since Lord Julian arrived,"
Hyperia said, the note of gentle reason still present. "Tampering with
the saddle and breaking up coach wheels are the behaviors of somebody bent on harassment rather than deadly harm."

"For now," Dalhousie grumbled.

"Or," I said, "the behavior of somebody willing to give you the
benefit of time to reflect. His Grace of Waltham is notably unenthusiastic about enclosures. Perhaps I am being given time to talk sense
into you."

"Waltham has done me the courtesy of sharing his opinion on the
topic. His arguments are sound, articulate, and entirely backward,
meaning no offense. He can afford to be backward, at least for the
present, but others of us must look to the future."

"You don't need to enclose the fen to drain it," I said. "You don't
need to put a bill before Parliament or build humongous walls. You
can increase your arable acreage year on year without stealing all of
the commoners' rights at one go."

Dalhousie hadn't considered half measures, hadn't considered compromise or an incremental campaign. "I'm not keen on raising cabbages for the delectation of the local rabbits, my lord."

"Rabbits don't eat maize," Hyperia said. "And yes, deer can be keen on it, so fence your deer park, hmm?"

Dalhousie had regained sufficient self-possession that he would not argue with her—wise man.

"Think about what you truly want, Dalhousie." I rose and returned the desk chair to its proper place. "Do you want generations of resentment and vandalism, or do you want cordial relations with the neighbors because your vision of prosperity and progress included them too?"

"It's not my fault Tom Davey has a dozen mouths to feed."

"Thirteen," Hyperia said, rising, "unless you expect Tom himself or possibly his wife to starve. It's not Tom's fault he was born into poverty on the land of a rapacious, greedy, strutting thief in fine tailoring, is it?" She smiled pleasantly and patted Dalhousie's shoulder. "I merely quote the talk that's doubtless floating about the inn's common, my lord. I know you to be a gentleman to your bones."

Her exit was exquisitely unhurried.

"I wasn't up to her weight," Dalhousie said, attempting to sip from his now-empty glass. "Bother." He put the glass down. "When I escorted her about Town for those few weeks, I was tempted, Caldicott. I will not lie. I was tempted to offer her marriage, lest you mistake my meaning. She put me in mind of a more gracious version of Mama, though. A woman very much in command of herself. Painfully well-read too."

One could not *be* painfully well-read. "She sensed that your intentions were merely friendly. You were never at risk for matrimony with her."

"She *told* you that?"

"We are engaged to be married and in each other's confidence. One does not approach the institution without having to offer a few explanations for past developments." My words left me feeling both supremely blessed—I liked even saying the words *engaged to be married*—and a touch hypocritical.

Parts of my past remained firmly undiscussed with Hyperia, and I hoped to keep it that way. Parts of Hyperia's past were going firmly undiscussed as well, and that was doubtless for the best too.

"You are up to her weight," Dalhousie said. "Too many years of managing my mother's high-handedness have left me unwilling to..."

He looked so downcast, so bewildered. "Yes?"

"Mama wears a body out," he said. "Suze agrees, and she is the kindest of souls. We can tolerate Tamerlane's flights of genius and folly, and we're inured to Lady Albert's sniping. Cousin Cressy has mostly left us in peace in recent years, but the marchioness is a stranger to compromise. Once her mind is made up..."

"She will build her enclosure, despite all common sense, sentiment, or arguments to the contrary. A genuine dilemma, I grant you."

His brows rose in a fashion exactly reminiscent of his mother. "A hit." He raised his empty glass to me. "A direct hit on my stores of righteous certainty, which are admittedly vast and honestly come by. Please explain to my mother what you found in Town, my lord. She will be less likely to argue with you. I am not going to Town until the whole messy business is resolved, and her ladyship had best resign herself to that fact."

"You should be the one to tell her, Dalhousie. You should enlist her wise counsel, appeal to her protective nature. She loves you. She carried you under her heart and brought you into the world at risk to her own life. You underestimate her maternal devotion."

I had underestimated my own dear mother in the same fashion, but let it be said, Her Grace had done some underestimating of me as well.

"Mama's version of love comes very close to dictatorship." Dalhousie pushed to his feet. "Right now, I could not vouch for my ability to remain civil to her if she embarked on more arguments. I am weary, my lord, and you can take the small, disagreeable task of explaining the situation to her off my plate. Please?"

I lacked charm. Harry had frequently told me as much, but perhaps what I truly lacked was a desire to manipulate people with false entreaties and displays of supplication.

Botheration. "I will speak with her ladyship and ask you to consider that her dictatorial streak bred true in her son. Nobody respects a tyrant, Dalhousie. Nobody will guard a tyrant's back indefinitely when trouble stalks him."

I would not desert my post at the Manor willingly, but the course of events was settling into a siege. Dalhousie would have his enclosure, come fire, flood, or celestial thunderbolts. His enemies—likely plural—would harass and thwart him until his new walls were periodically blown up, or his life was taken by miscalculation.

No wonder the marchioness was desperate for him to marry and beget some heirs, but what an unfortunate—if prosperous—legacy his children would inherit.

~

In Spain I had learned that hard riding was best done on a less-than-full tummy. I was thus famished, and desperate for a bath, and did not dare embark on a negotiation with the marchioness in all my dirt and peckishness.

I found the bath waiting for me in my quarters—bless you, darling Hyperia—along with a tray sporting five half sandwiches of ham and cheese.

"Atticus!"

He emerged from the dressing closet. "Aye, guv?"

"Dinner attire, please, though I know it's early." I untied my limp cravat and started on the buttons of my waistcoat. "Hessians instead of slippers. My errands might take me out of doors."

I heaped my clothing on the bed and climbed into the tub. Bliss upon ecstasy upon lavender-scented heaven...

"You aren't to fall asleep in there, guv."

"You may eavesdrop on the Archangel Michael himself, Atticus, but do not eavesdrop on me and Miss West when we are having a private conversation." Sleep dragged at me, promising sweet dreams and sweeter oblivion.

"I weren't eavesdropping. Miss West told me. Said you were ready to drop, that you've overtaxed yourself, and next thing, you'll be forgettin' your name again. You rode clear out from Town since breakfast, and you ain't no express jockey to be covering that sort of ground in a day."

"I am tired," I said, dipping my fingers into the soap dish. "Miss West is right about that. Take another half sandwich if you're hungry. Grab a biscuit or two."

"I'll spoil me supper."

"Not possible. If you grow any faster, we'll hear your bones stretching. I arrived to something of a battle in progress here at the Manor, else I'd already be napping. The marchioness was exhorting Dalhousie to remove to Town and has already ordered the London residence readied for the family's arrival."

Atticus swiped half a sandwich and disappeared into the dressing closet. When he reappeared, the sandwich had met its fate, and proper evening attire was draped over his arm.

"Her ladyship wanted everybody to know the marquess was on the way," Atticus said. "Part of making a grand entrance. Send the staff scurrying about, have Cook buy out half the market three days running, beat all the carpets where the neighbors can see... Better than a notice in *The Times*."

"She was creating expectations, you mean." I scrubbed sore muscles and dunked. "Dalhousie is very much a man attuned to expectations. Her strategy was sound." Washing my hair took but a moment. Atticus assisted me to rinse, and the time came to leave the warmth and comfort of the bath.

"You should nap." Atticus gathered up a length of linen he'd hung over the back of the reading chair to warm. "Miss West is right about your spells. They come when you're tired."

It was on the tip of my tongue to reply that I was always tired, and a year ago, even a few months ago, that would have been true.

I was doing better for having left the Hall. My every moment wasn't crammed with correspondence, neighborly calls, appointments with stewards, and consultations with the stable lads. My days as a guest at the Manor started later and ended earlier, and jaunts to Town notwithstanding, I was benefiting from reduced activity.

To get some consistent, proper rest, I had needed to leave the place where I felt safest and happiest. What an extraordinary thought.

"My spells come when they come," I said, referring to a temporary and complete lapse of memory. When in the midst of these episodes, I did not know my own name, nor the day of the week, nor the location I inhabited. I carried an explanatory card in my pocket at all times as a defense against complete terror.

The memories always came back, sometimes after an hour, sometimes after a night's sleep. The memories came back, and to that fact, I clung with the tenacity of a man dangling on a single rope above a deep, dark abyss.

I dried off and dressed as far as shirt and breeches, then did justice to the remaining sandwiches and the tankard of cider accompanying them.

"Your hair could use a trim," Atticus said, gathering up my dirty clothes.

"So could yours." My hair was a tender subject. Sharp blades wielded near my person was another tender subject. At present, my locks, which fell to my shoulders, progressed from golden near my crown to white for the last few inches.

"You look like some sort of badger." Atticus hung my dusty riding jacket on a hook on the bedpost, put my plain waistcoat over the back of the chair at the escritoire, and disappeared into the dressing closet with the rest of my small clothes.

"Badgers are fierce." I shrugged into the formal waistcoat, a burgundy affair subtly embroidered with fleur-de-lis and roses. Dalhousie's household dressed for dinner, but not quite formally.

The rest of my ensemble was black, my cravat a spotless white, and my cravat pin a discreet ruby.

"When are we going home, guv?" Atticus asked from the depths of the dressing closet. "I miss my pony."

"It's time we put you up on Atlas." Atticus was new to the art of riding, but had the natural seat most children brought to the endeavor and a tremendous sympathy for any domesticated beast.

He reappeared in the dressing closet doorway. "Truly? You want me to exercise him?"

"You do everything else for him, and you've sat on enough ponies to know what you're about. If the weather obliges, we can put you up tomorrow and see how you get on."

Atticus grew two inches taller before my eyes. "Tomorrow morning, guv. You promise?"

"If the weather allows. Spring is not quite upon us, and this is England." I queued my hair back with a black ribbon and prepared to deal with a dragoness. "Best polish your boots, lest you make a poor impression on my steed."

Atticus's smile would have blinded the angels. "We'll get on splendidly, me and Atlas. Always have. You should wear slippers with that get-up, guv, especially if you're making your report to Lady Ophelia."

I followed his advice, not because Godmama would take issue with my Hessians, but because the next call thereafter would be upon the marchioness, who would take issue with Saint Peter on the proper care and polishing of his halo.

"The village forays are odd," Lady Ophelia said, her traveling desk open before her on the escritoire. "I can usually ferret out a sense of the local feeling by appealing to the ladies who set the trends—the vicar's wife, the innkeeper's wife, the grandmothers of greatest provenance, the prosperous merchant's wives, the herbalist or midwife."

"They won't talk to you?" I asked, taking a seat opposite the desk. The chair was pretty, delicate, and only thinly padded, and my saddle-weary backside protested the lack of comfort.

"For heaven's sake, sit on a pillow, Julian. If you must impersonate a young fool by riding the whole distance from Town, then allow yourself to also impersonate an old fool and use pillows to ameliorate the effects of your rash excesses."

I remained where I was, because stubborn foolishness was available to any age. "Tell me about the ladies you've been canvassing."

"They all speak highly of the marquess, but in the most vague and general terms. Such a gentleman, takes his responsibilities seriously, a gracious host, patient with the elderly. A paragon of superficial virtues."

"Nobody grumbles?" At Caldicott Hall, the same litany would have been ascribed to Arthur, along with nigh-affectionate footnotes along the lines of *a bit too serious is our duke*, or *not exactly a colorful soul, though we appreciate his many fine qualities*.

Arthur was held in high regard for being an almost perfect exemplar of a duke. He was held in *warm* regard for having a few imperfections.

"I heard not one word against the marquess," Lady Ophelia said, pouring sand back into a folded paper envelope. "I heard no words at all aimed at Lady Dalhousie, though Susanna is apparently as well-liked as Tamerlane."

I liked Susanna too. Practical, adult, didn't take herself too seriously. Seemed to genuinely value her family in all their idiosyncrasies and tensions.

"What do you make of the diplomatic silence?"

Her ladyship ran her thumb over the blade of a letter opener intended to resemble a Scottish dagger. "They know something, Julian. Those people watch the Manor as a new governess watches her only charge. They have to. The best jobs, the biggest customer, the most influence, the epicenter of the neighborhood lies at the end of the Dalhousie formal carriageway."

"Are they merely being discreet?"

"Julian," Lady Ophelia said gently, "I am as good in my way at reconnaissance as you were in Spain. I listen. I know when to allow silence to become innuendo. I grasp how to modify my patterns of speech to make me more approachable. I have been smiling and shopping and strolling the green for nearly a fortnight, and... nothing."

"Are the local folk terrified?"

"No. Merely unwilling to take me into their confidence."

"And you can find no explanation for that pattern." I rose creakily and barely resisted the temptation to rub my backside. "What do you make of the fire in Dalhousie's London abode?"

She set her toy dagger into the burgundy velvet-lined desk compartment made for the purpose. "As fires go, it doesn't sound like much of an effort, the way you describe it."

"But substantial smoke and water damage resulted, and worse could have happened. I thought about offering Dalhousie the use of Caldicott House for the Season, but..."

Her ladyship peered up at me. "But? Your gesture would be seen as gracious. Lady Dalhousie would owe you a favor, and the Caldicott House staff would have a marquess to fuss over."

I did not tell her that when I'd abandoned the Hall more than a year ago to wallow in solitude and despair in my own London quarters, I'd made it a point to drive past Caldicott House whenever I'd gone out. In a closed carriage, I was free to gaze upon one of the family homes and recall happier times.

Going up to Town with my parents had always been an occasion for great excitement, and the dignified façade of the London dwelling housed many a boyhood memory, most of them joyous. The mere sight of the place had assured me that happier times were possible, that not all of life was torment and nightmares.

"I might want to use the town house myself later in the Season," I said, "and bringing Dalhousie's trouble to my own doorstep would be imprudent."

Her gaze narrowed, and she rose. "But first you will return to the

Hall, which you doubtless miss. When you are there, Julian, you mutter about mountains of mail, the demons of drainage, the fiends of foal watch, and the tribulations of tenants."

"I do not habitually alliterate. The Hall is my responsibility at present." To say the Hall was my home would have alliterated. "I am permitted a quotient of muttering about the tedious tasks those responsibilities entail." Though Arthur didn't mutter or alliterate about tedious tasks. Perhaps he muttered to Banter?

"I'm glad you miss it," Lady Ophelia said, putting ink, quills, and seal into their assigned desk compartments. "You probably didn't allow yourself to miss home the whole time you were in Spain and feared if you ever took leave, you'd abandon the regiment for good. I wish to God that you had."

Sometimes so did I, a sentiment at appalling variance with the dictates of honor. "I am off to discuss the situation in London with Lady Dalhousie. Wish me luck."

Godmama snapped the traveling desk closed. "I am missing the Season, too, you know. I can sympathize with Lady Dalhousie somewhat. You mustn't tell her I said that."

"I would not want to impose," I said, though having Godmama on hand was a comfort. "You think you've come up with nothing of use and are thus prepared to remove to fresh terrain, but you have revealed an interesting possibility that I would not be considering but for your delicate and determined efforts."

"I have?"

"If the local folk disdain to disparage Dalhousie, and they are not cowed by his power, and they will not overtly vilify his enclosure scheme to you even after subtle and repeated prompting, perhaps they are *loyal* to him."

"They hate his enclosure scheme, but hold him in high regard personally?"

"I don't know, but you've given me more to think about." As had the traveling desk, with its assortment of writing implements and horde of epistles received. "I think it's time I had a peek at Dalhousie's mail."

"You'll go behind his back to read his private correspondence? Not done, Julian."

"Then I will ask permission and have a look at his ledgers too. I warned him that my services can become intrusive."

"And you do so love to read correspondence."

"Cruel, Godmama." I kissed her cheek. "Until supper."

She twinkled at me, and as I made my way to Lady Dalhousie's suite, I sent up a quiet prayer that between Godmama, Hyperia, Atticus, and myself, we could resolve Dalhousie's situation in the immediate future.

Planting would soon be under way, and I longed to return to the Hall and resume my muttering and alliterating—longed to rather fiercely.

"We don't know what the fire means," I said as Lady Dalhousie plied her embroidery needle on what looked like a table runner. More roses fashioned from silk thread on cream linen, more tiny, exact stitches.

"A smoking chimney means the footman was lax," Lady Dalhousie retorted. "One should always check the flue before lighting a fire."

"The flue was open. He checked. He was not lax. Somebody arranged either for the chimney to catch fire or for a great deal of mess to befall the marquess's quarters. That's a very pretty piece you're sewing."

"Roses for remembrance. Messes can be cleaned up, my lord, and in the normal course should be. Dalhousie retained you to see about a mess that seems to be getting worse while you do little about it."

Dalhousie had not, in fact, *retained* me. No coin had changed hands, nor would it, for pity's sake. Her ladyship insulted me with the very notion.

"Does my lady dispute that since I've arrived, no further attempts have been made on Dalhousie's life?" My riding accident might have qualified as such, barely.

She considered her stitchery. "Fire takes many lives."

"True, but as Miss West has pointed out to me, the chances of this particular fire doing any harm to the marquess himself were practically nil. He would never be expected to content himself with rooms lacking heat. Far in advance of his arrival, the hearths would be blazing and the trouble in his suite evident—as it became evident —without him even being in London."

"Then your quarry is a man of low birth who would not think about the domestic obligation to keep one's titled employer warm."

"On the contrary, a woman familiar with the management of a household would have known precisely how harmless a lot of rags stuffed up the chimney could be—to the marquess himself. She would have a great deal of experience watching a household ready itself to receive the head of the family and been well aware of the schedule upon which the chimneys were routinely cleaned."

Her ladyship's hands descended to her lap, hoop, fabric, and all. "Are you accusing me of arson, my lord?"

I was thinking out loud, watching her reactions. "You put the Town staff on high alert, even as Dalhousie warned you that he was reluctant to leave the Manor."

"You think I staged this near tragedy? For what purpose?"

"I doubt you had anything to do with it, but your letter to the housekeeper would have sat out on the sideboard in the foyer, awaiting Dalhousie's signature as franking. Anybody here at the Manor would have known that you were warning her of the family's intention to travel."

The marchioness ran a manicured nail over her tiny roses one by one. "Tamerlane," she said, nodding once, vigorously. "He'd know all sorts of nefarious characters in Town. He nearly is a nefarious character, come to that. He's stupid enough to think that a stuffed chimney would earn him the title."

No, he was not—was he?

"We must consider all possibilities. It's also possible that some-body wanted suspicion cast upon you, my lady."

"To what possible end?" She set her needlework back atop her workbasket and rose. "All I want, all I have ever wanted, is my son's happiness, his contentment in the duties it is his honor to fulfill. You make these... these *allegations*, you discover nothing, you solve noth-ing, and I have had my fill of your poking about, Lord Julian. You are not good *ton*, and all you have proved—if anything—is that Dalhousie faces a lot of foolishness and no real threat. He must go to Town, take a bride, and put all this nonsense behind him. See yourself out."

I was already on my feet. "You are upset that Dalhousie did not explain the fire to you himself. He is upset that you don't take the risk to him seriously. All he wants is to see you content, but you criticize and carp and treat him as if he cannot reason for himself. Tell him you'd like me to leave the Manor. He is so devoted to giving you your way that he will doubtless send me packing, when my presence alone seems to have de-escalated the threats from deadly to merely menac-ing. Until supper, my lady."

I bowed properly and took my leave, though the interview had gone even worse than I'd predicted. The old besom was flustered, clearly, and she was right to want the succession secured. Every reminder that Dalhousie had a clever and determined enemy was a reminder that his heir was also, in the opinion of even that heir himself, unsuitable.

The solution to that conundrum was to marry and produce a son, though Dalhousie had no guarantee that his firstborn male offspring would be an improvement over dear cousin Tam.

I was sitting in Dalhousie's chair behind his desk, sorting through stewards' reports—the bane of any landowner's existence, surely—when it occurred to me that *Lady Dalhousie* would ensure that any son of the present marquess conformed to the mold necessary for the proper care and management of the family's holdings.

Ye gods of intrigue and mischief... She would take the boy in hand *most especially* if his own father was not extant to do so. I firmly ignored the ramifications of that speculation and tried with limited success to attend to the wonders of peas, beans, and turnips.

CHAPTER FOURTEEN

Supper was a tense affair, the Dandridge gift for pleasant conversation taxed to the utmost. Lady Ophelia probed delicately regarding the reticence of the village women, Lady Dalhousie sniffed and pushed her food about on her plate, and Lady Albert tossed out the occasional barb toward me, the marchioness, and even Dalhousie.

The marquess was uncharacteristically silent, and even Susanna seemed to have run out of cheerful small talk. Hyperia had remarked on the weather, the prospect of Easter bonnets on display at divine services, and the pleasure of lengthening hours of sunshine. When those gambits failed to engender much conversation, Perry busied herself with her ham and potatoes.

We'd made it as far as the sweet, a vanilla mousse topped with raspberry sauce, when the first mortar shell exploded across the table.

I greeted the opening barrage with a mixture of relief and disappointment.

"Tamerlane is likely even now planning more sabotage," Lady Dalhousie muttered, taking a martial grip of her dessert spoon. "Why he was left in Town unsupervised when we know what mischief he is capable of defies all understanding."

"The real question," Lady Albert countered, "is why *you* are left unsupervised, my lady. You would do anything to see my son's good name blighted."

Dalhousie looked not to his mother or Lady Albert, but to me.

"Bickering will solve nothing," I said. "Either Lady Dalhousie or Tamerlane could have arranged for that fire to be set, though I doubt either of them was involved."

"Enlighten us as to your reasoning," Lady Ophelia said. "Please."

"To make that fire happen from a distance would require colluding with the criminal element local to Town. Neither Tam nor the marchioness would risk the dodgy loyalties of such an accomplice. Her ladyship is too much of a snob, and Tamerlane is too aware that any such arrangement would set him up to be blackmailed for the rest of his life. Conspiracy to commit arson is a hanging felony, after all."

"Now we discuss capital crimes at table," the marchioness said, jabbing her spoon into her mousse. "See what a refining influence Lord Julian has on otherwise decent company."

By all the gracious cherubim, she was firing at random. "You raised the topic of arson at the town house, madam. The rest of us were struggling along with Easter bonnets and daffodils."

"Then who set that fire?" Dalhousie asked. "Why set it at all if the purpose was simply to make my quarters uninhabitable for a few weeks?"

"Whom do you plan to court when you arrive in Town?" Hyperia asked, holding a spoonful of mousse before her. "Somebody wants you kept in the shires, my lord. If that party is a rival for a particular heiress or diamond, they have motive and means where all your troubles are concerned."

I gazed across the table with something like awe. Hyperia had, in the space of one question, changed the topic, posited a credible if far-fetched new theory to explain the whole situation, and opened up all manner of new possibilities regarding a potential villain.

Or villainess.

"In the alternative," I said, "a young lady who has set her sights on the Dalhousie coronet might rather keep the marquess from Mayfair now, the better to charm him at some house party later in the year. So who are your candidates for the next Marchioness of Dalhousie, my lord?"

Dalhousie pushed his serving of mousse aside. "One does not discuss such a matter at table."

"Lady Venus Twillinger would do," the marchioness said earnestly. "I've spoken to you of her many times, Dalhousie. Decent settlements, papa is a marquess, brothers sound enough, and they're good Dorset stock. The family seat is a mere day's travel from here. Lady Annamarie DeHaven is similarly situated, and her father is a duke. Her maternal side boasts an earldom, and while she's a bit hard of hearing, she has a fine disposition and is one of eleven, *nine* of whom are boys."

Susanna was staring hard at her lap, though whether she was hiding laughter or horror I could not tell.

"Lady Harmony Weltzer is only an earl's daughter," the marchioness went on a little desperately, "but quite well dowered and very graceful on the dance floor. She is said to be accomplished at the pianoforte, and she has six brothers."

"Your ladyship," Dalhousie began. "Mama—"

"Her father is merely a viscount," the marchioness barreled on, "but Miss Honoraria Venable is exceedingly handsome and will inherit a fortune. Only three brothers, though her father was one of five sons. She is said not to put on airs, which is always a fine—"

"Mama, for the love of all that is dignified, *stop*. I will make my own choice in my own time, and while your comments are appreciated, the matter is one for me and me alone—"

"My comments? My *comments*? Sir, I'll have you know I have spent years—far, far too many *years*—gathering this information and choosing these possibilities. I have bored myself to tears collecting the gossip at a hundred at-homes. I have danced with gouty generals and lost hands of whist to prattling aunties. The lengths I have gone to on your behalf would make a more dutiful son—"

"Excuse me," I said, rising. "The exertions of the day seem to be catching up with me. Dalhousie, I can join you for a quick brandy in the library, but thereafter, I must seek an ignominiously early bedtime. Ladies, I bid you good night."

Hyperia's gaze hid a touch of humor. Lady Ophelia was cooly approving. Miss Susanna was engaged in a thorough examination of her mousse, and Lady Albert looked intrigued. Gentlemen did not plead fatigue. Gentlemen did not flee to the library following supper.

Gentlemen also did not sit by and idly watch as a peer of the realm was reduced by his very own mother to the status of stud colt on the auction block.

"Brandy would suit." The marquess rose as well, and so did his mama.

"Scurry away, will you? I point out again, Dalhousie, that Lord Julian Caldicott has been a bad influence. You refuse to do your duty by the title. You will cling to this enclosure scheme no matter what it costs us in terms of standing with our neighbors. You will make a laughingstock of my efforts to find you a suitable bride, and he,"—she gave a haughty lift of her chin in my direction—"abets you at every turn. I demand that you send him back to from whence he came."

Lady Ophelia abruptly rose. "I have a headache, Dahlia Dandridge, and you had best acquire one, too, in the next thirty seconds, lest I tell you what I really think of women who parade around in stolen coronets and then presume to insult their more honorable betters. Ladies, gentlemen, good evening. I will see myself upstairs."

She swept out on a tide of feminine dignity, off doubtless to draft a report to my mother. Lady Dalhousie tried for comparable bravado with her own departure, but one insulted a ducal heir repeatedly at peril to one's social future. If Lady Dalhousie's cause was seeing her son well matched, she'd just crossed the line that might ensure Dalhousie was forced to offer for the vicar's tittering pride and joy.

Susanna stood. "I'd best go to her." She'd made a statement that was nonetheless a question.

Dalhousie shook his head. "Let her consider the consequences of her actions for once. Lord Julian, shall we to the library? Ladies, you will excuse us, and my apologies for Mama's difficult mood. She is frustrated with me, and for good reason. We must accord her some latitude. Please do enjoy the mousse. It's quite good."

He had not tasted his. I snatched up my spoon and barely touched serving and again bowed good evening to the women.

Dalhousie ambled along the corridor to the library. The house was cold, but lacked the frigidity of deepest winter. In the library, fire screens kept one end of the room almost comfortable and afforded a sense of privacy as well.

"She's growing worse," Dalhousie said, going straight to the sideboard. "You mustn't blame her. Before you came upon us earlier, I'd told her I did not see how I could conduct any sort of courtship under the present circumstances. When I reached the part about skipping the Season altogether this year, she flew into a rage—for her."

"A vast silence," I hazarded, "followed by comments such as 'do as you think best,' laced with scorn and mortal affront? No brandy for me." I took a spoonful of sweet, rich vanilla mousse.

Dalhousie tossed back one drink and poured himself another. "Something like that. References to my late father's legacy reverting to the crown—what little Tam would leave unplundered—and the Dalhousie name living on as the butt of very bad jokes. She has it in her head that because she stole Papa from Lady Albert, she will be punished by an absence of grandchildren."

Dalhousie had not worked that out for himself. "Is that Susanna's reasoning?"

"The theory fits the facts, does it not?" He prowled to the grouping at the warmer end of the room, took one wing chair, and gestured me into the other. "Mama is wearing me out, my lord, but I honestly do not see myself succeeding at any courtship when I have no suitable London quarters, somebody for whatever reasons wants me dwelling at the Manor, and every lady Mama finds acceptable seems not to have a brain in her head."

He finished half his brandy and eyed the fire. "I apologize. I ought not to be insulting the ladies. They likely think I am an arrogant prig, and sometimes I am."

"Go easy on the spirits, Dalhousie. You will say something you truly regret, in company where an apology will not set the matter right. Your mother is concerned that you... cannot have children."

He peered at me by the flickering firelight and gestured with one hand. "Cannot?"

I finished my mousse and wished I could ask for seconds. "She thinks you are attracted exclusively to other men, and thus she is haunted by all manner of potential for scandal. A wife—any wife— would scotch the worst of the talk." Not all of it, of course. Arthur's devoted partner, Osgood Banter, had a lovely son to whom Banter was an excellent father figure.

Only as Lady Dalhousie had desperately enumerated her list of possible brides had the source of her panic come clear to me.

"Mama thinks me... unnatural? Oh, that is rich. That is... of all the ironies, of all the celestial jokes in poor taste. I like some men, I like some women, but when it comes to *desire*, I am as prosaically inclined as any son of Albion is supposed to be. Mama has yielded to dire fancies once too often, but I fear you have put your finger on some of the explanation for her ridiculous zeal."

What I observed between Arthur and Banter was far more natural than many a contrived Society union.

"You made your mother a promise, Dalhousie. Said you would take a bride this year, and that means going up to Town and doing the pretty."

"No, it does not. When Town empties out, as it will in a few short weeks, the house parties begin, then the shooting parties, and finally a few intrepid souls will host holiday parties. Mama won't see it like that. It's Mayfair or be damned, to her. She will have her enclosure, won't she? One marquess tucked behind the walls of the breeding shed of her choice. My head is pounding."

Dalhousie was in the philosophical phase of inchoate inebriation, and that suited my purposes well enough for the present.

"I have begun reviewing your ledgers and correspondence, something I should have undertaken sooner."

"You're reading my mail? How boring for you. The ledgers are a little livelier, thanks to Mama's occasional flights of decoration. Her sitting room is inviolable, but the rest of the house is subject to regular refurbishment. If I marry, the whole lot will be done all over again to my bride's taste. The merchants will sing odes to my marchioness."

If he married, not *when.* I beheld a man still fighting his fate—or his dear mama. "Lay off the brandy, my lord. You've told your mother you are declining to spend the Season in Town, and there's an end to it. Let that be known, back away from your enclosure project, and your enemy might well withdraw to winter quarters as well."

Or spring quarters.

"You should withdraw," Dalhousie said, taking his empty glass to the sideboard. "If I capitulate to Mama to the extent of sending you on your way, she will do me the courtesy of a temporary cease-fire. I might have to permit her a house party here this summer. One shudders. Heiresses popping out of linen closets and originals dragging me into the bushes. Tam will find it hilarious."

Tam, as the marquess's heir, would find himself dragged into a few hedges, too, if he wasn't careful.

"I have not identified the author of your trouble," I said, "and I am reluctant to leave without concluding that mission." Reluctant, but I could not insist on Dalhousie's hospitality indefinitely. "I don't believe anybody is trying to kill you at present."

But had they been prior to my arrival? I could not speak as confidently to that question, which raised the specter of worse trouble following my departure.

"I am off to commune further with your stewards' reports," I said. "You should seek your bed, Dalhousie. Her ladyship will appear at the breakfast table, ready to renew her siege, and you must be on your mettle if the walls of your familial authority are to withstand her sappers and artillery."

"The walls of my bachelorhood, you mean. What say you bide here for another week, Caldicott? Mama will like that you've set a date for your departure, and you can occupy yourself in some quiet corner with the ledgers. Tam will be back from Town by then, and he has always been one to guard my back."

Tam, in the opinion of the marchioness, had with lethal intent shot at that same back.

"I will consider your suggestion," I replied, though, in fact, Dalhousie had proffered a polite order to vacate, "and consult with the ladies. One does not surprise them with short notice of a change of venue."

Dalhousie would not argue with that point, not when he could instead pour himself a third brandy. He needed a wife, the poor sod. A lady to listen to his troubles and entrust her own to him in return. A friend, lover, and fellow conspirator against life's many vicissitudes.

Why the hell hadn't he found himself a marchioness years ago?

On that idle question, I made for the door, only to be greeted by Susanna, clad in a shawl and night-robe, in the corridor.

"One wants a book of soothing prose before bedtime," she said, smiling self-consciously. She was covered from neck to ankles, but I was not family, and she was a lady. "The soothing-er the better after that performance at supper."

"Dalhousie is still brooding. Perhaps you can encourage him to brood his way up to bed. He'll have a very sore head in the morning at the rate he's going."

"Oh dear. Gordie hasn't Tam's tolerance for spirits. Lady Dalhousie would drive a saint to drink, though. Forget I said that."

She dipped a curtsey, which in her night-robe came across as both an effective bit of propriety and a trifle humorous. I bowed in the same ambiguous manner.

"What are you two conspiring about?" Dalhousie called from the sideboard. "Suze, you must light me to my room, lest I take a notion to enlist in the Royal Navy. Join me in a nightcap?"

I left them to the brandy and brooding and made my way to the study. I built up the fire only to realize even before I took the chair behind Dalhousie's desk that I had reached the end of my tether. I could stare intently at ledgers for the next two hours, but I would see nothing and absorb even less.

Dalhousie was kicking me out. The whole semi-tipsy performance in the library might well have been his elaborate version of commanding me to leave. Sideways, pleasant, unconfrontational, and somewhat ignorable, but not entirely so.

I was being drummed out of the regiment for dereliction of duty and had only seven days to see the verdict overturned. Not at all how I'd envisioned my Hampshire project concluding.

I longed to return to the Hall, but on my terms and with answers in hand to all pertinent questions regarding the troubles at Dalhousie Manor.

"Dalhousie stood up with the DeHaven diamond at least three times last year," Lady Ophelia said as we stepped out onto the back terrace. "No waltzes, but it was her first Season. The Venable heiress was wafting about Paris over the winter and crossed paths with Dalhousie there any number of times. She's facing her third Season, but not for want of offers. She's said to have attracted the notice of some German princeling who owns two castles."

The morning sun was nigh blinding, at least to my weakened eyes. I unfolded my blue-tinted spectacles and donned them, though too late to spare myself an initial stab of agony echoed by a hint of queasiness.

Hyperia and her ladyship waited while I put on my eyeglasses. "And Lady Venus?" I asked.

"Out of action last year because her mother stuck her spoon in the wall, poor lady. Consumption. Saw her youngest daughter launched the previous year, expired, and in so doing, increased that daughter's already hefty settlements."

We struck out across the terrace, bound for the crushed-shell walkways of the garden below.

"What do you ladies suggest in terms of further initiatives? I cannot very well go to Town and inquire of these women if they've been trying to nobble their bachelor of choice. I honestly find that notion far-fetched." Keep Dalhousie in the shires, and... what? Waylay him on some dawn hack and spirit him off to Scotland for a wedding over the anvil? Wait to bag him like an oversized grouse at a shooting party?

I was growing fanciful in my frustration, also slightly bilious. Too much time spent with accounts, receipts, and unanswered questions.

"I agree," Hyperia said, slipping her hand around my arm. "The notion of a young lady wreaking havoc on Dalhousie's courtship itinerary is far-fetched, but some baron's second son knocking Dalhousie out of the running is more credible. All of the women Lady Dalhousie mentioned have enormous settlements."

"How do you know that?" Society was nosy, of course, but Hyperia was certain of her facts.

"I do not have enormous settlements, and thus the younger, wealthier women have all been cordial to me. I barely know Lady Annamarie, but one hears things in the retiring room."

Did they envy Hyperia now because she was engaged to a ducal heir, or pity her because that heir was my dodgy and disgraced self? I wanted to put the question to her, but felt I hadn't the right. He who longed to leave Spain in the past and all that.

"Who is Dalhousie's competition among the bachelors?" I asked as we passed a bed of daffodils making a cheerful splash against cold, damp ground. "Who must marry one of those ladies come fire, flood, or furious creditors?"

"Half the bachelors in Mayfair will be panting after the women on the marchioness's list," Lady Ophelia opined as she descended into the garden, "and most of those fellows won't even be fortune hunters."

"We should look at the misters and Honorables," Hyperia said. "The courtesy lords, heirs, and peers would see themselves as Dalhousie's equals."

"Earls and below deserve a closer look," Lady Ophelia countered. "They are not Dalhousie's equal, and few of them can match his wealth."

I let the ladies discuss bachelors of sufficient desperation, standing, and guile to merit suspicion, but I feared that Hyperia's theory of a jealous rival suitor had little to recommend it. True, Dalhousie had only recently declared his intention to take a bride, and matchmaking in Mayfair was a blood sport, or the nearest thing to it.

But the logistics of pinning Dalhousie down at his family seat, wrecking his personal quarters in Town, tampering with a saddle... too complicated, too much the work of a familial intimate. And that business with the tainted dessert, too risky on the one hand—dosing poison was notoriously inexact—and too expert, in that it required knowing the specific organization of evening meals under another man's roof and his favorite sweet.

Hyperia led me down the side of the garden that faced east, where the sun had been warming the garden wall for several hours.

"Jules, how are you faring with the marquess's ledgers and letters?"

I'd spent the previous four hours in that purgatory, which might explain my increasingly unhappy digestion.

"The ledgers are spotless and current almost to the hour. Nothing out of the ordinary that I can see. If somebody entered the purchase of a new chandelier in the ledger, then a receipt for that item is to be found in a file arranged by date. Tidy to a fault."

"One's books cannot be tidy to a fault." Lady Ophelia brushed a gloved hand over a patch of sheltered rosemary, the scent striking me as acrid rather than pleasing. "Unless one is embezzling?"

"Are we back to Tam in the dock?" Hyperia asked, moving us along to a patch of daffodils. "He's been fiddling the books somehow, or having a steward fiddle them, and any solicitors examining books prior to marital-settlement negotiations will find the fiddling?"

She plucked a yellow bloom and affixed it to my lapel. The scent of the daffodil should have been soothing, but the fragrance did not appeal. Too cloying, too heavy.

"Embezzlement is another hanging felony," Lady Ophelia noted. "Julian, dear, are you well? You look like you've just caught wind of rotten meat."

"If there's an embezzler in this house," I said, ignoring Godmama's question, "Dalhousie would not bring criminal charges. Not against Tam, not for dipping an occasional hand into the family till. Dalhousie cannot embezzle from himself, so let's set aside..."

I sank onto a cold, hard stone bench, my guts abruptly turning traitor on me. Breakfast had been merely buttered toast. I'd had no appetite for more, and the toast had not sat well. I'd attributed my initial lack of appetite to frustration, but frustration did not incline a man to cast up his accounts.

"Ladies, if you will excuse me. I need some privacy."

"You need a physician," Lady Ophelia said, putting the back of her bare hand to my forehead. "No fever, but you are pale, my lord."

"Come," Hyperia said, taking Lady Ophelia firmly by the arm. "Julian has said he needs privacy. We have been given our marching orders."

Hyperia apparently grasped what I truly needed, and while a footman's assistance might soon be involved, some mandatory indelicacy had become imperative. When the ladies had regained the back terrace, I ducked behind the nearest Greek statue, stuck a finger down my throat, and left the paltry remains of my breakfast in the dirt at Apollo's feet. I used my boot to cover the mess and felt marginally better.

Only marginally. I managed to get myself to the house, where I accepted the aid of a footman when faced with the main staircase.

"Lady Ophelia and Miss West are solely to be trusted to oversee preparation and delivery of any rations from the kitchen," I said as the door to my apartment loomed miles and leagues away down the corridor. "Atticus will attend me."

"The lad is in the servants' hall, milord. I'll send him up straightaway. Got into some bad eggs, did you?"

"That must be it, but let's not worry Cook or the rest of the household over a passing bellyache."

He nodded worriedly, and that told me if nothing else had that my symptoms mirrored the marquess's bout with poison. Whatever Dalhousie had consumed hadn't killed him, but he'd taken the poison on top of a full stomach and eaten only a small portion of the tainted item.

I had eaten every bite of my toast on an empty stomach and, worse, swilled an entire pot of unpleasantly strong tea. Bloody hell.

"Shall we send for the quack, milord?" the footman asked. "Mrs. Wachter would be faster, and she knows her remedies back to the Flood."

"Neither, but for God's sake, please fetch the boy."

The footman left me at my apartment door, which I managed to pass through and closed behind me before collapsing into the nearest wing chair. My belly was empty but threatening to heave anyway. My head pounded, my skin felt both hot and clammy, and my bowels were threatening to join the riot.

I pulled off my boots, got myself into silk pajama trousers and a dressing gown, and prepared to endure the siege to end all sieges. Dysentery hadn't killed me, despite making a good try. A thorough purging wasn't about to succeed where the unacknowledged scourge of Wellington's army had failed.

Atticus arrived. I gave him orders to admit no one under any circumstances and embarked on a course of suffering fit to torment the damned. Three hours later, every window of my apartment was open, the fires were roaring, and the enemy was in retreat.

"Stop fretting," I said to Atticus from the depths of a chair by the hearth. "I'll live."

"I might not. You were sicker than any dog I've seen."

Dry heaves, the shakes, the mother of all headaches, a rotten taste in my mouth that yet lingered... I twitched at the blanket covering my legs, and a thought occurred to me.

"You ate some of my toast this morning, Atticus. Did you have any of my tea?"

The boy had the grace to look self-conscious. "Took my tea from Lady Ophelia's leftovers. She has chocolate in the morning, but the kitchen sends her up a whole pot of tea anyway. Likes it strong, and so do I."

"Who knows that you snitch from her tray?"

"Nobody. I don't snitch from yours neither. You order me not to let good food go to waste."

The sass was reassuring, suggesting that Atticus wasn't as worried about me as he had been, and thus I need not be as worried about him.

"My question is investigative in nature, young man. A dose of poison that I could shake off might be enough to put period to your earthly adventure. Any servant carrying a tray back down to the kitchen can be expected to not let good food go to waste. Was poisoning you an acceptable risk to my enemy, or were you preserved from harm through happenstance?"

Atticus closed the sitting room windows and remained gazing out at the garden's afternoon shadows.

"You always send your teapot back empty," he said. "Down the lot, or as near as. That I've had a cuppa from the pot likely wouldn't occur to anybody. They aren't high sticklers here, but they watch their steps, especially with the ladyships."

Poison was usually considered a woman's weapon. Had I said that myself, or was I repeating one of Hyperia's observations?

"I need to sleep." I folded up the blanket and rose more steadily than I had for the past three hours. "I also need to consume a substantial quantity of clear liquid. Please let the kitchen know that Miss

West has ordered a pot of green tea with some more ginger biscuits, then bring the tray here."

The ginger biscuits I'd already consumed had quelled the riot more effectively than any tisane could have. Miraculous inventions, ginger biscuits.

"Aye, guv. I think one of them simmering lavender sachets might be in order too."

The boy sought to drive the last of the foul miasma from the rooms. "A sound notion for once I've quit the apartment. Let the ladies know that enemy forces have been routed and remind the kitchen that Miss West takes her tea with cream—not milk—and honey. I intend to be back on my feet by supper."

"Dicked in the nob, but then, poison can do that too." Atticus decamped, and I was left a short period of privacy to make my way to the bedroom. I left the windows open—Dalhousie burned coal, and the coal smoke offended my heightened senses—ran the warmer over the sheets, and tucked myself up against the pillows of my bed.

I slept in the usual fashion—half upright—for the sake of my nascent recovery and also because I was as inclined to do some pondering between catnaps.

I would puzzle over who had poisoned my morning teapot later, though Lady Dalhousie was the most likely suspect. She wanted me gone and had no idea that Dalhousie had already scheduled my congé. As the literal lady of the manor, she should know her way around the herbal, and fashioning an effective purge was a simple enough challenge.

My thoughts drifted to the Dalhousie ledgers. They balanced to the penny. They were astonishingly current. Seed, plow blades, lengths of iron for shoeing the horses, barrels by the dozen for the estate ale, fresh linens, boot black, and much more was all tidily cataloged, and yet... something wasn't right.

I could find nothing wrong, but something was most definitely amiss with Dalhousie's books. Would I need to bet my life to figure out exactly what?

CHAPTER FIFTEEN

"I didn't do it." Lady Dalhousie's tone was defiant and just a bit worried.

She'd accosted me during the predinner gathering in the family parlor, a toasty space recently done up in cheerful tones of blue and cream with green accents. Daffodils added a touch of cheer on the mantel.

I remained across the room from their scent. "My lady has me at a loss." I was weak, wrung out, and holding my preprandial glass of champagne merely for show, though I'd watched Dalhousie pour it from the decanter myself. I would eat and drink nothing that wasn't communally served. My belly simply could not handle spirits.

Hyperia had greeted me with a buss to the cheek and a hand on my sleeve, then glided off to accept her apéritif from the marquess. Her manner had been calm—her manner was nearly always calm—but I suspected she would chide me for leaving my bed when she had the opportunity to do so.

"You've been ill," the marchioness said, sipping her drink with a great show of composure. "My lady's maid had it from the first footman, which means the entire staff knows of your malady. I don't suppose we can attribute this unfortunate weakness to your years racketing about Spain?"

"My symptoms were exactly the same as Dalhousie's, and he was never privileged to serve in uniform. My morning pot of tea was apparently poisoned. I drank the entire contents. It's a mercy my tiger—a mere lad—didn't touch a drop."

She scowled at the glass in her hands. "I want you to leave. I have no wish for you to die."

"Why do you want me to leave?"

"You are determined to be tiresome. Dalhousie has promised me that he will wed this year. The Season has begun, and he is missing the best weeks for selecting and courting an appropriate bride. He said at lunch that a house party wasn't out of the question, but house parties are tedious and expensive. You have convinced him that he is safer here at the Manor, but you cannot even keep yourself safe here."

"The frontal assault lacks subtlety, but I do applaud your boldness. You have galloped straight to the point that supports your agenda most strongly."

"I state facts. You were poisoned. You said it yourself. Dalhousie might well be next, and the Town household is much smaller, much easier to manage closely."

"So small and manageable that somebody easily set the scene there for arson *in the marquess's apartment*."

The head footman appeared in the parlor doorway, suggesting the meal was ready. Lady Dalhousie had her back to the door, though, and was too interested in throwing me from the parapets to notice.

"My lord is insufferable."

"I merely *state facts*. Is my lady suggesting I should remove to London with the marquess?"

I expected my suggestion to horrify her. She glanced around, saw the footman, and set aside her champagne.

"Come to Town if you please to. Lady Ophelia will doubtless

join the whirl, and Miss West deserves a chance to gloat over her engagement, such as it is. Do me the courtesy of biding at a Caldicott property, though. I have seen enough of you to last me a lifetime."

"You did not poison me," I said quietly when the marchioness had paused to reload her verbal cannon. "You could not intrude belowstairs yourself, and you could not trust the staff to do your bidding and keep quiet about it. They obey you because they are loyal to their pay packets and to your son. However generous their compensation, it doesn't cover the capital crime of poisoning a ducal heir. Your lady's maid could not credibly condescend to carry the tray up two flights of stairs to my room—snobbish by association, poor dear—and she is the only possible minion you might rely on."

In other words, the marchioness lacked the infantry to have accomplished this latest mischief, and mercenary forces weren't to be relied upon in battle.

"You suspect Lady Albert, then?" The question was aimed with undisguised relish.

"One gathers information in the course of an investigation and allows the facts to guide any eventual conclusions. Your unenthusiastic support among the staff exonerates you. Beyond that, I have formed no other conclusions."

More to the point, Atticus had brought up my tray, taking it from a customary location on the kitchen worktable. The tray had been waiting for him, as had become the morning routine. Had the marchioness or her lady's maid been hovering anywhere in its vicinity, the staff would have been abuzz with curiosity.

Whoever had dosed my tea with a purge traveled regularly belowstairs or had loyal allies on the staff.

"Tamerlane is the most popular member of the family among the servants," Lady Dalhousie observed. "They positively dote on him, what doting his own cousin doesn't do. His mother would burn the village church for him, and she thinks nothing of intruding on the kitchen simply to vex me."

Lady Albert likely vexed the cook exceedingly with that behavior too. She stood across the room in conversation with Susanna, and the malevolence in the marchioness's eyes as she beheld that pair was appalling.

"Let it go," I said, without intending to speak, much less to tell this arrogant besom how to order her affairs. "Life is short. We have but a passing span on this earth, and you waste that gift in pride and antagonism. No sensible man would willingly bring a bride home to this elegantly appointed battleground. If you cannot put down your weapons for your own sake, then consider a cease-fire for your son's."

Lady Dalhousie glowered at me as if I'd spouted treason, blasphemy, and scandal at one go. She then crossed the room and took the marquess by the arm.

Dalhousie, who had been chatting with Hyperia, bent his head, his expression one of fixed geniality.

"Dinner is served," he said as the footman opened the double doors to the informal dining room. "Ladies, Lord Julian, shall we be seated?"

The numbers were hopelessly lopsided. I escorted Lady Albert and left Hyperia, Susanna, and Lady Ophelia to manage on their own. For once, everybody—meaning Lady Albert and the marchioness—was on good behavior. I ate a few bites of buttered potatoes and allowed myself a taste of the beef and barley soup. At the end of the meal, I took a cautious nibble of bread pudding, but eschewed further indulgence when I encountered spirits in the sauce.

At the conclusion of a quiet meal, the ladies retreated in polite order, leaving Dalhousie and me at his end of the table as the footmen began tidying up.

"I keep a fine selection of brandies in the game room," he said. "Let's leave these good fellows to their appointed rounds, shall we?"

I followed the marquess up the steps to a predictably masculine chamber that boasted a billiards table, dartboard, chess set, and a pair of card tables. The fires had been lit in both hearths in time to ensure the room was warm, and a selection of cheeses and fruits sat on the sideboard.

Dalhousie had planned this meeting, in other words, or this cordial ambush.

"You were poisoned," he said without preamble. "As your host, this troubles me deeply. As somebody who has recently endured the same ordeal, I am all commiseration. Whom do we suspect?"

I had spent the best part of the afternoon alternately heaving, sweating, cramping, and cursing while I'd considered that question. My latest theory would get me banished of a certainty, and yet, the marquess must be warned.

"The perpetrator fits a particular mold," I said. "A knowledge of herbs—for example, of their effects and dosing—is central to the question."

Dalhousie examined the cue sticks gleaming on a wall rack. "We have a very competent herbalist in Mrs. Wachter. Anybody could consult her."

Resistance at the first fence. We'd be a long time cantering over the terrain I sought to cover. "And Mrs. Wachter, who likely lives on your land, would answer you honestly if you asked her who had procured a substantial dose of a purgative that causes further symptoms you and I know only too well."

"Very well, but anybody can read a pamphlet, and I know we have them in the herbal by the dozen. Gout, headache, female complaints, depression of the animal spirits, fading memory, rashes... They all have their remedies."

Depression of the animal spirits? I made a mental note to visit the Dalhousie herbal before being ejected in disgrace.

"Let us assume Mrs. Wachter was not consulted. I will establish that fact first thing in the morning by interviewing the woman myself."

His lordship chose a cue stick. "If you must." He rolled the cue stick on the table, then replaced it on the rack.

"The second fact we can imply regarding my poisoner is that they are a regular visitor belowstairs."

"Or they are employed belowstairs."

"We come again to the question of an accomplice, Dalhousie. Who on your staff would risk a noose for coin? I am the Waltham heir and the sole safeguard to the title's succession. In the event of my murder, my brother would not rest until somebody was brought to justice."

"You yourself have told me that my enclosure project will cost me the regard of the village and the gentry both. We might well be looking at an embittered footman whose family will lose access to the common land."

I schooled myself to patience. "Your staff has no direct motive for poisoning *me*. You are correct that I have argued against imposing the enclosure scheme on the common land. Anybody averse to your ambitions—your employees, your neighbors, your tenants—would want to keep *me* in excellent health so that I could continue to advocate for moderation, compromise, or retreat. Motive matters, Dalhousie. Why take the enormous risk of harming me?"

He chose another cue stick, rolled it on the table, found no flaws, and replaced it. "Mama doesn't like you. I admit that freely. She has her reasons, some of which are shared by others in polite society, but not by me."

"Your mother could never have slipped poison into my morning pot of China black. The staff watches her as rabbits watch a crabby hound. She had no opportunity to poison me."

"She's tenacious as a hound, too, unfortunately." Dalhousie left off playing with cue sticks and pulled a trio of darts from the thick square of cork surrounding the dartboard. "Lady Albert intrudes belowstairs at will, claiming she wants a word with the cook, or her cook at the dower house has a new recipe to share... Any pretext for trespassing. But I ask you, my lord, what would Lady Albert's motive be?"

"I don't believe she has one. She might know her purges and laxatives, but she has never been responsible for managing an entire household, unless you count the dower property. The traditional chatelaine's role of household nurse would hold little appeal for her."

"She might want to make the point that bad things happen in Tam's absence." Dalhousie tossed the first dart and came several inches from the bull's-eye, but perhaps that's where he'd been aiming.

If Dalhousie were a horse, he'd have tried to buck off his rider by now, but I persisted.

"The London fire happened in Tam's absence. Her point was made without poisoning me."

The second dart hit the board with more force. "Tam has a motive for prying loose any sort of bodyguard, investigator, or ally from my side. I don't like to admit it, but he's the obvious suspect, though perhaps his mother acted on his behalf."

Now my lord was shying and curvetting before a puddle. "Lady Albert has no knowledge of herbs, and if having me underfoot annoys the marchioness, then it delights Lady Albert."

"Out with it, my lord. You are intent on reaching some clod-pated conclusion that I will positively loathe, despite Tam's obvious motive for wreaking havoc."

Now he was insulting me, he who had insisted that I leave my home, travel frozen roads, and install myself under his roof.

"Susanna knows her remedies and tisanes. She moves freely belowstairs. She will lose status and possibly her home when you take a wife. She might well be reduced to keeping house for Tamerlane, in much humbler circumstances, and that is not a prospect to fill any woman with glee."

The third dart hit the cork surrounding the board. "You are insane. This is what I get for ignoring Mama's opinions. The fellows in the club said you'd be discreet, whatever else is true about you. Wellington insisted you served honorably. One of the best intelligence officers ever to grace the ranks. And now this outlandish, unbelievable, ridiculous... I brought you here in good faith, my lord..."

Dalhousie fell silent. He hadn't brought me to the Manor in good faith. He'd all but dragooned me into giving up weeks of my time when I'd rather have been at the Hall. I had been put at risk of at least a bad fall from the saddle and had suffered real harm on Dalhousie's behalf.

And only now was he well and truly spooked.

"You are safe," I said to him as gently as I could. "If Susanna is determined to prevent you from marrying, then if you continue to pretend you are content with your bachelorhood—"

"I *am* content in my bachelorhood, more's the pity."

He was lonely, tired, longing for respite from the constant dunning of his unhappy family, and in need of children. Not for the blasted title, but children for his heart, for his old age, for his personal legacy. Middle age had come up on his flank, with Dalhousie all unsuspecting, and now he likely looked for gray hairs every morning and dreaded what they portended.

For an awkward moment, I understood why the marchioness was so desperate to see her son settled. She did not want him to end up as she had—aging, friendless, lonely, and irrelevant to Society's greater aims while she serially redecorated a house she would never own.

Perhaps Dalhousie's enclosure scheme was driven by a need to establish a legacy—a misguided need—which was just too rubbishing bad.

Now was not the time to be swayed by pity for mine host. "Susanna had means, motive, and opportunity to poison me and to poison you. She was present at the shoot. She has access to the saddle room. She is competent with a firearm. She is capable of wielding a hammer with sufficient force to smash through wooden spokes. She could certainly stash a note among your correspondence. She personally nursed you through your ordeal with poison and likely offered the exact teas and tisanes to ensure you recovered. More to the point, she is proud of her role in this household."

Susanna was not proud of Tam, precisely, but she liked reviewing menus with the marquess, making peace with the elders, doing the rounds with the neighbors. She was the unpaid housekeeper, manager, accountant, nurse, ambassadress to the village, and consultant to the senior staff.

Settlements were important, but what Susanna had at Dalhousie Manor was a kind of power, and for a woman in her position—past her marriageable prime, looks unremarkable, connections few and attenuated—that power was precious.

The longer I'd considered her as a suspect, the more details had fallen into place, even to the lowering realization that I'd overlooked the obvious for the entirety of my investigation. I seldom hit the bull's eye on my first throw, but in this case, I'd badly missed the mark at every turn.

Dalhousie pulled his darts from the board. "Caldicott, I thank you, truly I do, for all your efforts here. I know you have tried your utmost to resolve a vexing situation, and now my enemy has apparently become yours. My enemy, who could not possibly be Susanna, whatever your logic and evidence might tell you to the contrary. I will understand if you decide to depart on the morrow. In fact, in view of the misery you endured today, I must insist that you seek the safety of your own home with all due haste."

"I cannot leave tomorrow."

"Still not feeling quite the thing? I sympathize, but I cannot have you bruiting about ridiculous and insulting theories regarding a family connection who has devoted her life to the happiness of others."

"I have not yet mentioned my theories to even Miss West, who is very much in my confidence. I wouldn't bruit them about. *I am discreet*, please recall. I cannot leave tomorrow because it's Easter, Dalhousie. Of all Sabbaths, that's the one I am least likely to disrespect with nonurgent travel."

I took the darts from his hand and stepped back some eight feet from the board. "I will depart on Tuesday, after the ladies have had a chance to pack, and my health is sufficiently recovered. I wish you the joy of your circumstances, though I also wish you'd reconsider that blasted enclosure."

I pitched the darts into a tight grouping at the center of the board, bowed, and left mine host to his excellent brandy and to his stubbornly, even dangerously, closed mind.

～

The hour was not yet that late by Society's standards, though I was tired, discouraged, and overdue for a report to the ladies. I stopped by Hyperia's sitting room on the off-chance that she'd excused herself from scandal-broth duty. I found my beloved reading.

"Dalhousie has issued a writ of eviction," I said, taking the place beside her. "We are not to have even a week's grace. What are you reading?"

"Mr. Addison's play. The Americans are very fond of it, though they seem to forget that for all his rousing speeches, Cato never did confront the tyrant or do a blessed thing to save Rome from the tyrant's vile ambitions."

I did not want to debate the politics of ancient Rome. "Hyperia, Dalhousie has given me the sack."

She set the bound volume of plays aside. "Then he has given *us* the sack, hasn't he?"

I was too consumed with my bungled disclosures to Dalhousie, with his nigh predictable reaction, to at first catch the cool note in Hyperia's question. I should have been more patient with him, should have laid out the evidence more carefully, should have suggested Susanna's culpability as a mere theoretical possibility considered only out of excessive thoroughness.

"We have until Tuesday," I said. "We'll accomplish nothing tomorrow, save to admire a lot of new bonnets and consume a quantity of ham. I am nonetheless determined to consult with Mrs. Wachter regarding purges and laxatives even if I have to do it in the very churchyard. Mrs. Wachter is the herbalist. She's apparently very competent and much trusted."

"I know who Mrs. Wachter is. Susanna and I met her outside the dry goods shop."

Only as I reached for Hyperia's hand did I realize that she hadn't hugged me, hadn't touched me, hadn't even smiled at my arrival.

A skein of foreboding threaded through my frustration. "Will you be relieved to quit this place, my dear?"

"Will you keep your promise to look in on Healy with me when we leave?"

I hadn't exactly made a promise. "If that's your wish, of course. Hyperia, is something amiss?"

She gave me back my hand. "Why is Dalhousie dismissing us?"

"Because Susanna has engineered this whole debacle, and Dalhousie won't admit it. If he takes a wife, she loses what little consequence she has, along with considerable influence as the de facto manager of the Manor, its tenants, its denizens, and—not a detail—its marquess. She's subtle about it, but her hand is omnipresent, and she had means, motive, and opportunity at every turn."

Why did I then feel no sense of triumph at having caught her out? I still wanted the villain to be Tam. "She herself tried to cast blame on Tam," I went on. "All roundabout and earnest, she said I must investigate his involvement if for no other reason than to exonerate him. The woman is clever."

"Some women are."

The foreboding roiling in my vitals became dread. "Hyperia, have I given offense?"

"Julian, you come here at a questionable hour to discuss your frustrations with the investigation. At the holidays, you read to me. You left poems on my pillow. You toasted me at supper before your family, and... I had hoped that our courtship was developing into the sort of friendship that could withstand all shocks."

I was shocked. My darling was informing me that I'd bungled badly, despite our earlier conversation about the past. I had consigned that discussion to a duty done, put a line through it, and heaved a sigh of relief.

"Hyperia, I do apologize. I have been preoccupied, and I promise I will be more attentive in future."

Her gaze dissuaded me from taking her hand, much less assaying any placatory cheek kissing.

"Dalhousie should trust you," Hyperia said. "You accuse Susanna based on logic, evidence, and your considerable experience solving difficult puzzles. You are correct that she treasures her place here at the Manor above all else. Despite her attempts to remain invisible, you see that she is quietly running the staff, managing the tenants, keeping relations with the neighbors in good repair, and otherwise enjoying a vital role, all without causing offense or earning notice. That is a more impressive motive to keep Dalhousie from going to London to take a bride than most men would credit."

She offered not a compliment, but more evidence against me, though I still did not know with what I'd been charged.

"What's wrong? Whatever it is, I will address the problem to the very best of my ability."

"I fear you already have, Julian."

Hyperia merely glanced at the mantel clock, but that was enough to devastate me. "Hyperia, please don't be coy. I have apparently mis-stepped, and I will do anything in my power to put matters right between us."

"*You* do not trust *me*, Julian, and I fear you cannot put that right simply by interviewing a dozen neighbors, having a good gallop on Atlas, and noting who was over-imbibing at last Tuesday's card party."

Hyperia was not only wroth with me, she was hurt. Very, very hurt, to be denigrating my investigative skills.

"I am sorry," I said, sliding to my knees before her on the sofa. "I am abjectly, desperately sorry, Perry. I have transgressed, and—"

"Do get up. Begging becomes nobody."

What did I care if begging flattered me, *provided it worked?*

Except it hadn't. I resumed my seat beside my intended, though in her present mood, Hyperia could easily set me aside.

"Julian, when you were so ill, did you even once think of sending for me?"

Julian, not Jules. Only Hyperia called me Jules now. Harry had, too, but he was dead.

"Yes, I thought of it," I said, bewildered. "But the ailment affected my bowels and guts, and the whole apartment bore the stench. You haven't had dysentery, Hyperia. The sheer, reeking shame of it is nearly as deadly as the malady itself. The infirmary was always set up downwind of the camp itself, and one learned not to visit the afflicted because they were too humiliated to receive... Suffice it to say, I did you a favor by leaving you to pass the afternoon in peace."

"No," she said, picking up doomed Cato's story. "You did me no favors. You did *us* no favors. For all I know—for all *you* knew—you were fatally and maliciously dosed. I am a competent nurse. I nursed both of my parents in their final illnesses. If we married, I'd expect to nurse you from time to time, and if I fell ill, I'd hope you wouldn't abandon me over a little stink. I've visited the jakes on occasion, Julian, and lo, I have not fainted from mortification as a result. Do you suppose the ladies' retiring room is uniformly scented with roses?"

While she paged through the book, my mind became a chaos of misery, despair, rage, and confusion.

I had meant to preserve her from... *me*, in all my reeking mess.

"I am sorry," I said again, rising. "Please find it in your heart to forgive me. The next time I am ill, I will entrust you with my care, assuming circumstances allow me that boon."

"It's late," she said, running her finger down the margin. "I will be here in the morning, Julian, and make a decorous departure with you on Tuesday, but don't convince yourself that all is well between us. It isn't. You have valid and serious reasons for withholding your trust from life at large, and any couple must weather some mutual disappointment, but this goes beyond disappointing me, Julian."

She looked up from her book, eyes glittering by the firelight. *"Your life was in danger,* I was in a position to give aid, and you never even thought to ask me for it. You relied exclusively instead on one very worried boy. You have disrespected me, and that, I cannot abide."

"I am sorry." I bowed and left, nearly colliding with the doorjamb on my way out.

I was guilty as charged. The complaint was not that I'd decided against relying on Hyperia's care, but that I'd never seriously considered summoning her, not in the sense I'd automatically assumed I would have Atticus's loyalty and support.

A very worried boy... *Ye gods and flaming failures.*

I felt again as I had when I'd learned of Harry's death. Wartime provided constant reminders of human frailty, and being taken captive by the French had brought my own vulnerability into constant view. But when the punctiliously polite commander of the French garrison had condoled me gravely on the loss of my brother, I'd been unable to believe him. Not unwilling, but rather, *unable.*

No. Not Harry. This must be another of Girard's diabolical games. Never Harry. Harry is alive and being told a foul lie about my demise. Girard is fiend enough to wield such weapons against us.

Some realities were too awful for the mind to absorb, and I still, on occasion, expected Harry to emerge from his dressing closet, cursing because he could not find his favorite pair of cuff links or singing some naughty ditty in anticipation of a night of carousing.

Harry was dead, and Hyperia could leave me. She would be kind about it, but implacable. As I sat on my bed, knowing I should undress or build up the fire or do some damned thing, all I could think was, my behavior, the evidence I'd given her, justified her decision absolutely.

CHAPTER SIXTEEN

I greeted the most joyous day of the Christian liturgical year with profound despair. The ladies had to a woman taken trays in their rooms for breakfast. Dalhousie, after offering me a terse good morning, had enjoyed his eggs and toast from behind the ramparts of the financial pages.

A bit of chat wouldn't have gone amiss, but the marquess was intent on banishing me from conversation even before banishing me from his acres.

To blazes with him, and I wished him the joy of his bachelorhood. Susanna would not harm a hair on his head, not on purpose. Hale, whole, and unmarried, he was her ticket to years and years of quiet dominance over the Dalhousie household.

While I had all but lost the woman who mattered most to me in the whole world.

"That's the herb lady," Atticus said, falling in step beside me in the churchyard. "Mrs. Wachter, with the purple reticule and purple ribbon on her bonnet."

Why would I...? Oh right. "My thanks. You can take Atlas back to the Manor. I'll walk."

"Ride him back to the Manor? Myself?"

How well I knew that combination of glee and dread. Every boy wanted to ride like a Corinthian, but getting there took courage.

"He likes you. You have done your maiden voyage under supervision, and he knows where his bucket of oats awaits him. If you get lost, give him his head and keep him to the trot. He'll get you home." God knew, the horse's sense of direction had been the lone safeguard between me and disaster often enough.

The distance back to the Manor by the lanes was perhaps a mile and a half. Atticus, I was sure, would ride halfway across Spain, through the Pyrenees, and off into darkest Peru before trotting into the stable yard.

"We'll send out a searching party if you come a cropper," I said, untying Atlas's reins from the back of the Dalhousie carriage. "Do try to stay aboard, though. Nobody wants to spend Easter poking about the hedges, looking for an unseated jockey."

"And I don't want to miss the feast," Atticus said as I adjusted the stirrups to fit his shorter legs and took the girth up two holes.

"No galloping, and canter only on flat, dry stretches of road. If Atlas tries to scamper off, you rein him in immediately. Otherwise, he learns that he can pull naughty tricks."

"Right. Pull his head to my knee and make the poor blighter walk."

Given his size, Atticus wasn't capable of pulling a horse's head to his knee, but one imparted the theory in aid of future skills.

"Up you go." I tossed him into the saddle, though he wasn't as toss-able as he'd been even a few months earlier. Good food, adequate rest, and time were working magic on his frame, and as quickly as he was gaining height, he was also putting on weight and muscle.

"C'mon, horse," he said, nudging Atlas onto the lane before the church. "Get us home." They left at a sedate walk—the beast had been standing for more than an hour, and Atticus knew better than to demand brisk activity immediately—and I watched them go with another increment of despair.

That dear, maddening, brave, and loyal boy would one day leave me. My stalwart steed would die. I could not bear either thought in my present frame of mind.

You might leave them first. Stop wallowing. The voice in my head was Harry's. He should have been alive to enjoy this sunny spring morning, though to be honest, the day wasn't as mild as it looked. The breeze was nippy. The sunshine watery. Mud puddles on the shady side of the churchyard had sported needles of ice before the service had begun.

"Mrs. Wachter." I approached the lady, bowed, and tried for a genial smile. "Lord Julian Caldicott at your service. I do apologize for introducing myself, but I understand you are the herbalist in these surrounds. Might I put a few questions to you?"

Like any medical professional, she had an instinct for patient privacy. She was a woman who had likely been pretty since earliest childhood, with large brown eyes, flawless skin, and a kind smile. She would be pretty into old age, and strangers would doubtless be accosting her for medical advice then too.

"My lord, good morning. I met your young lady when she was out with Miss Susanna. One understands good wishes are in order."

One wanted to crawl in a hole and whimper. "We are engaged to be married, and that is cause for rejoicing. I suppose you heard about my recent bout of dyspepsia?" I offered my arm as I posed the question, and being nobody's fool, Mrs. Wachter allowed me to escort her to the edge of the nearby green.

The sun was stronger, away from the shade and granite edifice of the church, and the distance allowed me to take in the tableau of the churchyard after Easter services. People stood in small groups, a more colorful palette than would have been in evidence in the previous weeks. Lenten grays and browns had been exchanged for spring green and lavender, and bonnets were awash in new trimmings.

Hyperia in that moment stood apart, apparently content to survey the passing scene. She was so damned lovely, and so damned alone. I was no prize, but surely I was better than spinsterhood and solitude?

"What were your symptoms, my lord?" Mrs. Wachter asked gently.

I enumerated the indignities and left off the sheer terror that had filled me. Dysentery and its dread accomplices had killed as many soldiers as the French ever did, and had our regiment not fallen under the care of a particularly ferocious and knowledgeable medical volunteer—French himself, of all things—I might well have died in a noisome infirmary.

"That could have been food poisoning," she said, brows knit. "I am inclined to think not, though, because nobody else fell ill with the same symptoms, not even belowstairs."

"You're sure of that?"

"Miss Susanna has made it plain to the housekeeper that I am to be sent for at the first sign of illness among the staff. We have only dear Dr. Mattingly otherwise, and he is the old-fashioned sort. Strong spirits and bloodletting are his preferred remedies. If it's good enough for the Regent himself... and so forth."

"Strong spirits are still beyond me," I said. "The malady affected bowels and belly both, the headache was ghastly, and yet, I was able to eat a few bites within hours."

"Ah." Her brows unknit. "Did you also have a foul taste in your mouth?"

"Exceedingly. Like brass and dirt with notes of sulfur."

"You were dosed with a combination of remedies and at little risk of lasting harm. An emetic and a purge are almost never administered at the same time, though, unless the patient has already been poisoned. It's a harrowing practice, usually reserved for emergencies." She went off on a flight of Latin names and speculation involving weeds, flowers, bark, and heaven knew what else.

"Are the symptoms I described to you consistent with those experienced by Lord Dalhousie on the occasion of his bout of food poisoning?"

"Yes and no. Food poisoning usually follows a progression. Not all sufferers are fortunate enough to start with upheaval in the belly, though some do, and the bowels are involved only as the situation progresses, along with sweating, tremors, weakness, and vertigo."

Her litany had me feeling queasy all over again. "Was the marquess dosed with a combination of remedies, as I was, or did he truly come across some tainted food?" At a family meal where nobody else fell ill.

"Miss Susanna and I weren't sure. She asked me to support the food poisoning version of events, so I have, but the progression of symptoms, and their variety and number, weighed equally in either direction."

Mrs. Wachter looked at me steadily while dancing around that diplomatic mud puddle. She'd kept her word to Miss Susanna and all but assured me that the same hand had precipitated both my malady and the marquess's.

"Who has sufficient knowledge to deal in the concoction that I was served?"

She waved to some other ladies across the lane. "Anybody can read a pamphlet, my lord, and heaven knows reading a few pamphlets turns most of us into experts these days. Mrs. Northby is very competent with herbs. You could walk into her herbal, pluck a few clearly labeled tinctures from the shelves, and send the whole household to the privies for the afternoon. The same could probably be said for the vicarage, where we keep extra stores for families who can't afford their own medicinals. The innkeeper's wife keeps a good supply on hand, travel being notorious for precipitating illness."

The vicar had not poisoned me, and I had yet to meet the innkeeper's wife. Mrs. Northby's stores might have been raided, but there again, Susanna had means, motive, and opportunity.

"Thank you, Mrs. Wachter. You have been most informative."

"Drink good quantities of watered cider," she said. "The treatment you endured deprives the body of fluids, and replenishing them can take days. Avoid tea or coffee, avoid wine and spirits."

"Meadow tea?"

"A very good choice, if you stick to the mints and chamomile. Ginger and lemon are your friends. Nothing exotic. Another two or three days, and you'll be right as a trivet."

Such was her confidence in her own prognostication that I should have believed her, but as long as I was in Hyperia's bad books, I would never be truly right.

I rode back to the Manor on the box with the coachman, a blessedly taciturn fellow. The thought of the holiday feast left me nigh bilious, but then I spotted Atticus and Atlas, trotting happily one field away along the bridle path parallel to the road.

He had a fine seat, that boy, and Atlas was enjoying the outing as well. I was pleased for them both, in the corner of my mind still functioning despite my own misery and despair.

If only regaining Hyperia's favor was as simple a task as putting an eager boy on a willing horse and turning them loose on a chilly spring morning.

I nibbled at the Easter banquet, though to my abused palate, the ham was too salty, the potatoes needed more butter, and the Italian cream cake—I tried one bite—failed to impress. I took no wine with the meal, instead asking the footman for a pitcher of mint tea, which did not arrive at the table until the cream cake was already served.

Had the marquess's displeasure with me become common knowledge belowstairs, or was the kitchen simply too busy with a major meal to accommodate an unusual request?

All around me, chat escalated to chatter. Lady Albert criticized half the parasols and bonnets on display in the churchyard. Susanna gently changed the subject to the bravery of the tulips pushing into bud among the daffodils.

The marchioness favored quoting Vicar's sermon, which had emphasized the need for a thread of solemnity in all the most meaningful celebrations, for life on this earth was fleeting, et cetera and so forth. Hadn't I told her much the same thing? Life was short. Don't waste it on pride and appearances...

Hyperia was quiet, Lady Ophelia full of sly asides mostly for the benefit of the marquess. Tam arrived in the middle of the meal, much to the delight of the company, despite the fact that he'd traveled on the Sabbath to rejoin his family.

The marchioness predictably chided him for that, while every-body else was too pleased to see him to bother with high stickling. A visual exchange transpired between Dalhousie and Tamerlane once a place had been laid for the prodigal between Hyperia and Susanna.

Those glances were easy to translate: *Talk later*.

I dealt with my own postponed conversation by offering to escort Susanna to the parlor for the ladies' session with the teapot. She accepted with good grace. Rather than accompany her directly to the family parlor, I steered her into the same alcove she'd once occupied with the marquess. She tolerated that detour with her usual good cheer as well.

"If I might be blunt," I said, "I will ask you to attend my words closely. I do not mean to give offense. I mean to share my observa-tions, which are as follows: You had the means to effect every bit of mischief the marquess and I have endured. You had opportunity in each case. You are the de facto lady of the manor, though you are so clever about it that neither Lady Albert nor the marchioness realizes what you're about. I have called all of these factors to the marquess's attention."

She put a hand on my arm, concern in her eyes. "Lord Julian, are you well?"

"I am recovering. Dalhousie has turfed me out, effective the day after tomorrow, because I brought the foregoing to his attention. If I thought you wished him real harm, I'd never allow him to drum me out of the regiment. As it is, I will be pleased to leave the lot of you to your silly intrigues, but should any harm befall Dalhousie in future, I will speak up loudly regarding my suspicions."

She was a talented actress, a skill that had been critical to her successes thus far. Her concern deepened to confusion then to dawning indignation. She snatched her hand from my sleeve.

"You accuse *me* of trying to harm Gordon?" She'd hit just the right note, halfway between disbelief and ire.

"I make no accusations. I make observations. Given enough time, others—the marchioness, Lady Albert—might make the same observations. In each instance where the marquess, his possessions, or his property has come to grief—or where I have come to grief in his stead —you have had the ability and knowledge needed to cause the trouble. As a result, the marquess has not gone to Town to take a bride, and he has informed his mother that he will not make the journey this year.

"He remains a bachelor," I went on with quiet emphasis. "You remain on your shadow throne here at the Manor. I am assured by knowledgeable sources that many women would go to great lengths to preserve such a reign."

A lesser woman would have begged me to understand, to keep silent, to please not damn her without all the facts.

She needn't have bothered. I was no one to judge anybody. Susanna lacked great beauty, a vast fortune, and noble birth. She'd been shunted aside by Society and told to content herself with good works and humble service. Heaven forbid anybody should notice a spare, aging female cluttering up the assembly rooms.

Susanna had fashioned a better fate for herself and done what was necessary to safeguard her future. The result was a household running more smoothly than it would have otherwise, a neighborhood and a large estate running more smoothly.

Until recently.

"My lord, you have apparently mistaken the matter." She spoke slowly and evenly, as if to a dimwit. "I would never allow harm to come to the marquess, never. He has been so kind, so generous, and tolerant, of me and my family. You cannot know how absurd your conclusions are."

"Dalhousie had stronger language for me than that, you'll be pleased to know. The marquess told me to pack my bags before I'd even completed my recitation. You and he are both warned, and what you do with the knowledge is your business. I'll leave you to find your way to the family parlor."

"You poured this spite into Gordon's ear?"

I was abruptly tired, thirsty, and so homesick I ached with it. "I shared my observations with him, as I have shared them with you. He all but begged me to upend my life to sort out his situation here. I have done as he asked to the best of my ability."

Into the bargain, I'd inadvertently offended my beloved, possibly past all bearing, and some of that frustration leaked into the rest of my diatribe.

"You and Dalhousie may assure each other that I have, indeed, lost what few wits I ever possessed—Society was right about me all along. If you please to go about discreetly assassinating what remains of my character, I will not be surprised. I could have done without the bellyache, though. You frightened my poor tiger witless, and the boy has been through enough."

"I'll send Miss West to you, my lord. Clearly, you are suffering some sort of megrim or a relapse of yesterday's fits, or—"

"I do not have fits, and Miss West's *kind offices* will not be necessary. I have nothing more to say."

Susanna spared me one more annoyed, puzzled perusal, then ducked out of the alcove, leaving me face-to-face with Hyperia herself, who had likely heard at least the last, indignant pronouncement.

My intended shook her head when I would have launched into explanations. Hyperia then followed Susanna down the corridor and left me in the chilly alcove, sick with regret and unable to do a thing to put right what I had just put even more impossibly wrong.

∾

By Monday afternoon, I was all but pacing the metes and bounds of my sitting room, ready to kick any random chair. Lady Ophelia found me in this state, upon which she was sure to comment.

"Where's your shadow?" she asked, closing the door behind her.

"Atticus has taken Atlas for a hack in the company of the head groom. My skills as a riding instructor are no longer needed." Surplus to requirements, again.

"Sit down, sir. Your unseemly pacing will give me a megrim." Lady Ophelia took one wing chair. I tossed myself into the other.

"I gather your ladyship finds my theories outlandish?"

"Not outlandish enough to dismiss them out of hand. Susanna will be deposed when Dalhousie takes a bride, no question about that. She is clever, determined, and in her way, formidable."

Much like Hyperia, who shared with Susanna an ability to keep her strengths from notice. "Thank you for that much." Atticus in a towering pout could not have sounded more aggrieved than I did.

"Julian, whatever is going on here, you are no longer welcome. We are no longer welcome. For the sake of your pride, please resign yourself to a dignified exit tomorrow. Dalhousie will attempt to be cordial, and you must humor him."

"I would like to humor him to the tune of best out of three falls."

She arranged the elegant drape of her skirts. "I am torn between rejoicing to see you displaying some temper and dismay over the nature of your anger. You were incapable of anger when you came home from Waterloo. All the wrongs you had suffered, all the harm done to you, and you could muster no outrage. That worried me terribly."

My apathy should have worried *me*, but at the time, I'd been so depleted, so far gone into melancholy... "A rough patch, I agree, and I am sorry you were given cause to fret over me. I will fret over Dalhousie, and that annoys me. I've put him wise to Susanna's machinations, and his response is to question my sanity. Susanna took the same tack."

"You are doubly insulted, then. Dalhousie scoffed at your keen insight and scoffed at you personally."

I bestirred myself to inspect her ladyship and found no smugness in her expression. "Perceptive of you, Godmama. If they had simply dismantled my conclusions with contravening facts, if they had posited alternative explanations or produced alibis for Susanna... but instead they attacked *me*. While that underscores the accuracy of my deductions, it also gives offense."

"Touches a nerve. I'm the same way when anybody criticizes me as a grandmother or parent. Very sensitive about my flaws, defensive even."

Godmama exuding gracious regret bothered me sufficiently that I shifted the topic. "Disprove my theory, Godmama. If Susanna did not orchestrate this whole production for the sake of her personal ambitions, then what is going on here?"

I raised the question in part to avoid discussions of touched nerves, sensitivities, and shortcomings, but also because in the normal course, Hyperia would have challenged my conclusions and tested all the counterarguments with me. We excelled at that sort of adversarial cooperation, and I usually delighted in it.

"The London fire puzzles me," Lady Ophelia said, shifting in her chair.

I passed her a pillow, which she stuffed behind her back. "Puzzles you how?"

"How did Susanna bring that about, Julian? She's the hand silently guiding the staff here, but I doubt she enjoys the same status in Town. She's not there nearly as much as the marchioness is. Short of a besotted footman, I don't see how she could have brought about the actual deed."

"Might Tam have aided her?" I asked.

"He is fond of Susanna, true, but I suspect he is loyal to Dalhousie first, to the extent he bothers with quaint notions like loyalty. Arson is in some regards taken more seriously than murder. One might land an unfortunate blow in the course of a heated moment and thus take a life. A jury would likely sentence such a one to transportation. Setting a fire, by contrast, takes premeditation and the willingness to devastate an entire city."

In the privacy of my thoughts, I admitted that Susanna, while determined, had no cause for desperation of that magnitude.

"Tam," I said, "might have assured her the whole matter could be safely managed, which it was." Even I was growing weary of pointing fingers at Tam, though.

"What does Tamerlane gain from conspiring to commit arson, Julian? If I were a betting woman, I'd say he truly does not want to become the marquess, nor would he like visiting that fate on his son. He has means, a place of his own, and private pursuits, however frivolous."

My ire was dissipating, in part because Godmama had put her finger on the disrespect fueling my anger. I'd accomplished my assigned mission, despite more than a few challenges. My thanks was a dishonorable discharge and a rift with Hyperia.

"When I was ill the other day," I said, "was Susanna at all concerned?"

"She was out making calls with Lady Albert for most of Saturday afternoon. Word of your suffering took time to filter up from the servants' hall, but I wouldn't say anybody found the situation unduly alarming—anybody save myself, Hyperia, and the boy. You should not have served Atticus such a fright, Julian."

"I should not have been poisoned." Though the poisoning suggested I had been poking too near the truth, which should have bolstered my confidence in Susanna's culpability.

"Given the harrowing events of your past, young man, that poison could have had a much more dire effect on your constitution than it had on Dalhousie's. You are lucky to be alive, and that's another reason why I find it hard to suspect Susanna, or Susanna alone, of wreaking all this havoc. Sooner or later, Dalhousie will marry, and for that matter, Susanna herself is hardly ancient, destitute, and hideous. Why settle for unacknowledged contributions here with a pair of bickering besoms when she might be some younger son's doted-upon wife?"

Exactly the sort of point Hyperia would have raised that I could not have come up with in a thousand years of pondering and ruminating.

"She's liked and respected here," I murmured. "You're suggesting she could be loved and respected in her own household." Was there a greater prize in all of life? "Godmama, you cast doubt on my theories despite yourself." Doubt on the strength of the motive involved, and upon that nail, I hung my whole kit bag of evidence.

"Good," she said, patting my knee. "I have distracted you from your injured dignity. Now I will distract you further by very nearly violating a confidence."

I dragged my focus away from the possibility that I'd leaped to a conclusion justified by the facts, but not by the *motives* involved.

"You have my entire attention, Godmama."

"Matters between you and Hyperia are troubled."

"We are engaged. That remains untroubled, to the best of my knowledge."

Her ladyship rose and took the seat at the table by the window. "Young people can be so dramatic. When Hyperia pretends to read, she forgets to turn pages. She stares at nothing for twenty minutes, then reaches for the bell-pull even as an untouched tea tray sits before her. When I catch her in her distraction, she pretends she was merely stretching, then she finally turns a page."

Oh, my poor beloved. "I disappointed Hyperia when I did not summon her to tend me in my illness. She says I do not trust her. Trust comes into it, I grant you, but my dignity deserves some consideration as well."

"Have you told her that?"

"We are in neutral corners for the nonce. She has assured me we will depart from the Manor with every semblance of civility." And then—heaven help me—would the gloves come off? Would her engagement ring come off?

I recalled all the times Hyperia had asked me what I was thinking, to prod me to share observations and opinions on the present
situation. I considered her insights and instincts vital to any investigation, but what partner had to constantly importune her supposed
equal to simply confer with her?

Her ladyship tapped a nail on the table. "You confirm my decision to raise old news."

Oh glory, not the past again. Not personal history and demons
and regrets. Please not that, not now.

Though deflecting Lady Ophelia from a fixed objective was nigh
impossible. "Say on, Godmama."

"Do you recall when I dragooned you into escorting me to the
Makepeace house party all those months ago?"

She'd stormed into my gloomy town house like the wrath of
Athena and demanded that I brave bright sunshine, Society's sneers,
and England's dubious roads to accompany her into the Kentish
countryside.

"I recall the occasion, not exactly fondly."

"Did it occur to you, Julian, that I have been traveling about
unescorted for more than half my life?"

What was she getting at? "You made a case for demanding my
services. I am a gentleman, and I executed the duties assigned
adequately." I'd also stayed on at the house party long enough to
untangle a serious plot to defraud one of Lady Ophelia's widowed
friends—and to defame my hapless self into the bargain, when my
reputation was already in tatters.

"Julian, I well knew the state you were in. Your housekeeper kept
me informed, and I passed along relevant summaries to Arthur. We
feared for you, and—"

"And that justified invading my privacy?" Any fellow raised with
a nosy older brother and a gaggle of enterprising sisters learned to
value his privacy dearly, but my inquiry barely qualified as
indignant.

They'd been right to be worried about me. I had been waiting for death and calling days of unending despair and ennui a gradual recovery in case anybody asked—which they hadn't bothered to do.

"You were press-ganged into putting in an appearance at the Makepeace house party because *Hyperia* demanded it of me. She could not intrude on your privacy when you were determined to keep the shades down and the knocker buried in the garden, but she knew she could drag you into the figurative light by appealing to your honorable nature."

Perry had insisted that I bide for a few days at Makepeace so as not to appear to shun her, my former almost-intended. The ploy had worked. I'd become entangled in the ongoing intrigue and been unwilling to leave until I'd found the culprit responsible.

"Why tell me this now?" That Hyperia had resorted to subterfuge to aid me all those months ago... that she'd *had* to resort to subterfuge served to lower my already abysmal mood.

"Doubt that the stars are made of fire, you dunderhead, but never doubt that Hyperia West loves you. Make it possible for her to preserve her dignity in your present battle of hearts, or you shall regret the consequences for the rest of your life. So will she, and you do not want that on your conscience, young man. Trust me, you do not."

Godmama rose, bent to kiss my cheek, and left me sitting thunderstruck in my wing chair. She'd hit my self-respect broadside and knocked me into a useful shift in perspective. My difficulty with Hyperia was a puzzle to solve, and I excelled at solving puzzles. Convince Perry that I loved her and respected her, guard her dignity as fiercely as I guarded my own, and build a foundation for mutual trust.

I remained in that chair, staring at nothing in the grand tradition and contemplating not despair, not defeat, not even pride, but rather, hope.

CHAPTER SEVENTEEN

My optimism was short-lived, while my frustration grew by the hour. When Tuesday morning rolled around, Dalhousie did indeed bestir himself to play the cordial host. He assisted the ladies into my traveling carriage, then offered me a hand.

"Safe journey, my lord, and my thanks for your efforts here." *Misguided though they were.*

The qualifier remained unspoken. The hand of civility remained extended. We shook, I bowed, and yet, I hesitated to leave.

"You'll be careful, Dalhousie?"

He glanced back at Tamerlane, who had joined us on the front terrace despite the early morning hour.

"I will be careful," Dalhousie said. "I am not without allies, my lord, and now that I am resigned to bide here in the country for the nonce, I wonder how the place ever managed in springtime without me. Much to do this time of year, is there not?"

A gentlemanly nudge to get my arse into the coach and back to Caldicott Hall.

"A busy season, I agree. Please extend my thanks and farewells to the ladies, especially your mother."

None of the ladies had come down to breakfast, but then, the sun was barely up, and gracious words of parting had been offered by Lady Albert and Susanna the previous evening.

I was reluctant to leave Dalhousie in a situation where he refused to acknowledge who his foe was—or had been—but he was a grown man, and I was no longer welcome. I ducked into the coach, and Dalhousie closed the door firmly behind me. The carriage rocked slightly as Atticus climbed up to the box beside John Coachman.

Lady Ophelia rapped on the roof with the handle of her parasol, and the vehicle lurched away from the steps.

I sat with my back to the horses, facing the ladies. Lady Ophelia's coach had been sent on ahead to her rural domicile. Our itinerary would take us to the West family seat, where Hyperia could look in on her brother, and then to Lady Ophelia's country residence, and then I could return to Caldicott Hall, there to resume my feeble impersonation of Arthur in spring.

Planting, plowing, lambing, foaling, calving... brooding, regretting, resenting. I had bungled the investigation even though I'd solved the mystery, and I'd also bungled with my beloved, an intolerable state.

We'd made the first change, and with every mile, I felt more displeased with the situation. Between Hyperia and me an awkward silence stretched that broke my heart, and my best sleuthing efforts had met with scorn.

Beneath both of those failures lay an insidious miasma of self-doubt.

"Your expression," Lady Ophelia said, "would leave one thinking that your digestion, a gouty toe, and a flock of determined creditors were all troubling you at once, Julian."

"I am wrestling with the possibility that Dalhousie was right, and I am wrong."

Hyperia shifted her gaze from the greening countryside to me. "Wrong in what regard?"

"When the matter of the London fire comes up, my tidy theory of

Susanna guarding her fortress falls apart. Then I invent facts to support my theory—Tam assisted her, a footman has lost his heart to her, she has the London household wrapped around her finger—despite having no observations to support any of it. I am inventing evidence that does not exist when I should be questioning my pet theory."

"Julian," Lady Ophelia said, shaking a finger at me, "let it go. The investigation is concluded. Put it behind you."

My tenacity was clearly alarming her, perhaps shading into obsession in her eyes. Where, after all, was the line between obsession and honor?

"Questioning your theory how?" Hyperia asked.

"Susanna has options," I said slowly. "Godmama has pointed out that the lady is well dowered, attractive, and by no means doddering. She could marry a doting swain. She could remove to Tamerlane's residence and run the whole household indefinitely, without having to mediate between Lady Albert, Lady Dalhousie, Mrs. Northby, and the neighbors. She isn't powerless."

Hyperia shifted to sit beside me. "And all this sabotaging of coaches and tampering with saddles is the behavior of somebody who feels powerless, isn't it?"

"I don't know." I was damned certain, by contrast, that I reasoned more clearly with Hyperia beside me. "Tamerlane also has alternatives. If he wants to move up in the world, he could marry advantageously, he could publish learned treatises, he could circulate in fashionable Society, but he spent less than a week in London just as the Season was launching. Not the behavior of a man determined to displace his powerful cousin."

"Keep thinking," Hyperia said, patting my arm. "The whole business at Dalhousie Manor felt rushed to me. Rush you up there, set you loose with a whole neighborhood potentially involved in the intrigue, then run you off when you spot the first credible pattern that could explain all the trouble. Like a dress rehearsal that's running much longer than the play was supposed to last."

"Lady Albert," Lady Ophelia said, "has alternatives. She could have remarried—she's quite comfortably fixed. She could bide with the Northbys, establish her own household, and take Susanna with her, travel abroad. She need not remain locked in battle with the marchioness simply to maintain whatever relationship she has with Tamerlane."

Who, then, was *stuck*? Who was cornered by circumstances, unable to maneuver freely? Chained figuratively to the elegantly decorated walls of the Manor? The marchioness to some degree. The staff, probably. Northby was also bound to his situation, though he seemed abundantly content with his lot, and well he should be.

The coach rattled along while a thoughtful silence reigned. With Hyperia at my side, my thoughts ranged freely over what I knew and what questions remained. My mental peregrinations were both unstructured and orderly, much like reconnaissance in good weather.

The second change came up. I donned my blue spectacles and handed the ladies out to stretch their legs in the sunny, cobbled courtyard.

"I'm for the jakes," Atticus announced, climbing down while the spent team was led off to enjoy their oats.

Out of habit, I accompanied the boy around to the back of the innyard. He used what facilities there were, and finding them thoroughly limed, I did as well.

"How does John Coachman do it?" Atticus asked as we returned to the innyard proper. "My proverbial parts are sore already. That box gets harder with every mile. Hard as rocks,"—he stomped his booted foot on the unforgiving cobbles— "and why his arms don't fall off is a wonder of the modern world."

We'd come closer to London in the past twenty-four miles, and the innyard testified to that increased proximity to civilization. The whole space was surrounded by a high wall of golden sandstone, a wrought-iron rendering of the inn's name—The Wild Geese— arching over both entrance and exit gates.

"Cobbles are noisy," Atticus observed, "but the yellow stones look bright in the sun."

"Cobbles are noisy, but they keep us from the mud. The high walls also make the innyard noisy, trapping sound rather than absorbing it. It's hard to sneak into a cobbled innyard."

Atticus gave me a measuring look. "You'd know about that, wouldn't you, guv?"

I knew that a horse who'd let me calmly wrap his shod feet in thick leather to muffle his hoofbeats was a horse to treasure.

"Miss Hyperia hates it when you do that," Atticus said, slapping his cap onto his head.

"Do what?"

"You were thinking about Spain just then. I mention sneaking about, you get a look in your eye that says you're recalling some particular occasion of sneaking, but you say nothing. She knows when you do that, and it makes her mutter about stubborn jackanapes and masculine vanity."

Atticus enunciated the last few words carefully, an imitation of Hyperia's precise diction.

"Why don't you count all the rocks on that side of the wall?" I suggested.

"Because John Coachman will leave without me. He's told me so a dozen times."

"He used to tell me the same thing, and yet, here I am."

"You leave Miss Hyperia behind," Atticus said, gaze on the far wall. "She musta knocked ten times to ask how you were managing when you were sick. Is he any better? Any worse? Would he take some ginger tea or ginger biscuits? She had the kitchen send up both, and you disappeared them biscuits when you wouldn't eat nothin' else."

I was being scolded, thoroughly and appropriately. "I had no right to rely on you when I was ill. You have my earnest thanks for your attentiveness." *Admit no one,* I'd said, and the lad had for once followed orders to the letter.

"My nose deserves more than your earnest thanks, guv. How many rocks do you think it took to build that wall?"

I seized upon the change of subject and launched into an explanation of the estimation process: measure about one-tenth of the length of the wall, count the rocks, multiply by ten. Not perfect, but a well-informed guess.

"A ruddy lot of rocks," Atticus said. "And they have to be the right kind of rocks. Dalhousie's head lad explained it to me. The commoners can take the rocks from the fen, but they have to take the right kind and the right shapes for making byres and walls and cottages, and the rocks have to be lying in plain sight. No digging allowed, though people do. Masons know a lot about rocks, but I'm glad I'm not a mason. Rocks are hard and heavy."

Ten times Hyperia had knocked. *Ten times* she'd been turned away on my orders.

I took off my spectacles and welcomed the familiar stab of pain in my eyes. Hyperia felt exactly as slighted and dismissed by me as I felt slighted and dismissed by the marquess: She'd had skills and abilities necessary for dealing with my situation, as I had skills and abilities Dalhousie had needed.

She'd been willing to help when help was needed, and she'd been rejected repeatedly, her suggestions never reaching me. She'd nonetheless succeeded in providing me some relief, even though I'd never acknowledged her *right* to care for me.

Worse yet, I had faulted Dalhousie for being unwilling to confront his womenfolk regarding thorny topics. I had shut Hyperia out of my past for essentially the same reason: I lacked the fortitude to grapple with a particular set of difficult issues. My hypocrisy was all the more spectacular because Hyperia was not a prickly, self-centered besom, but the most sensible and compassionate of ladies.

If she'd fallen ill, I would not have been content to pace outside her door, making suggestions to a worried lady's maid. I'd have broken down the door and flattened anybody who stopped me from keeping guard at her bedside.

I was in serious trouble.

Atticus remained beside me, silently counting rocks, his finger shifting minutely from left to right while he moved his lips without sound. The fresh team was backed into the traces and fidgeting restlessly. John Coachman ascended to the box and took up the reins.

"I give up," Atticus said, jogging off toward the coach. "Too many rocks to count. Tons of rocks, and this is just an innyard. The thought of a castle boggles the mind."

"Ride inside if you like," I called after him. "The benches are cushioned, and the company is excellent."

Lady Ophelia emerged from the inn, a brown paper parcel in her hand. Hyperia, walking beside her, had never looked more dear to me. The bright sun caught every fiery highlight in her hair, the perfect texture of her skin, the pride in her bearing, and the ferocious intelligence in her eyes.

I cannot lose her. I considered going down on bended knee, but as Atticus had pointed out, cobbles were hard. Besides that, my sentiments were for her alone, not for echoing from one wall of the innyard to the other.

I handed the ladies up, took one last look around the sunny expanse of activity and bustle, and in the next moment, felt as if the Hammer of Truth had smacked me over the head.

"About-face, John Coachman," I called up to the box. "We're returning to Dalhousie Manor."

John Coachman, whose name was Luke Cameron, like his father and grandfather before him, touched a finger to his hat brim. "Forgot something, did you, milord?"

"Overlooked a matter of significance. We'll not be staying the night, but to Dalhousie Manor, we must go."

I sprang into the coach and took my backward-facing seat. "Sorry, ladies, but we're for a slight detour."

Lady Ophelia passed Atticus a hot cross bun. "A slight, fifty-mile detour, Julian? In the name of all that is sensible, why?"

"Forty-eight miles round trip, and we can spend the night at this very inn, if you like. The Wild Geese looks commodious in the extreme. We're turning around because Dalhousie hasn't bought a single, ruddy rock when he means to build miles of stone wall. A bit inconsistent, wouldn't you say?"

"No rocks?" Hyperia said, accepting a bun.

"No rocks, no mules, no masons, no rope, no wagons, no shovels. No correspondence to procure same, no surveyors scheduled, no letters to other peers seeking their support for a bill in the Lords. Not one shred of evidence to support the possibility of enclosure walls, other than a lot of talk originating with Dalhousie himself. I thus conclude no enclosure was ever seriously intended."

I plucked a bun from Godmama's hoard and munched with quiet satisfaction. Means, motive, opportunity, and *evidence* all began to assemble themselves in a logical fashion.

"Why such haste to return to the scene of the crime?" Lady Ophelia asked, tearing off a small bite of sweet. "One grows weary of racketing about in even the most commodious coaches with even the best company."

"No, one don't," Atticus muttered, mouth full.

"We make haste because a great tragedy will take place if I don't put matters right at Dalhousie Manor. A life wasted, years spent in lonely yearning. Bitterness, regret, the whole sad works, and we cannot have that on our conscience, can we, Godmama?"

She looked puzzled. "I suppose not. Though I do wish you'd gift us with the particulars, Julian. One wants to ride into battle properly armed."

We demolished our buns, and I aired my revised conclusions. No matter how we questioned, tested, and challenged my latest theory, the whole hung together, and with the aid of my trusted associates, we planned our march upon Dalhousie Manor.

～

Five miles from the marquess's demesne, we changed not only horses but coaches, arriving at the Dalhousie village as just another conveyance full of weary travelers. The ladies wore their veiled bonnets, and I, who had not made the acquaintance of the innkeeper's wife, arranged a private parlor for my party.

I also ordered a generous midday meal, the hot cross buns being but a distant and fond memory.

Atticus, by means into which I did not inquire, had a note written by Hyperia delivered to the Manor. After the last of our dishes had been taken to the kitchen and a pot of daffodils placed on the center of the table, Dalhousie himself rapped on the parlor door.

"Miss West." He bowed formally, though his consternation was evident in his eyes, despite a carefully polite expression. "I came as soon as I could."

"Then get in here," I said, grabbing him by the wrist and pulling the door closed behind him. "You, my lord, have a great deal of explaining to do."

He glowered at me down the length of his patrician beak. "Caldicott, have you taken leave of your senses? I put you in your coach this very morning and sent you on your way. I owe you no explanations."

"Tiresome attacks on my sanity will get you nowhere with me and might annoy the ladies. You owe me no explanations, I quite agree, but you'd best rehearse what you'll say to Susanna."

He took a visual inventory of the room's occupants—Hyperia and Lady Ophelia, veils drawn back to reveal patiently encouraging gazes, and myself, feeling anything but patient.

"I have nothing to say. I wish you all a safe journey back to your respective domiciles. Now, if you will excuse me—"

I stood in front of the door, and though Dalhousie had me for brawn and height, he would not be as fast or as determined.

"Have a seat," I suggested. "The time has come to own your feelings, Dalhousie, in all their messy, inconvenient glory. You are besotted with Susanna, but you don't dare court her. Of all the women in the world, she is the one your mother would never, ever accept, or so you've convinced yourself. You are the one prospective husband Lady Albert would never, ever grant permission to court Susanna. You have assured yourself that your love is doomed, and yet, you have resorted to drastic and highly inventive measures to avoid marrying where your Mama would approve."

Dalhousie sank into a chair on the side of the table opposite the ladies. We allowed him a moment to rearrange his defenses, to accept that retreat would be his best option. Once we'd begun considering possibilities, we'd realized that Dalhousie *had no alibis*. Dalhousie was an affectionately tolerated interloper belowstairs—witness, those apples he daily pinched from the larders for dear old Blenny. Dalhousie had shot a hole in his own hat and dosed himself with medicinals, he was so determined to thwart his mother's matrimonial schemes.

A man in love would pursue measures more desperate than any sensible criminal might consider. This explanation had the very satisfying quality of being obvious in hindsight and only in hindsight.

The marquess stared morosely across the table. "Mama will make Susanna's life hell if I so much as mention a passing fondness. I know that."

"You don't know that," Hyperia said. "You fear it, and with good reason."

"You've seen Mama," Dalhousie retorted, setting his hat on the table, an odd counterpoint to the cheerful daffodils. "She's relentless, a force of nature. Mama will turn all of her spite on Susanna if I show any marked favor in Suze's direction. Lady Albert will return fire, of course, though she won't aim her guns at me. She will blame Susanna for attracting my notice, much less for accepting my suit. I've had years to watch those two maneuver, and as much as I do esteem Susanna—abundantly, lavishly—I cannot ask her to be my wife."

"Yes," Lady Ophelia said, rapping on the table, "you can, and you must."

Dalhousie touched the brim of his hat, a modest, brown affair, the brim only slightly curled. "For the sake of others and even for my sake, Susanna will reject my suit."

He had thought through all the possibilities and come to a logical —if wrongheaded—conclusion. So easy to do.

"Why would she reject your suit?" I asked.

"Because if we marry, the marchioness and Lady Albert will make our lives hellish. The hostesses will be poisoned against Susanna. Her presentation at court will be awkward. There will be talk. The loyalties belowstairs will be divided, and the staff at each of my properties will feel bound to take sides. You've seen pitched battle up close, my lord. I will have the domestic equivalent on my hands if I try to court Susanna, and she will preserve all of us from that fate by simply refusing me."

Love might not be blind, but it could certainly be gloomy. "She will accept you if you sort out the besoms. Did your dear papa formally grant Lady Albert a life estate in the dower house, or have you simply indulged her claim for the sake of your mother?"

"The solicitors can find no record of such a claim."

Meaning he'd looked for one. An encouraging sign. "The marchioness wants Lady Albert in the dower house because as long as her ladyship bides there, your mother is left to run the Manor, at least to appearances. You would never expect the two beldames to bide together, and thus Lady Albert's claim suits the marchioness's purposes."

"Tam suggested something like that over chess a few weeks ago. Said I should boot his dear mama from the dower house under the guise of making extended repairs to the roof. He offered to ensconce her at his house."

"Let the repairs begin," Lady Ophelia declared. "Lady Albert has wrought enough discord to last several lifetimes. You managed to send Julian packing when he was only trying to help, and he is not a man easily dismissed. Banish Lady Albert."

I'd left without a fight, but here I was, back amid the affray. Perhaps I wasn't so *easily dismissed.*

"That still leaves my mother," Dalhousie said. "I could not ask Susanna to embark on married life with my own mother determined to sabotage Susanna's happiness. Mama means well, most of the time, but she takes a notion and won't let go of it. I'm to marry one of her handpicked ninnyhammers, a biddable, sweet ornament, and the very notion... I cannot contemplate such a fate. I've tried, and though I love my mother, I simply cannot. Not when I am in love with another."

Saying the words seemed to settle something in him. His posture on the hard chair became more relaxed, his features less severe.

"You should tell Susanna that," I said, moving away from the door to prop an elbow on the mantel. "Tell her often and show her. Not just flowers on her pillow, but her favorite flowers."

"Give her your trust," Hyperia said, glowering at me. "Give her that, and you won't have to spend half a week interrogating her friends, her lady's maid, and her acquaintances to determine what her favorite flower is."

"Give her both," Lady Ophelia said, "and for pity's sake, do it soon. You've managed to dodge this Season, but then you gave back most of the ground you'd won by agreeing to a summer house party."

Dalhousie was not a weak or indecisive man, but he was torn between competing demands of the heart. His mother was owed every respect, but he longed to give Susanna the rest of his life.

What a coil.

"How did you deduce that I was bent on avoiding the Season?" Dalhousie asked.

I took the chair beside him. "I nearly didn't. The whole thing has to do with rocks. You haven't bought any. Haven't asked for estimates, haven't corresponded with any quarries, and yet, you wanted me to believe you were dead set on building an enclosure and that that project had put your life at risk. I also wondered why somebody close enough to pot your hat didn't discharge the second bullet more lethally. Nearly every pistol has two barrels, and firing only the one made little sense. Then too, the angle was peculiar. To put a bullet through only the brim suggested a stray bullet, a ricochet, or a very odd firing angle."

"The situation had to be dire," Dalhousie said. "I needed a substantial reason to haul you up from Caldicott Hall, a reason why somebody would wish me ill enough to threaten my life. Mama could brush off a stray bullet as an accident, but not when Lord Julian Caldicott was taking it seriously.

"Then," the marquess went on, "all I had to do was mention an enclosure scheme, and my reception in the churchyard dimmed considerably. My plan worked too. You caused quite a stir, the 'threats' continued, Mama accepted that this was not the year for me to go courting in Mayfair."

"You bought yourself one Season," Hyperia said, "and to do that, you had to poison a man who was only trying to help you. You put him at risk for a lethal fall from a very tall horse. Bad form, my lord."

Hyperia's ire was all the more devastating for being stated quietly, and yet, I felt a mild defense of the marquess was in order.

"Dalhousie knew I was a capable horseman and ensured we stayed off rocky ground when mounted. I did not, in fact, take any sort of tumble from the saddle. Please recall as well that he poisoned himself, too, and that's how he knew I would come through the same regimen unscathed."

My darling was not amused. "If you were unscathed, then Napoleon is enjoying a holiday by the sea."

"I am sorry," Dalhousie said. "Very sorry, but his lordship was growing too persistent, and Mama had capitulated to the notion of sitting out the Season. It was time to persuade you to leave, and I reasoned that if you were imperiled, the ladies would talk you into quitting the field."

Lady Ophelia's harrumph to the contrary could have been heard halfway to Town.

"I am glad for a chance to express my remorse," Dalhousie said, taking his hat from the table, "but I don't see what has changed just because you've exposed my scheme. I have wasted your time, put you at risk for a bad fall from my horse—that was supposed to be my fall, but the point was made even with you in the saddle—and subjected you to a trying afternoon. I have much to atone for. You have only to indicate how, and I will exert myself on your behalf."

"Save your honorable speeches for Susanna," I said. "You can atone for your considerable mischief by marrying Susanna, if she'll have you."

"She will have you," Hyperia said, a touch of humor in her words. "She looks at you the same way Atticus regards his hot cross buns."

"Who?"

"My general factotum, conscience, and the king of spontaneous good advice. He's a mere lad, but you don't dare come between him and his well-earned sweets."

Dalhousie rose. "Susanna is fond of me. Beyond that, I dare not hope..."

The poor sod hoped, prayed, and begged the Celestial Match-maker for a scintilla of encouragement. When it came his way, he was delirious with unspoken joy.

One knew the look. "You are right, Dalhousie," I said, getting to my feet as well, "that significant aspects of your situation have not changed. The marchioness will bitterly resent your choice of a wife, or pretend to. I suspect her objections will mostly be a matter of form in the ongoing battle with Lady Albert."

"Tam will support dislodging his mother from the dower house," Dalhousie said. "He'll go with her to his own property if I ask it of him."

"Ask it of him," I said. "You and your bride deserve peace and quiet as you embark on the splendors of married life."

"Splendors, my lord?"

Had he no imagination? "Splendors, by heaven, such as quiet mornings cuddling in the library, peaceful strolls holding hands in the garden, and lively arguments over politics, to say nothing of bound-less affection and the comfort of a true ally."

I did not dare look at Hyperia as I held forth. Where trust fit in that medley of blessings, I wasn't sure, but Hyperia had the right of it —one needed trust to truly share a lifetime with one's beloved.

"How do I deal with my mother?" Dalhousie asked, circling his hat in his hands. "She will not relent. I've tested her resolve, and she's the sort who takes strength from being thwarted. She digs in her heels and gains purchase the harder you try to tug her away from her fixed notions."

The ladies and I had considered this aspect of the situation at length on our return journey. They had provided the critical insight and the solution.

CHAPTER EIGHTEEN

"Think, Dalhousie," I said. "What has your mother longed for almost as dearly as she longs to see you settled?"

"To take her proper place in Society," he replied immediately. "To be accepted with the respect due her rank. I believe she hopes that serving as hostess at a summer house party will aid her in that cause, but I foresee refused invitations and gossiping guests turning the whole business against her."

Lady Ophelia allowed a dramatic silence to build, then offered Dalhousie a monarch's indulgent smile. "I shall attend. I will recruit my handsomest godsons and my most accomplished nieces and goddaughters. If your mother will for once do the sensible thing and accept matters as they are, she will have my unstinting and ever-lasting support with Mayfair's snobs."

I felt as Wellington might have felt when he'd rolled his big guns into place and put the fear of eternity into a French army that had been anticipating an easy victory. Hyperia had come up with this strategy: Dangle before Lady Dalhousie the very acceptance she'd been denied for decades and make that prize contingent upon supporting the marquess's chosen bride.

Dalhousie looked thunderstruck. "Mama will try to resist the lure."

"That is just too bad for her," I said, "because you will have the ultimate ace up your sleeve."

"What ace is that?"

"You and Susanna will be blissfully married before your mother can say one word against it. Present the marchioness with a fait accompli, and she will be faced with the loss of the one devoted ally she has—you—versus the possibility of her dreams coming true. All she has to do is pretend that Susanna would have been her choice all along, but for Lady Albert's inevitable objections."

Dalhousie stared hard at the blooms on the table. "That is... perfect. Mama could do exactly that. She'll sniff and murmur and sit up very straight, but she will... A fait accompli, my lord?"

"Buy a special license," Hyperia said, rising and slipping her arm through mine. "You can be married by this time next week if you send a pigeon to your solicitors today."

"Susanna hasn't said yes." Dalhousie clapped his hat on his head and then tilted it a half inch to the left. "By God, she hasn't even been asked if I might pay her my addresses. That is an oversight. I will—"

"You will be patient awhile longer," I said. "Susanna might suspect your hand in the whole campaign to keep your bachelorhood, Dalhousie, but of your affections, she likely has little inkling."

"One tries not to be ridiculous," Dalhousie said, very much on his dignity.

"Poison is ridiculous, my lord," Hyperia shot back. "Tampering with a saddle, smashing your own coach wheels, sending yourself notes, inveigling Tamerlane into carrying the brunt of suspicion, rousing the whole village with fears of an enclosure... All because you would not stop the squabbling in your own household. Were you not a man in love, we'd find your scheme exceedingly ridiculous. Susanna has to know the whole of it, or you embark on married life with a false foundation."

His expression became so bleak, so daunted, that I wanted to kick him, but then... I knew the feeling of being unequal to a simple task, of being faint of heart in the face of a mundane challenge.

"Let's send another note," I said, "and, Dalhousie, you can spend the next half hour drafting an express for your solicitors regarding the need to dispatch a clerk to Doctors' Commons. If you hurry, they'll receive it today."

"Another note?" Dalhousie asked.

I looked to Hyperia and Lady Ophelia, both of whom nodded. "We'll ask Susanna to join us here," I said. "We'll assure her that the whole business you orchestrated was intended not only to keep you out of the clutches of the ninnyhammers, but more significantly to clear the way for a union with the woman you esteem above all others. Even above your misguided mama. You will go down on bended knee, hand over your heart, and make a complete cake of yourself for the sake of true love."

He had the grace to look abashed. "You are casting me as the hero when all I have been is a frantic fool, beyond desperate to keep my foot out of the marchioness's mousetrap."

Hyperia withdrew her arm from mine. "Heroes can be rash at times, and what looks like desperation to others might simply be unstoppable determination. I'll ask the innkeeper for paper and ink, shall I?"

Lady Ophelia departed with her, and Dalhousie and I were left alone in a parlor redolent of daffodils and hope.

"Will she have me?" Dalhousie asked.

"A question for the ages, man, but if she won't, then you must cede the field with good grace and know that you did your utmost to win the battle fairly. If she refuses your suit, I promise to get you drunk for a week, and your mother can blame me as the bad influence of record—again."

"And if Miss West sends you packing?"

"I am partial to Armagnac."

"Fair enough."

We resumed our seats, the start of something that could be true friendship budding between us, and awaited the return of the ladies.

~

"My lord, my lady, Miss West." Susanna curtseyed politely. "I admit you have me at somewhat of a loss. Is anybody ill?"

She wore an everyday bonnet, a gray cloak, and muddy boots, but when she caught sight of Dalhousie standing to the left of the parlor door, she became subtly luminous. Why hadn't I noticed the transformation on other occasions? Hyperia certainly had.

"My lord." Susanna curtseyed again.

Dalhousie bowed. "Susanna, thank you for coming on short notice and with little explanation."

She looked at him expectantly, but the hero of the piece was taking on the aspect of a cornered hare. Immobile, alert, silent.

"Miss West's note said a matter concerning Lord Dalhousie's welfare required my immediate attention. Gordon, are you well?"

I held out a hand for the lady's bonnet. "He hasn't poisoned himself again, if that's what you are asking. Hasn't poisoned me either, I am relieved to say. Why don't we all have a seat?"

Susanna passed me her bonnet along with a guarded glance. Dalhousie roused himself sufficiently to take her cloak and hang it on a peg on the back of the door. He held her chair for her, and because the ladies had scurried into their own chairs, the marquess by default seated himself beside Susanna.

"Dalhousie has some explanations to offer you," I said, "but first, miss, I owe you a profound and sincere apology. I related to you certain observations I'd made, and I related them to you in an admonitory manner."

"But you did not *accuse* me," Susanna said. "Not quite. You merely mentioned that I might poison a man I esteem highly, shoot at him, bash his coach wheels, send him nasty notes, and tamper with his saddle, all for the privilege of counting linens by the hour."

I plucked the relevant item from among the list. "You esteem Dalhousie highly, and as it happens, he returns your regard."

The members of the besotted couple both regarded the daffodils as if I'd just suggested Napoleon really wasn't a bad sort. Doubtless fearing for my wits, the both of them.

"When the ladies and I," I continued, "considered all the evidence, we had the hardest time explaining the London fire." *I* had had the hardest time, to be painfully honest. "That was a clever bit of work, not as dangerous as it first appeared, but impressive as a deterrent to lodging in the affected abode. Even if Dalhousie had wanted to bide in Town, his quarters were sopping wet and reeking of smoke."

"I did not set that fire," Susanna said, showing the first sign of true temper. "Tamerlane did not either. Chimneys are notorious for clogging. London is rife with birds who build nests. The whole business has been sorted to Gordie's... to *his lordship's* satisfaction, and I see no need, no need whatsoever to rehash—"

"Suze," the marquess said softly. "I contrived to lay that fire."

She blinked and resumed staring at the flowers. "Perhaps we should change the subject."

"He laid that fire," I went on when Dalhousie remained silent, "on his way home from Paris. The sweeps had just been through, nobody would be using his quarters for weeks, but Dalhousie was already determined to avoid another Season in Town, and this Season in particular. He took careful pains to ensure that the result would be smoke and stink rather than a genuine house fire, and quickly discovered by the staff. His scheme worked."

Susanna nodded. "An effective ruse, necessary because the marchioness hounded his lordship into making that silly promise and because the marquess is too gallant and devoted a son to break his word to his own mother. It's not fair, to hold a man to assurances given under duress, and the marchioness's verbal bludgeoning never ceases."

All the while the marchioness had been flailing away at his lordship's bachelorhood, Susanna had listened quietly, hopelessly, and planned the menus. I was abruptly glad I'd not continued on to Caldicott Hall and left the denizens of the Manor to sort themselves out.

"Have you any idea, Susanna, why the marquess went to this bother, even to the point of having me investigate the situation?"

She sat up as straight as the marchioness ever had. "All what bother? If Lord Dalhousie sabotaged his own chimney to avoid the Town whirl, that is his business. That somebody resents his enclosure scheme enough to do him harm is another matter altogether."

Dalhousie took a flower from the bouquet and passed it to Susanna. "There is no enclosure scheme. Never was. Caldicott worked it out. I was afraid you would, too, as much time as you spend with the ledgers. I needed to convince Mama that I was in sufficient peril that I could not safely leave the Manor, and the London fire was only supposed to be further proof. Enclosures are universally despised by the commoners losing their rights, hence I could credibly be despised."

"Nobody despises you," Susanna retorted. "Nobody. You are liked, respected, and worthy of the regard in which you are held."

And that explained the reticence Hyperia had found among the neighbors, and the ladies in particular, when it came to the local opinion of the marquess. He *was* liked and respected. He'd never put a foot wrong in his locally scrutinized life. The ladies had been reserving judgment, weighing evidence rather than being taken in completely by gossip.

"As it happens," I said, "Miss Susanna, you, too, are liked and held in very high esteem."

She jammed the flower back in among its confreres. "I am nobody. The not-quite-poor relation. If Lord Dalhousie resorted to elaborate measures to fend off his mother's meddling, we can only marvel at his cleverness and determination."

"Lady Albert," Dalhousie said, "will dwell with Tam at his property. The marchioness, after the house party, will remove to the dower house. My bride and I will have peace and quiet at the Manor, or I will have peace and quiet there in which to enjoy the rest of my life as a bachelor."

Susanna, blinking repeatedly, used a single finger to nudge one daffodil apart from another. "You should not be a bachelor, Gordon. You are marvelous with children, and the title must not fall into the crown's hands. You've done so much with what you inherited, and not all enclosures are the same. The fen creates foul miasmas and mosquitos and... and..."

And would somebody please propose to this dear, brave, loyal woman? Any handy marquess would do.

"Lord Dalhousie," I said, rising, "went to extraordinary lengths, not simply to preserve his bachelorhood, but to preserve the heart he'd already given to another very deserving party. I feel a need for some fresh air. Ladies, will you join me for a stroll?"

Hyperia and Lady Ophelia were already out of their chairs.

"Don't bungle this," Hyperia said to the marquess. "Julian did not risk his neck on your behalf just so you could fall on your sword after a lot of empty speeches."

I patted the marquess on the shoulder as I held the door for the ladies. "Bended knee, my lord. Bended knee."

Susanna sent me a dazed look. "I'm nobody. The marchioness will never, ever... Gordon, what's going on?"

I answered her. "You are not nobody. You are the glue that has held a squabbling family together through difficult years. You are the manager who keeps the staff happy in their work and the entire neighborhood cordial. You are the reason Dalhousie has carried on when lesser men would have descended into debauchery or dishonor. *You are somebody of exceeding worth.* Dalhousie has been smart enough to realize it. I hope you can find it in your heart to reward his steadfast love with an admission of your own regard for him."

I drew the door closed, pleased with my little homily. When I swung around to escort the ladies into the innyard, I found Hyperia looking at me most solemnly.

"What they need," she said, "is the courage to trust one another."

"They also need privacy, as tempting as it is to actually lurk at a keyhole for once. Let's enjoy the fine afternoon weather, shall we?"

Matters between Hyperia and me could not be resolved by stirring declarations and theatrical genuflections. I knew that. Unless I came to a more trusting relationship with her, I would be the one trudging through an endless bachelorhood, and that prospect threatened to make all my previous fits of the dismals pale to insignificance by comparison.

"I do not understand young people," Lady Ophelia declared as we set off on a circuit of the village green. A pair of stately oaks provided a semblance of shade beneath a gauzy pink canopy of leaf buds, and the fountain on the inn side of the green was ringed in red and yellow tulips, half of them yet to blossom.

A peaceful spring afternoon, though Lady Ophelia seemed anything but calm.

"You refer to Dalhousie and Susanna?" I asked.

"Of course. Why didn't the marquess simply declare himself to the lady three years ago? They are of age, distantly connected— Society likes that—and Susanna has some means but not enough to obscure the fact that it's a love match. Society likes those, too, in moderation. I do not understand all of these sighs and subterfuges."

Once I'd grasped the pattern of events, I'd seen Dalhousie's motives immediately and understood them intuitively. I could not explain the combination of determination, frustration, and honor that had resulted in Dalhousie's scheme, but I comprehended what had driven him.

"The marquess," Hyperia said, strolling on my right, "kept his sentiments to himself because he is proud—what if Susanna did not reciprocate his affections?—and also because he is kind. What if she did? His mother would have disapproved of the match and made

Susanna's life wretched, much as Society has made the marchioness wretched. Lady Albert would have agreed with the marchioness—a moment for the history books—and declared the marriage an intolerable mésalliance. They would have pecked away at Susanna without mercy. Tam would have patted shoulders and gone back to playing scholar."

She stopped opposite the churchyard. "The whole business would have rolled on forever had not Julian intervened."

Hyperia was saying that she understood pride. Maybe she even understood that I kept many memories to myself so they would not contaminate happier minds with glimpses of hell. Or was that more of my pride talking, hoping that if I never spoke of my demons, I would not summon them nigh?

"I still think Dalhousie borrowed a leaf from his mother's book," Lady Ophelia said. "He convinced himself his love was doomed and ran amok when a bit of plain speaking might have won him the day."

"Or cost him the war," I murmured.

Godmama did me the courtesy of ignoring my aside.

"The chandler sells candles shaped like roses," she said. "I restrained myself on previous occasions, but regret not purchasing a few. If you two will excuse me..."

Before I could protest, Godmama was sailing across the green, reticule at the ready, leaving Hyperia and me to accept some privacy whether we wanted it or not.

I did... and I didn't. I wasn't ready for the required discussion and probably never would be. I should have been court-martialed for how severely I had castigated Dalhousie for a similar unwillingness to confront thorny issues.

"Let's sit," Hyperia said. "Dalhousie and Susanna deserve as much time as they need, and I am loath to ever again set foot in a coach." She perched on a weathered wooden bench that had likely occupied the same spot since the Druids had pretended to cede the shire to the Romans.

I came down beside her, mentally preparing myself for a severe, if inevitable, blow. "I have seen enough of Hampshire to last me for some time, though I suspect we will be invited to the wedding." If there was one word I should have avoided, it was—of course —*wedding.*

"Jules, I've been thinking..."

I did not want Hyperia picking her way through a delicate explanation of why no wedding would ever befall us, of that much I was certain. I took her hand and, with all the resolution of the Scots Greys charging to their doom, kept talking.

"I dwelled in hell, Hyperia. Part of hell yet dwells in me. You want my trust, my confidence, and you deserve it, and I yearn to yield all to you. I am nonetheless afraid—terrified—that if I mention those dark depths, that if I share them with you, then you will be so horrified, so bewildered and revolted, that you will leave me to dwell in my personal pit once again, this time without the hope of a future that includes you."

Whatever I'd planned to say, it wasn't that.

"Julian, you were ill. What has that to do with...? Ah. You were ill in Spain?"

"Our medical man once remarked that dysentery was invented to stop wars. The French were as besieged as we were, and you have never known such a medical indignity, my dear. Men longed for death simply to end the humiliation."

"Did you?"

The temptation to dodge, to change the subject, to leap off the bench and run all the way home to the Hall was a physical ache in my chest. I held Hyperia's hand and marshaled my courage.

"I did not long for death then, but at times, when I was held prisoner, I did not know if I was alive or dead. I was often kept in complete darkness and deprived of food and water, and the mind takes odd flights."

She moved, and I wanted to shout at her not to leave me, but she was merely shifting about on the hard bench.

"Hell," she said. "You were subjected to exactly the aspects of hell we all dread, save for the fire. The darkness and eternity and isolation and yearning."

Might we change the subject? But if I wanted to sit on more hard, ancient benches with Hyperia at my side, I had to learn to stand fast in the face of my fears. Every soldier knew the urge to run, and I had never fancied myself a coward.

The thought fortified me.

"I don't want anybody to see me when I'm ill," Hyperia said. "I have never had dysentery or even food poisoning. I was so worried, though, Jules, and you shut me out."

"I am sorry." I rummaged around for olive branches and fig leaves. "You advised Atticus anyway. He told me. The ginger tea and ginger biscuits. They helped. You did not accept your banishment without protest. If ever again I am afflicted, you have my word you will manage my care directly to the extent you wish to."

Her fingers tightened around mine. "Do you promise, Julian?"

"You have my solemn word, but in return, Hyperia, I want your word."

"Say on."

"If you should ever be brought to childbed, I want to be at your side, counting the pangs or mopping your brow or whatever other comfort the brewer provides for his wife and the blacksmith offers to his. If you fall ill, you will allow me into the sickroom."

"Julian, you are a man."

"The very best medical authority I know is very much a man, also French. More to the point, I am a man who loves you to distraction. When I denied you the opportunity to tend me in my illness, I was acting out of pride. I have apologized for that. You remained loyal anyway. I would be just as loyal to you, if you please."

"I don't intend to find myself in childbed."

"One understands that. My point was hypothetical for illustrative purposes. We will both grow old, my dear. Our faculties will diminish, our frailties multiply. I am expressing a hope that we grow closer with time despite those developments."

"Atticus would say you are going toplofty, Jules."

And my darling Hyperia was evading my request.

"Julian, what was the worst thing? I am not being ghoulish. I am hopeful too. I hope that if you tell me the worst thing and see that I am right here, listening, not flying off with a case of the horrors, that you might find it easier to believe in my loyalty."

Why must my beloved be so rational? So shrewd? So wonderfully devoted?

I sorted through my catalog of terrors and regrets. "Losing Harry like that. Not knowing if he was truly gone, fearing he was, knowing I was to blame for the fact that his life had ended as a prisoner of the French, likely in pain and full of rage—at me. The guilt, Hyperia, the terrible, crushing guilt. I lived. He did not. Why? My bewilderment sometimes rushes up on me, like a biblical tempest, and I can barely breathe."

"Nightmares?"

"Oh, my dear..." I told her then about wanting to die, about cold so penetrating it froze thought, about living like an animal on bitter mountain slopes, and dwelling in a mute beast's fear of all creatures on two legs. I told her about despair so encompassing that movement, much less eating or speaking, had eluded me for days.

"The knowledge that I had failed and would be regarded as a traitor has tempted me to end my existence, Hyperia. I am no prize. My thoughts disgrace me frequently. If you expect me to trot out every regret and foul element of my past for your inspection, I tell you right now, I lack the fortitude. Some of the memories ambush me, leap at me out of nowhere, things I haven't dwelled on or thought of since Spain, and there they are in all their ghastly, vivid menace. It's all I can do in such moments to remain upright, much less coherent."

I was being as honest as I knew how to be, and still Hyperia kept her hand in mine.

"All I ask, Jules, is that when the demons hover, tell me, and I will stand at your side while we wait for them to pass. When the recollections drop from your mental trees like highwaymen of old, let me know so I can stare them in the face with you. When you are haunted by memories of dysentery and fever, tell me, because I will fight for you as fiercely as ever you have fought to stay alive for me."

A nigh permanent knot of dread in my chest eased a degree. Hyperia wasn't asking me to bare my soul. She was asking me for such trust as, moment by moment, I could manage to give her. Asking me to *try*. I owed her that, and I wanted to be worthy of her.

"When I am haunted, I will tell you where I see the ghosts. When I am felled by memories, I will tell you from whence they arise. I will try, Hyperia, and you must be patient, and you might occasionally have to lead by example."

She let the last comment pass, but I'd made it knowing that my beloved had been through battles of her own and that I'd not yet been entrusted with the details. We would muddle on, closer and braver, hand in hand, investigation by investigation. Consolation enough for a day that had already been long and fraught.

Lady Ophelia emerged from the chandler's shop, clutching a sizable parcel. At the same moment, Dalhousie and Susanna, hand in hand, wafted down the inn's front steps.

"Lord Julian, Lady Ophelia, Miss West." Dalhousie bowed, though the man could not seem to stop smiling. "Please congratulate me. You are the first to know that Susanna has made me the happiest man in all of creation by agreeing to be my wife."

He'd given her a ring, the devious sod. He'd been up to more than sabotaging his own chimney on his latest pass through Town. Susanna blushingly displayed her new accessory and explained that Dalhousie had agreed to include his half of the fen in her marriage settlements—a brilliant ploy for rallying the neighbors behind the new marchioness, who was staunchly opposed to any enclosures, of course.

The ladies kept up a lively chatter while Dalhousie beamed like the happy swain he was. "Have you sorted matters with Miss West, my lord?"

"That's Caldicott to you, sir, and yes, we've come to an under-standing regarding certain irksome matters."

"Sent for a special license yet? I have it on the best authority that a small, sudden wedding can solve a host of difficulties."

"I will forgive you that sally, Dalhousie, because you aren't sane at the moment. Happy, handsome, and deserving of every joy, but not quite sane."

Dalhousie's smile became yet still more fatuous. "Not sane because I am to be married to the most wonderful woman in the world?"

"That too, but mostly not sane because you have been liberated from your worst fears and granted your most treasured boon. Unnerves a man, so I'm told." And if I was smiling a bit fatuously at Hyperia, well, spring air could have that effect.

Dalhousie went back to grinning and beaming and tenderly regarding his prospective marchioness. "I owe you, Caldicott. Wellington will hear that I am in your debt, depend upon it."

An unlooked-for kindness that meant more to me than Dalhousie could possibly know. "My thanks. If your wedding is to be discreet, you'd best nip over to the vicarage and have a word with the parson."

"Suppose I ought to." Before my eyes, Dalhousie's good cheer expanded to surpass all bounds. "I suppose *we* ought to. Susanna, might you accompany me on a call at the vicarage?"

They strolled off, not a whisper of daylight between their sides.

"Young love." Lady Ophelia sighed. "So lacking in dignity, so full of charm. I suppose we'd best return to the Manor and set off again in the morning. I will say I misplaced my favorite bracelet and didn't want it entrusted to the mail. Will that serve?"

"That will serve," I said, for want of any better ideas. "Hyperia?"

"They will be fine," she said, tucking her arm through mine. "Dalhousie and Susanna. The marchioness won't part them, and they will be fine."

They were obnoxiously fine. The ceremony took place less than a fortnight later, though Dalhousie relented and informed his mother of the nuptials the morning of the wedding. Lady Albert had by then already been established on Tam's property, and without a foe to battle, the marchioness had capitulated to the inevitable with stoic calm, if not with good grace.

Hyperia and I did not attend the Dalhousie Manor summer house party, but we did return to the Hall in fine charity with each other. We had barely unpacked our trunks before the next adventure befell us, but that, of course, is a tale for another time!

Printed in Great Britain
by Amazon

59059285R00139